'*The Lingering* is a gripping read, full of creeping menace and insidious dread, perfectly paced and guaranteed to cause you sleepless nights for all the right reasons. Fans of Susan Hill and Andrew Taylor, take note. One of my favourite authors' David Mark

'*The Lingering* is Susi's best book to date. Creepy, unsettling and all-consuming, Holliday tackles fascinating psychological issues in a narrative that will stay with you for a long time after the last page. I devoured this book in a weekend – loved it' Jenny Blackhurst

'*The Lingering* cements Holliday's position as one of the most gifted and entertaining psychological thriller writers in the business. It's simply superb' Steve Cavanagh

'Fascinating fusion of murder mystery and ghost story. Blood-chilling from beginning to end' Paul Finch

'A relentlessly unnerving mystery – like shuffling footsteps from a long-locked attic' Matt Wesolowski

'All kinds of awesome. Perfect modern-day Hitchcockian suspense!' Steph Broadribb

'I was lulled by the stunning prose and then BAM, shit myself. A serious spine-chiller from an exceptional talent' Chris Whitaker

'What a great read! A fascinating premise, strong writing and creepy AF. Loved it!' Michael J. Malone

'This book unnerved me right from the start. Haunting and chilling to the very last page. Not your average ghost thriller. It lingers in the mind long after you've finished reading. For all sorts of reasons' June Taylor

'Eerie and unsettling, with a bittersweet beauty that won't let go' Fergus McNeill

'Tense, chilling and with a creeping sense of unease, *The Lingering* will linger long after you finish the final chapter. Brilliant stuff from S.J.I. Holliday and another hit from Orenda Books – bravo!' Neil Broadfoot

'Ooh, spooky, compelling and chilling, I couldn't put it down!' Jane Isaac

'A brilliantly creepy story with a vivid setting, stunning twists and surprising, unsettling characters who will stay with you long after the book is finished. The best ghost story I've read in years' Louise Voss

'A story that gets under your skin – and stays there' Quentin Bates

'Loved *The Lingering* by S.J.I. Holliday. Quietly unsettling it quickly builds to full-blown chills as the tragic past of Rosalind House and the secrets of newcomers Jack and Ali are revealed. A beautifully written thriller / ghost story, this dark delight is the perfect winter read' Lisa Gray

'I could NOT put it down! It's brilliant – like Stephen King meets Thomas Harris. The claustrophobia, the tension, and the sense that there was worse to come were brilliantly maintained. Bravo!' Derek Farrell

'The creepiest book I've read in a long time! Witches, ghosts and an old psychiatric home make for a brilliant, spine-tingling read!' Laura McCormick

'God, this was creepy. I felt like a thirteen-year-old reading *Rosemary's Baby* under the covers again. I loved it. LOVED it' Louise Beech

'S.J.I. Holliday is the queen of creepy storytelling and keeps the pathos going throughout the novel' TripFiction

'Just finished *The Lingering* by S.J.I. Holliday. Finally a fresh and unsettling story! Loved each creepy page of it, though there might have been a tear or two at the end...' Nic Parker

'Beautifully written and perfectly plotted, *The Lingering* is a book that will stay with me for a very long time. The tension is almost unbearable at times. It's nerve-shredding and genuinely chilling' Random Things through My Letterbox

'*The Lingering* is a brilliantly chilling tale and Susi Holliday is on top, top form, delivering a story that feels like an instant classic. Get your copy ordered early for this one – dark as the blackest night and wonderfully disturbing. Captivating reading and a five-star shoe-in' Grab This Book

'Strange occurrences are putting everyone on edge in a book you'll want to read with all the lights on' Crime Fiction Lover

'Creepy and disturbing in equal measure. I've really enjoyed her other books but this takes things to a new level for me … It's deliciously gothic and supernatural, while focusing on a dark relationship with an added coercive edge' The Book Trail

'*The Lingering* is a dark, creepy story delving into the true nature of evil. Is it born, taught or guided? Nature or nurture? And can you ever escape from your past mistakes? Susi Holliday has created a brilliant combination of psychological thriller and ghostly mystery – a "chiller thriller" or "ghostly noir"' Off-the-Shelf Books

'A beautiful array of characters … five stars!' Donna Hines, GoodReads

THE LINGERING

ABOUT THE AUTHOR

S.J.I. (Susi) Holliday is a pharmaceutical statistician by day and a crime and horror fan by night. Her short stories have been published in many places and she was shortlisted for the inaugural CWA Margery Allingham prize with her story 'Home from Home', which was published in *Ellery Queen Mystery Magazine* in spring 2017. She is the bestselling author of the creepy and claustrophobic Banktoun trilogy (*Black Wood*, *Willow Walk* and *The Damselfly*) featuring the much-loved Sergeant Davie Gray, and has dabbled in festive crime with the critically acclaimed *The Deaths of December*. Her latest psychological thriller is modern gothic with more than a hint of the supernatural, which she loved writing due to her fascination with and fear of ghosts.

Follow Susi on Twitter *@SJIHolliday* or visit her website: *sjiholliday.com*.

THE LINGERING

S.J.I. HOLLIDAY

**ORENDA
BOOKS**

Orenda Books
16 Carson Road
West Dulwich
London SE21 8HU
www.orendabooks.co.uk

First published in the United Kingdom by Orenda Books, 2018
Copyright © S.J.I. Holliday 2018

A catalogue record for this book is available from the British Library.

ISBN 978-1-912374-53-3
eISBN 978-1-912374-54-0

Typeset in Garamond by MacGuru Ltd
Printed and bound by CPI Group (UK) Ltd, Croydon CR0 4YY

For sales and distribution, please contact *info@orendabooks*
or visit *www.orendabooks.co.uk*.

To Sue and Doc Holliday ... parents-in-law and fenland sweethearts, who are very much missed.

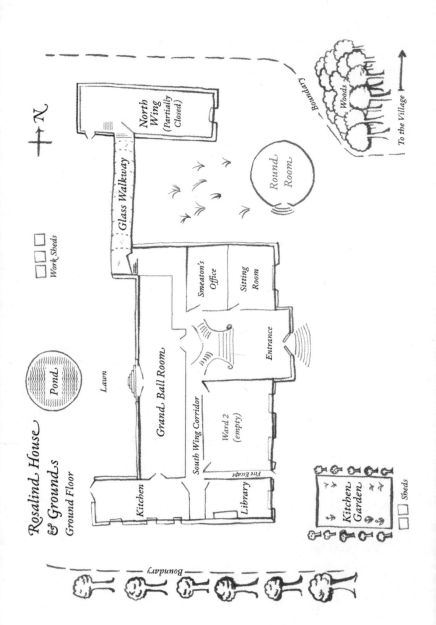

Rosalind House & Grounds
Ground Floor

N

Pond

Lawn

Kitchen

Grand Ball Room

South Wing Corridor

Fire Escape

Ward 2 (empty)

Library

Entrance

Smeaton's Office

Sitting Room

Work Sheds

Glass Walkway

North Wing (Partially Closed)

Round Room

Boundary

Woods

To the Village

Boundary

Kitchen Garden

Sheds

Rosalind House
& Grounds
First Floor

Boundary

ECT

North Wing (Partially Closed)

Glass Walkway (below)

Cyril's Room

Smeaton's Room

Empty

Entrance

Ward 1 (Empty)

South Wing Corridor

Ali & Jack's Room

Empty

Turret room above

Stairs to turret

Lucy's Room

Rose's Room

Richard & Julie's Room

Fergus's Room

Ford's Room

Angela's Room

Boundary

'*Certain dank gardens cry aloud for a murder; certain old houses demand to be haunted ... Within these ivied walls, behind these old green shutters, some further business smoulders, waiting for its hour*'

—Robert Louis Stephenson

Prologue

Angela

There's an unfamiliar smell in the air today. Something like wet pine cones and mulched earth. A hint of old sweat, something sweet, like a lily, and the sticky ripeness that comes with unwashed bodies. The Family like to tease me for my overactive imagination and my exaggerated sense of smell. I like to believe that I have a mild and unusual form of synaesthesia – certain smells triggering sounds and feeding my mind with wild possibilities. As for the imagination, it might be overactive or it might just be that I've attuned my senses to pick up things that others choose to ignore. I can hear Cyril tapping his walking stick on a fence post from the other end of the flower garden, but perhaps it's the still air that's letting the sound travel. Usually I can hear the birds nesting in the trees down by the entrance to the long driveway. Blackbirds or Chiffchaffs with their distinctive melodic tweets; and sometimes squirrels as they patter through the undergrowth, in the hedgerows that border the vegetable patches. But today there is silence, apart from Cyril's stick. And the air is filled with smells, not noise. I breathe it in, waiting, realising that I am the only one out here in the grounds, awaiting their arrival. Wondering who they are and why it is that they have managed to secure a place here without any of us meeting them before, without them learning about any of our rules and ways.

I hold my breath, close my eyes, focusing everything on my ears. Waiting. Waiting. Until I hear the distant sounds of a car engine, and my eyes fly open as I gasp in a breath and understand what it is I can smell in the air. Something dark. Something old.

Something bad is coming.

And there's no way to stop it.

Part 1
THE LIGHT

'A house is never still in darkness to those who listen intently; there is a whispering in distant chambers, an unearthly hand presses the snib of the window, the latch rises. Ghosts were created when the first man woke in the night.'

— J.M. Barrie

Extract from *The Book of Light*

The Essence of Us

The Rosalind House Community Project was formed by
Smeaton Dunsmore in 1995. Smeaton comes from a strong
community family, having been born and raised in
the world-famous Sweethope Commune in the north of
Scotland, and continuing his learning and experiences
of life at the Makaranda Love Ranch in Southern
California and in several smaller collectives in
Southeast Asia. Smeaton always hoped to carry on
the teachings of the Sweethope founders, his mother
and father, and saw Rosalind House as the perfect
location for his new family home. With community
members of all ages and from all walks of life, Our
Family wishes to welcome you to our happy home, and
hopes that it will soon feel like your happy home
too.

Guidelines for a Light & Bright Existence

'Embrace the light'

We all have one thing in common: the desire to live
in peace, harmony and freedom – away from wrongdoers
and those who take pleasure in the discomfort of
others. We have one key aim: for only goodness to
exist. By embracing goodness, we help it to grow.
Help it to grow here amongst us. All you need to do
is embrace it.

'Join hands, join minds, live as one'
The joining of hands has long been a method of
ensuring community engagement, without making anyone
feel that any boundaries have been crossed. We make
a simple vow to engage with one another in this way
before and after completing any group tasks. Although
we remain individuals and of free minds and spirits,
Our Family shares their love through this simple
ritual of platonic touch: *the blessing of light.*

'Do good and live within the light'
There is only one thing that can be controlled here,
and that is our own impulses. This is our only rule –
do good, be good – always be light, continue the fight
against the dark.

'Do not fear change, for the change is within you'
Change is inevitable. None of us can live as we once
did, as an individual in a too-wide world. To join
Our Family you must accept and embrace the changes
that are inevitable. Never fear. Never stop. Become
who you are.

'Respect this house, and live in peace'
This is an old property and it has its own ways
of existence. Do not question these, but accept
them with grace. Help us to keep this house happy.
Work together to improve what we have. Avoid petty
squabbles and you will exist in harmony. Always offer
to help.

'Bring in the dark, and live with the consequences'
Always be kind. Always be truthful. This is a happy
house, and all residents have been absolved of their

past wrongdoings. We must keep it this way, in order to remain in a synergistic, loving environment. When someone does wrong, they are not the only one affected. Protect this house and the wider environs by BEING GOOD, always.

Our Group Activities

6.30 a.m. daily: *Morning Singing.* Join us in the round room for thirty minutes of uplifting Taizé singing – wake yourself up with a smile!

7.30 p.m. Mondays: *Guided Meditation.* Join us in the living room for a peaceful break from your activities – take an Angel card and work towards dealing with your core issues in a quiet, contemplative setting.

6.30 p.m. Fridays (bi-monthly): *Formal dinner and party.* Let your hair down, enjoy some of our chef's special herbal concoctions and free your body and your spirit through dance.

Advisory Notes

The following are things that we advise you let go, in order to claim the peaceful existence that you have come here to find. As always, these are not rules, but they are things that we have come to believe you will benefit from removing from your lives. The following things are not advised:

- Mobile phones
- Internet use
- Regular contact with friends / family on the outside
- Visiting the village
- Purchasing unnecessary material items
- Illegal drugs

- Over-consumption of alcohol
- Television and radio
- Driving
- Swearing

Our Family

Smeaton Dunsmore

Ford Swanson

Richard Latham

Julie Latham

Fergus Jones

Rose Curtis

Cyril Mead

Lucy Worthington

Angela Fairley

~~Annie Palmerston~~

~~Lawrence Palmerston~~

Ali Gardiner

Jack Gardiner

1
Ali

As the road dips into the flat, bleak fenland, a burning ball of sunlight drops down in front of them and they both raise a hand to shield their eyes. Jack swerves to the left, almost ending up in the drainage channel that runs along the length of the field.

'Jesus,' Ali mutters from the passenger seat. She flips the sun visor down in front of her. 'Pretty spectacular. Can we stop for a minute? I just want to snap a pic on my phone.' Jack slows, turns to look at her. His look says the same thing that's just slid into her own head. 'Yeah, you're right,' she says. 'What's the point of taking a photograph now? It's not like I can send it to anyone.'

Jack adjusts his own visor and speeds up again. 'Well you could ... but it's not *advised*.'

Ali sighs. 'Do we have to go through all this again? It really will be easier if you embrace it with an open mind. You might even enjoy it.'

'I doubt that,' he mutters.

She wants to carry on. Pick a fight for no real reason. But she stops herself. That's what the old Ali would do. With the old Jack. Despite everything, she does still love him and she wants this to work. She glances around at the back seat of the car, jammed with what remains of their worldly possessions.

They've sold the rest. They don't need much where they're going. Not much of the stuff they used to need anyway. Technology. Gadgets. Fancy gold satin pumps and a Chanel clutch bag in the same shade, both far more expensive than her salary allowed. The girl who bought them looked like she'd won the lottery when Ali sold them at the car boot sale for a tenth of the price. She knows they could've made more money if she'd sold things on specialist websites, maybe even got a company to come round and do a valuation. But what was the point? They had their savings, and that was enough to secure their place. What would they do with more money? Would they be persuaded to give that away too?

Practically nothing from their old life is required anymore.

She feels liberated and petrified in equal measure.

Jack leans over and flips open the glove box. Ali swivels back around and bats his hand away. 'Keep your eyes on the road. What do you want? I'll get it.'

'I think there's a map in there. Can you check? I thought I'd memorised the route but I'm starting to think that we're going in circles. All these roads look the same. I'm sure we've passed that house three times.' He slows down.

Ali looks out at the small cottage on their right. It's crooked, as if it is slowly sinking into the marshes beneath it.

'That's definitely not the same cottage as the last one. The last one had a blue gate, and there were other cottages further along the road. This one's on its own, and the gate's not even painted.'

'I'm glad you're keeping an eye out.'

She rummages in the glove box and finds a crumpled Ordnance Survey map. She straightens it out on her lap. A faded coffee ring obscures part of the image on the front – a cathedral. Ely, maybe?

'*The Cambridgeshire Fens, 1998*. Wow. Was this the last time you used a map?' She unfolds it and a musty scent fills the air in front of her face. 'Shame we had to get rid of the sat nav.'

'I suppose we didn't need to do that, did we? It wouldn't do any harm left in the car. Are we even going to need the car after this? I'm still not totally clear about what we can and can't do in this place.'

'Me neither, but we'll find out soon enough. From what it said in the letter, I don't think we're actually banned from doing things or going anywhere, it's—'

'It's just *not advised*,' Jack cuts in. He has the hint of a smirk on his face.

Ali ignores it and runs her finger down the map. 'Got it. We're still on track. In fact, we're nearly there.'

He mutters something that she can't hear.

She stares at him now. Looks at the paleness of his skin, the dark circles beneath his eyes. He looks like he's barely slept. He's too thin, and a faint sheen of sweat sparkles on his brow. She lays a hand on his knee, fighting the urge to pull it sharply away again.

'It's going to be OK, Jack. I promise you.'

Jack doesn't reply.

He doesn't believe her. He's made that crystal clear over the last few weeks, since she set the plan into action. She's tried her best to reassure him, explaining in the best way that she can that there is no other choice. It's this, or ... she doesn't even want to contemplate the alternatives.

'Everything is going to be OK,' she says once again, just as the copse of high trees comes into sight – the first of the landmarks for them to follow to reach their destination.

She wonders who she is trying to convince.

She stares out at the bleak but beautiful landscape. She's read about this area of reclaimed land, where dead plants never decay and strange grasses sprout from the permanently saturated peat.

Ali takes the sheet of folded paper out of the bag in the footwell. 'Nearly there,' she says. 'After the trees it's only another mile, then we'll see the entrance to the driveway.'

Jack sniffs. 'I think I see it.'

The driveway is long and straight, the land on either side flat and scorched by the sun. The building grows in front of them, as Jack drives too fast over the potholes until, at last, they are there. He stops the car.

The main building is exactly as she has imagined it: an oversized front door with a stone archway, flanked by long narrow windows. She can make out some of the smaller buildings at either side. They are less impressive, and obviously built later, as the hospital expanded.

Hospital.

That's what Rosalind House had once been. Built in 1845 on land that had lain barren since a grand family home burned to the ground in the seventeenth century, it was once the largest asylum in the county. Residents were sent here for all manner of medical conditions, many of which weren't medical at all; such patients were mostly women, who were often sent away by men who wanted to silence them for having opinions of their own. The place had been self-sufficient back then, according to what she'd dug up during her research. The Victorian doctors had believed that activities such as tending to vegetable patches and churning their own butter would help soothe troubled minds. In the years that followed, though, the focus had changed, and in the 1940s it had become the local state psychiatric hospital, housing victims of wartime trauma as well as other members of society who had somehow lost their way.

It isn't a hospital now ... but Ali hopes that living a self-sufficient life of simple meals and soothing, repetitive manual activities will soon become as commonplace to them as ordering pizzas online at eleven p.m. and having non-stop movies on demand. It might even be enough to mend what has broken between them. She glances at Jack. He is staring at the building. His knuckles glow white from where he is gripping the steering wheel so tightly, as if he is holding on for dear life, hoping that someone will save him from falling off a cliff. She lays a hand on his knee and feels his leg relax. He sighs. His grip on the steering wheel loosens.

'We'll give this place a month, OK? That's what you said, isn't it? And if it doesn't suit us, we move on again, right?'

Ali nods. 'Yes. That's what I said. Only...' He turns to face her. Lifts her hand off his knee and squeezes it. 'Only what?' She squeezes back. 'I'm just not really sure what we're going to do if this doesn't work.'

He drops her hand and restarts the ignition. 'Let's think about that later,' he says. 'If we have to think about it at all.'

A scowl is etched onto his face, his brows are knitted. She hovers a hand back towards his knee, but changes her mind and folds it into her lap. On her left, outside, she sees the arched canes of a kitchen garden. Beyond that, a wheelbarrow parked next to a pile of dark soil.

She glances at the clock on the radio console: 10:30. There's no one around. Tea break? She'd loved tea breaks in her old job. Taking time off the wards, putting her feet up. She'd enjoyed being a psychiatric nurse but it was tough and it was draining. She relished those breaks simply because they gave her the chance to talk to people whose problems weren't pathological. She would miss her colleagues and their mundane little gripes about the world, but she wouldn't miss the job. She knows that she got too close to it. Became far too involved. Besides, she has enough to concern herself with now.

Jack pulls into a parking space near the entrance and Ali opens her door. There's a slight breeze, and she's sure she can hear the sounds of music drifting out of one of the side buildings. Something choral, uplifting. She steps out of the car and crunches across the loose stones and broken concrete. The music is coming from a small round building on the edge of the car park. It takes her longer than it should to realise that it's not a recording; it's live. It's people singing. Something in Latin, or maybe Spanish. The four voices of the group make a soothing harmony, from the low bass drawl to the tinkling melody of the sopranos, the tenors and altos keeping the steady rhythm in between:

De noche iremo, de noche que para encontrar la fuente,
solo la sed nos alumbra, solo la sed nos alumbra

They stand for a moment, listening as the same words are repeated over and over, as a chant. She has a sudden urge to jump back into the car, to tell Jack to drive away from this place, back to where they came from, or to somewhere else. Anywhere else. She turns around at the sound of the car door slamming shut. Jack is leaning against the bonnet, waiting. He almost looks as if he is smiling. She takes a breath. She can do this. They can do this. It's just music. It's singing. It's happy.

They can be happy. Here. In this place. This place is the answer to all of their problems.

She'll make sure of it.

2
Ali

'Ah, you've been listening to our attempts at something musical...' A man strides towards them, a wide smile on his face creating an array of crinkles at the sides of his eyes. He pushes a long flop of greying hair away from his face with one hand, and extends the other towards them. Ali and Jack step forwards at the same time, crashing against each other. Ali pulls back, lets Jack shake the man's hand.

'Smeaton Dunsmore,' he says. He looks confused for a second, glancing around. 'Was no one here to greet you? I thought...' he shakes his head. Smiles again. 'Never mind.' His accent is neutral – cultured but impossible to place. From the information he's sent her, and what she could dig up online, Ali knows he was born in Scotland, but there's barely a trace of it in his voice. Or his looks, for that matter. He is tall and slim, with a face that is all sharp angles. His eyes are the same shade of grey as his hair, and there's something vulpine about him that Ali is drawn to immediately.

'Jack Gardiner,' her husband says in reply. 'Pleased to meet you.'

Dunsmore holds Jack's hand for just a moment too long. Ali watches him as he locks eyes with Jack, trying to read him. Good luck with that, she thinks. Jack is a master at keeping his thoughts and emotions locked up tightly.

'I'm Ali,' she says, stepping forwards. She stretches out her hand, but Dunsmore steps in and holds her in an embrace. He smells of wood smoke and sweat. It's not unpleasant and she lets herself be held until he pulls away.

He lays his hands on her shoulders and smiles down at her. 'It's wonderful to meet you, Ali. I almost said "at last" but it really has been such a short time. It's very unusual for us to have anyone move in so soon after the first contact, but when you explained your circumstances to me and I discussed it with the others, how were we to refuse? An ex-policeman and an experienced nurse? We couldn't hope for more worthy additions to our little family.'

Sure, Ali thinks. *The money we offered to bypass all the usual evaluations might've helped a bit too, right?*

He winks at her, as if reading her mind.

'OK,' he says. 'Let's go inside. We need cups of tea, lots of cake, and a good chat before we move on to all the logistical bits. Am I right?' He nods at Jack. 'Perhaps you can park your car over there beside the low block? We like to keep the front of the building as free a space as we can manage.'

'Sure.'

Jack walks back to the car. Ali feels cold, suddenly, and hugs herself. Dunsmore disappears inside, just as a trickle of bodies starts to wind its way across from the circular building to the main entrance. There is a chorus of hellos and hi's and welcomes, but no one stops. They vanish into the building, and Ali feels herself shrinking inside. She's confident enough when she knows people, but she struggles with pushing herself into new groups. Jack appears by her side and squeezes her hand. She wonders if he realises just how much of a battle this is going to be for her, never mind him. The idea of living in a community where everything is shared and her life is no longer just for her fills her with absolute terror. But the thought of losing Jack is that terror magnified by one thousand. She squeezes her hands into fists then stretches them out and shakes her arms. 'OK', she says. 'Let's do this.'

Ali and Jack walk together through the imposing main entrance, then through a small foyer, with built-in seats on either side and an open frame with a cricket bat mounted inside it and bearing a small brass plaque saying *'Osborne James: 1947'* – an ex-patient, maybe? Or a benefactor? They follow the stragglers of the group at a safe enough distance to see where they are going but not so close as to crowd them.

Ali's slightly surprised at the muttered greetings; she was expecting a bit more fanfare at their arrival. But maybe they aren't quite as important as she thought they might be. Maybe newcomers aren't that rare. Or maybe this myth of a friendly community is just that: a myth. Or, more likely, she's tired from the three-hour drive from London and already regretting the decision to come here.

She stops and holds out a hand so that Jack stops too, whirling round to face her.

'You're right,' she says. 'I don't know what I was thinking. I can't do this. We can't stay here—'

'Ali...' Jack gives a tiny shake of his head. He looks at something somewhere over her shoulder, and Ali understands. She feels the heat of Dunsmore standing next to her.

'Don't worry,' he says. 'It's natural to have doubts. Unless you've been brought up in this kind of environment, it's bound to feel strange to you. Weird, even. I've heard most of the adjectives that people have come up with to describe us. We used to do open days, when we first started. We had a couple of barbecues, that sort of thing. Thought if the locals knew what we were doing and that we weren't a bunch of crazy Manson-esque whack-jobs – their words, not mine – that it would make things easier for us. We want to be fully self-sufficient here. That's the goal. Selling things would've helped with that. But you know what people are like. Besides, it's not only us the locals seem to be wary of, but the place itself. This house and the land it sits on has a very ... chequered past. You know what I mean?'

She senses he's not expecting her to respond to his final question, so she doesn't. Although she doesn't really understand what he's getting at. What chequered past? It was an asylum, and before that just the site of an old family home. She knows a bit about this landscape: often it's not possible to use it for much. There are expanses of empty fields, seemingly without purpose, and yet there is something *different* in the air here. Perhaps it's just the change from being in the city. She takes a breath and lets herself be guided into the room the others have entered. There are various sofas and armchairs, the décor clean but faded. On a chipped wooden sideboard there is an enormous, ornate brass gong, complete with a fluffy-headed mallet, hanging by a string.

'Javanese,' Smeaton murmurs. 'Got it on my travels. Beautiful, isn't it? We use it for guided meditations, and very occasionally if I need to summon everyone here fast. The sound reverberates quite remarkably, especially if you take the soft part off the mallet.'

Ali smiles, unsure of how to respond. It's a beautiful instrument. The singing she'd heard when they arrived was soothing and peaceful. Smeaton is nothing but friendly, so she has no idea why she feels so nervous. It was her idea, after all – as Jack reminded her in the car, several times. Yes, it *was* her idea. And it's a good one. At least it will be, once she comes to terms with it.

Jack seems miraculously unfazed by it all, despite being the one who protested ever since she'd set the plans in motion. She watches as he strolls confidently across the small sitting room to the sideboard on the other side, which contains an urn, cups and saucers and a plate piled high with chocolate-chip cookies. She watches as a young woman hands him a cup, and he smiles as she drops a teabag inside.

She has to ball her hands into fists to hold back her sudden pique of rage. How dare he be so calm about all this? After everything he's put them through? How fucking dare he? She's always been there for him, the dutiful wife, looking after him, doing everything for him, keeping him calm and happy, until ... She pushes the thought away. Refuses to think it.

Ali watches as the young woman moves away from him, takes a seat on one of the worn, overstuffed sofas. Jack doesn't follow. After pouring milk into his cup, he steps back to the far side of the room, blowing gently on the tea. His eyes flicker as he scans the space, the inhabitants, taking it all in.

She's about to get her own drink when Dunsmore appears at her side again. He has the uncanny knack of disappearing and reappearing without making a sound. He's one of those soft-footed, whispering types, who seem to almost float from place to place without anyone noticing where they have been or where they are going. He hands her a cup: something pale yellow with a hint of woodland dirt. Her nose wrinkles.

'Chamomile,' he says. 'Good for the nerves, I find. But if you'd prefer coffee?'

She takes a sip. 'This is fine. Thank you.'

They stand in silence for a moment, her sipping at her tea, him radiating heat beside her. Around the room, people are chattering, drinking and munching on cookies. At the back of the room, Jack is still watching the gathered crowd, and Ali is watching him – on whom his eyes fall, the cast of his face. If he has sensed her gaze on him, he doesn't show it.

Dunsmore claps his hands. He's standing next to the sofas now. Ali has barely registered that he has moved. 'OK,' he says. 'I think our new guests are suitably traumatised by our incredibly bizarre singing and tea drinking habits...' He pauses, allowing a tinkle of laughter to spread around the room. 'So to make things a bit easier on them, how about we all say a little bit about ourselves: where we've come from, what we're doing here...' He pauses again, glancing around the room. 'I know we're not all here, but I think this is a decent enough welcoming committee, no? Don't want to scare them off.' Another ripple of laughter. Dunsmore beams at Ali, then turns to face Jack. He lifts his hands out, palms upward. 'Come then, Ali and Jack, sit; make yourselves comfortable. Enjoy the show.'

The girl who handed Jack his cup stands up. 'I'm Fairy Angela,' she says.

Ali sucks in a breath and blinks slowly. When her eyes open, the young woman is grinning at her.

'You're shocked, and I'm not even wearing my wings.'

Everyone smiles.

Ali wants to run out of the room and jump into the car. Get away from this place and its cheerful hippy inhabitants. She looks across at Jack, but he doesn't look back at her. He's looking at Angela. Gazing at her. Ali's irritation dissipates into a flickering anxiety, as if someone is pricking her repeatedly with a pin.

'Sorry,' Ali says. 'I just wasn't expecting you to say that.'

Angela smiles wider. 'No, I'm sorry. I did it to provoke a reaction. It's not often I get a new audience. My name's Angela Fairley. My nickname started at school – you know, when they say your surname first ... anyway, it kind of stuck, and to be honest, I quite like it—'

'And she does have wings, actually,' says a voice from the corner of the room. A middle-aged man who looks like her old maths teacher: brown trousers, diamond-patterned jumper; wild hair like he's been standing in a force-ten gale.

'Well, yes,' Angela says. 'I do have wings ... but I only wear them on special occasions.'

Ali senses a swirl of energy from this odd young woman and she can't help but smile. Her earlier negative thoughts slide away as she realises that she likes the look of Angela. She can imagine what it might have been like for Angela at school. How she might have been treated. A girl like her often struggles. Pretty, but fragile. Naïve; too trusting. Too nice. All this from a few words? Ali thinks to herself. Well, yes. That's what it's all about – reading people, analysing people. Trying to work out the best way to deal with others while making sure to protect herself. It's what she's been doing since she was a child. It's what she's best at.

'I worked in a shop before I came here,' Angela continues. 'But I used to fantasise about being a pole dancer in one of those dark, smoky bars...' She smiles shyly and lets her sentence trail off. 'Here, I like to grow herbs and look after Alice and Agnes.' She pauses then releases a small girlish giggle, then her expression changes slightly. 'They're the eldest of our chickens. And, of course, I...' Her words drift off again. She looks down at the floor, and when she lifts her head again it's as if a cloud has drifted across her, distorting her features. She's travelled from flippant to fear in one glance. 'I'm sorry,' she says. Ali opens her mouth to speak, but Angela dismisses her with a small wave. 'I was supposed to be outside to meet you, but something came up.' She glances at Smeaton and he gives her a tiny shake of his head.

Ali feels a prickling under her skin.

Angela sits down and drops her hands into her lap.

Ali turns to Jack. His gaze is fixed on Angela.

Ali swallows down a lump in her throat. She doesn't like the way he's looking at her. Doesn't like it one little bit.

3

Angela

I fold my legs beneath me, and shuffle back into the depths of the sofa. I remove a cushion from behind my back and bring it around to hug against my chest. It smells mildly unfresh and I make a mental note to remove the cover and add it to the wash basket later. I look down at the floor, glad that my few moments in the spotlight are over. For now.

I can feel his gaze on me. I wonder what he makes of me. I should be unnerved by his stare, but I don't find it threatening. Curious, maybe, that's all. I lift my head just enough to see that the woman is staring at her husband with an expression that could be ... fear? No, not fear. Perhaps wariness. They have no need to be wary of me.

It's the house they need to worry about. What it was built on. The memories that lie here, hidden deep in the foundations...

I smile to myself and close my eyes. What has he done? I wonder. Why are they here? It's been a while since anyone new has moved to Rosalind House, and although I know the process, understand why Smeaton does it this way, it doesn't dispel my curiosity. *Patience, Angela*, I whisper to myself. All will be revealed soon enough.

Someone claps their hands and I am back in the room.

I recognise the sound. I can tell everyone in the room's individual claps, coughs and mutterings even with my eyes closed. We spend a lot of time with our eyes closed when we get together as a group. It's the best way to hone the other senses, Smeaton says. Sight is not the only way to learn what you need to about something. Not only can I recognise people by the sounds they make, I can identify them by their scents, too. Smeaton is wood smoke and something earthy, deep below.

The new woman is sharp sweat and faded rose. Her husband ... I take a breath, sucking warm air from the room. Her husband is something hot, metallic: burnished copper and smouldering ashes.

Something flutters deep in my chest. I smile, but keep my eyes closed.

Smeaton claps once more. 'Thank you, Angela,' he says. 'Now. Who's next?'

Someone clears their throat, a gentle gurgling sound accompanied by a waft of menthol in the air.

'My name is Richard Latham. I've been living here for seven years. I came here with my wife, Julie, after we lost our home in a flood. Everything we owned was ruined by the mud that filled the rooms of our riverside bungalow. We thought we'd lost it all, and our insurance was invalidated because we'd missed a couple of payments.' He pauses and I open my eyes. I glance across at Richard, who is squeezing Julie's hand. I catch a hint of rosemary and sage on the air, and then it disappears.

'It was clear that our families didn't want to put us up. Not for any length of time. Our children...' He pauses again and swallows. His Adam's apple bobs above his open-necked plaid shirt. 'Our children are more interested in material things ... We didn't want to burden them, so we came here. With nothing but our love for each other and our openness to experience this new way of life. We are very grateful to Smeaton for letting us stay. We look after the vegetable patches – managing ours and helping others to make their own patches thrive. Julie...' He pauses again, and Julie squeezes his hands and beams at him. 'Julie has become very attuned to the lives of the plants. She has a magic inside that she never knew she possessed, until this place opened our eyes and our minds.'

Julie dabs at her eyes with the sleeve of her cotton dress. 'We're grateful to be here,' she says. 'Here in the light.'

A series of murmurs spreads across the room.

'Embrace the light,' I say. Almost a whisper. I hold my hands up, steepling my fingers and pressing the tips together, and then let them spring apart, as if releasing an invisible balloon into the air. I look upwards. Blink. Everyone does the same, except for Ali and Jack, of course, who are standing side-by-side now, looking mildly alarmed.

Smeaton claps once more, then he laughs.

'Ali. Jack. I'm so sorry. This must all seem very strange to you. Our little rituals. I'm afraid that sometimes they just happen spontaneously, when people want to give thanks: to embrace their lives here and what we have achieved. Of course we'll run through all this later on. For now, the objective is for everyone to tell you a little about themselves.' He glances around the room. 'Thank you, Richard and Julie. Now ... perhaps, for the others, we could keep this a bit shorter. Just the basics. I'm sure our new guests are desperate to see their new home, have some quiet time to reflect before our welcoming ceremony later on...'

I look straight at Ali and see the terror flashing in her eyes. I smile, holding Ali's gaze until, eventually, she smiles back. I wonder if I might be able to confide in her, soon. About what I do here. About the cameras and the EMF meters. About all the tests I have to conduct on a regular basis, to make sure that we are all safe.

But more than that, I wonder if she might confide in me.

Dr Henry Baldock's Journal – 2nd March 1955

While initially pleased about the way the hospital has been run prior to me taking up my engagement here, it has becoming increasingly apparent that there are a few nagging concerns that cannot be dispelled. Although this is not an official document, and certainly not something that will be filed with my patient notes and findings, I feel compelled to record these concerns in some way, even if their only purpose is to convince myself that the issues are entirely in my own head. I am fully aware of the irony of this statement, as a psychiatrist within a mental hospital, but I am a strong believer in the power writing diaries and journals – they gather one's thoughts into some semblance of sense.

Many of the staff here have worked at the hospital for a number of years. Some were brought up in the grounds, the children of staff themselves – not just medical staff, but groundsmen and cooks and all matter of other things. Some of these fellows will have seen things move on a lot, and some might be resistant to so many changes – the advances in medicines, of course, but also the abandonment of certain practices that were used in the past but that no longer have a place here.

Mistrust among the staff of new medicines doesn't concern me. Persisting with the other treatments does, though. Seclusion and restraint are commonplace, here, but it's not even those that disturb me. It's the other interventions of which I've been made aware. Things that happen a lot more often than they should. Things that shouldn't happen at all. Things that aren't documented.

It is these things that trouble me most.

4
Ali

'You're probably wondering what I'm doing here, aren't you?'

Angela's voice is light, uplifting. She is obviously desperate for someone to talk to. But Ali can't muster the enthusiasm, not right now. She is walking alongside Angela, down a long dingy corridor. The lights flicker occasionally. The walls look like they were painted in the 1950s, with a shiny yellow paint, and not redecorated since. There is a slight smell of mould. But Ali is less concerned about the girl, than she is about herself, right now. What exactly are she and Jack doing here? Is it really going to help? She can hear Jack's footsteps close behind them, shuffling slightly. Reluctant. She knows he is tired and hopes she can convince Angela to leave them alone for a while. Of course she wants the whole tour at some point. There is much to be explored in the old hospital. She has to remind herself sometimes that *this* is why they are here, after all – to be part of this community. To be involved. She forces a smile into her voice.

'I'm more interested in you saying you wanted to be a stripper...'

Angela laughs, high-pitched and girlish. 'I wanted to be a glamour model, first—'

'What, like Jordan? Or those ones in the lads' mags?'

'Page three, actually. I first saw one of those photos when I went to the garage with my mum, to collect her car. The mechanic was reading it when we arrived. Left it lying on the table, wide open. Put his mug down on it and I could see that it was going to leave a brown ring across the girl's body, and I didn't want that so I lifted the mug off. Had a good look at the photo while the mechanic was talking to my mum, something about brake fluid and washers. I was fascinated by her smooth, pale skin. The perfect mounds of her breasts. She looked so ... serene, I thought—'

Ali snorts. 'You couldn't see the backdrop of exploitation behind her then, eh?'

Angela shakes her head. 'I'm not sure I agree with you, actually. If you've got a beautiful face and a beautiful body, why shouldn't you show it off?'

Ali feels a tightness in her chest, her vison distorts and she stops walking. An image swims in front of her: blurred edges; a heart-shaped face, baby-doll eyes; hair swirling around. Skin too pale, not smooth though. Although it would've been once. The mouth is like a raised scar. Ali blinks, and the image disappears. She clenches her fists, forcing it back into her subconscious.

Not. Real.

She sucks in a breath and carries on walking. 'I'm sorry,' Ali says, hoping that her voice sounds normal. 'I'm tired, so I'm a bit grouchy. Maybe we can have a bit of a lie-down before the welcoming party later. Do you think that would be OK?' She can still hear Jack behind them, although he hasn't said a word. His breathing is heavy. He's exhausted, too. Tiredness, that's all it is, plus a bit of dehydration. Those things can make your subconscious work overtime. She just needs to get a grip, have a rest. She probably imagined Jack staring at Angela earlier on, too. Surely he wouldn't be so blatant. Not so soon after they arrived?

Angela opens the door with a heavy brass key. It swings open. 'I've tried to make it nice for you,' she says. 'I'll come back and get you later, OK?'

'Thank you,' Ali says, genuinely grateful. She drops her bag on the floor and surveys the room. There's a large ironwork bed with layers of blankets; long sash windows with curtains made from what looks like stitched-together hessian sacks. There is a low bookcase, a dressing table with an old mirror and a battered-looking wicker chair. An old wooden wardrobe, and a hanging rail beside it. A door that leads off to what she hopes is a bathroom.

Jack follows her inside, pulls the door shut behind him. 'I'm just going to lie down for a minute,' he says, flopping onto the bed and kicking his shoes off. 'Then I'll unpack.'

She walks into the bathroom, taking in the beauty of the old claw-foot tub in the middle of the room. Perfect. Maybe it won't be so bad here after all, she thinks. As long as the water *is* hot. Ali turns on the taps and after a moment, water starts to creak and gurgle and judder through the pipes. She sits on the edge of the bath, watching it spurt out of the taps, foamy and brown. After a while, it settles and starts to flow, clear and hot now, steam billowing. She leans into the bath and drops the heavy metal plug in quickly, trying to avoid burning her hand. Smeaton wasn't lying then, about the water being hot and in plentiful supply. The bath, too, looks perfect. Wide and deep and just right for a good long soak. She stands and stretches, feeling her muscles popping in protest. How long has she been so tense, so coiled? This place will be good for them. She knows it. They just need a bit of time to adjust.

'Any idea where the toiletries are?' she calls out. 'I've got that jar of lavender bath salts that Mrs Edmonds from next door gave me. I'm sure she bought it in a charity shop. I thought it might be just the thing for here...' She leaves the bath running and closes the door to keep the warmth of the steam in the room. Jack is lying flat out on the bed, half of the blanket under him, the other half over the top, so he's folded in like a sandwich filling. She smiles to herself, gazing at the peaceful expression on his face, and marvels at the innocence of sleep. Do you dream about it, she wonders. Do you dream about *them*? Are your unconscious thoughts as dark as your heart? Her expression hardens. *Forget it, Ali*. She tries to tell herself. They can move on from this. If they allow themselves.

She picks up the leather hold-all that lies at the foot of the bed, and the contents half spill on the floor: shampoo, soap, flannels. Razors. She rummages quietly, glancing up as Jack snorts and rolls over in his sleep. She finds the jar of purple crystals and goes back into the bathroom.

The bath is half filled now. She dips a hand in and checks the temperature. Then turns off the cold tap, leaving the hot running as she unscrews the lid of the jar and tosses in a handful of the scented salts.

Lavender steam fills the air, and she breathes it in deeply as she takes off her clothes.

She turns off the hot tap and gently climbs into the bath. She leans back, letting herself sink down into the soothing depths. The room is filled with steam. No ventilation, no fan. But she likes it. Feels safe, cocooned in the warmth.

She sinks further, her hair swirling around her. Then further still, submerging her face under the water. Bubbles escape from her nose, and she opens her eyes, watching them disappear on the surface.

Peace. This is peace. She closes her eyes.

The cold hits her first. And then the hands. Strong hands, pressing down on her body. The ice-cold water is in her shocked mouth. *No*, she tries to scream. She thrashes, struggles, arms and legs flying. The cold. It's so cold. She can't catch her breath. Terror grips her, like rough hands on her soft skin. Pinning her down. Gripping her. Drowning her. Her eyes fly open.

And then it stops.

There is no one there.

She sits bolt upright, hands gripping the sides of the bath. Her heart hammers. Her lungs burn. She coughs, tasting the lavender in her chest.

'Jack,' she tries. But her voice is a croak. *'Jack...'*

With shaking hands, she pulls herself up and manages to climb out of the bath, grabbing a towel from the rail nearby. She is shivering. She wraps the towel around herself but she can't warm up. The water ... She dips a finger into the bath, and finds the water is still hot. Confused, she opens the bathroom door, and sees that Jack is still lying on the bed. Still sleeping. Oblivious.

It wasn't real.

She climbs onto the bed beside him, pulling the cover off him and over herself. She doesn't want to touch him; she's not ready for that yet. But has no choice. She can't stop shivering, and she needs his body heat.

With a grunt, he shuffles himself under the covers, turns over and hugs her close. She lies there on her back, staring up at the ceiling, not hugging him back. Not daring to move. Trying to breathe in and out – long slow breaths. After a few moments, she turns towards the bathroom door. In her haste to leave, she'd left it open just a crack, and she imagines she can see something moving in the room beyond.

Shadows, Ali. Just shadows.

'Jack … are you asleep?' She knows he is, but she yearns to hear his voice. She needs to know that everything is going to be OK. 'Jack?' she says again, turning her head back to face him. 'Something happened in the…'

Her words catch in her throat. Jack's eyes are wide open, staring straight ahead – straight to the bathroom door.

'Jack … Oh my God. What is it?'

She turns over again, pulling herself away from him. But there is nothing there. No one is in the bathroom. She imagined it. Didn't she?

She turns back. 'Jack?' she tries once more.

His eyes are closed again now, his chest rising and falling. He is in a deep sleep. His eyes can't have been open at all. Just something else that she's imagined.

She slides closer to him, and his arm flops over her like a dead weight. She's warm now, but there's no chance of sleep.

She stares up at the ceiling.

There is a creak of a floorboard up above, and she wonders who is there; whose room is directly above. She reminds herself why it is that they are here. She knows it's all going to work out. It has to. But that doesn't stop her wishing that she could go back to her old life, even just for a moment. She didn't even tell some people that they were leaving. But she knows that it will never be possible. They are here now. She tries to relax, to imagine that maybe things will be OK. Keeps trying to convince herself that nothing happened in the bath, that no one pushed her down, that the water didn't turn cold and then hot again. Tries to convince herself that she imagined it. That she is overtired – which is hardly surprising considering everything that's gone on. Everything that's gone on with Jack. She lies there, wrapped in his arms, feeling alternately trapped and scared, then hopeful and safe. Wild thoughts buzz around her like a manic fly, until finally she falls asleep.

5

Angela

I don't really know what to think of the newcomers. Not yet. I tried to be engaging, interesting … maybe a little controversial, with my talk of stripping and dancing. But I didn't get through to her, not really. Not yet. As for him? Not a word. He looked a bit worn-out, though, so maybe it was just that. Maybe I'm expecting too much. They've only just arrived. I listen at their door for a few minutes but I don't hear anything particularly interesting. I'm curious about them. I can't get a any sense of them. They seem confused, conflicted. I wonder if they'll settle in this room. If they'll settle here at all. I hear the creak of the bedsprings as one of them lies down; the screech of the taps as someone runs a bath. I catch a faint whiff of lavender, and then I walk away.

I'm still in the middle of setting things up. I had hoped for longer in their room, but Rose had insisted on helping me clean, even though I wanted to do it myself. I wasn't able to put any of my equipment in there, which is a shame, but not the end of the world. I might get another chance, once they're settled and not hiding out in their room, but for now I'll have to make do with the room above.

I've been through all of the rooms with a fine-tooth comb, so I know the best places to put things, and I know which floorboards to avoid. The room above Ali and Jack's is empty, except for a filing cabinet containing empty cardboard binders. There are lots of gaps between the swinging files, presumably because the authorities took the case notes away with them and put them in a proper place. But they didn't take everything away. There's all sorts of medical equipment lying abandoned around the building, but Smeaton has made it clear that we're not to go near it. He and a few of the others cleared quite a bit of it away when they first arrived, put it into one or two rooms, out of the way. The doors are locked, but I have been in there, once or twice. I've seen hard examination beds with straps and shackles attached, clunky electrical equipment swirling with wires. It reminds me of those medieval instruments of torture that I have read about in books, and makes me wonder what went on in this place. I shudder to think.

But this room is one of the saddest in the main block. Empty, dusty. The window dirty and smeared and only letting in a dull yellowing light. No lightbulb in the fitting, but that's fine because I've got my torch, plus a load of candles in jars, just in case. I want to get this done before the last of the daylight goes because, despite everything I am trying to do, I really don't like being in this part of the building when it's dark outside. There's a strange, heavy feeling in the atmosphere here. It presses on my chest, pushes bubbles of panic into my throat. Besides, it won't take long.

Stepping as lightly as I can, I creep across to the far side of the room, where the chink of light from below escapes upwards, though the gap in the floorboards. I've already prepared the camera, attached it to a longer cable than usual, and I have the other end joined to the heavy battery pack.

I can hear her down there. Her voice is full of fear. She is telling Jack about the bath. That something happened to her in there. Interesting, I think. I might have to try and get in there for a look. See if there is something I've missed. I've long suspected that the bathroom is the source of the strange activity in that room.

I slide the tiny camera through the gap and switch it on. I wish I could watch it in real time, but the wireless link never seems to work properly. I need better equipment, but I work with what I've got. There's only so often I can collect things from the village without arousing suspicion. Smeaton has warned me before – told me what I can and can't use. So I have to be careful with the cameras. But they're the only sure-fire way for me to prove anything. Just because I haven't seen anything yet, doesn't mean I won't. I just need to find the right place, and hope that, eventually, something will trigger some activity.

This hospital is definitely haunted. The villagers have told me the stories – about what it was before, long before … about what happened here with the witches. The old house where they kept them before trial might be gone, but we're right on top of the land on which it stood, and that land is tainted. And I've found things too. The room below this is the one I'm most sure about. I can sense it. I'm so close. I just need to keep trying, and one day I'll find proof.

I switch on the EMF meter. The lights usually flicker when I use it in their room, but today they are a steady green. I wait, trying not to breathe too loudly, in case they hear me.

Ali is still talking to Jack. 'Are you sure you didn't come into the bathroom when I was in the bath? I'm sure I felt hands on me…'

'You imagined it,' he says.

The lights on the meter stay at green. Nothing is happening. No electromagnetic disturbances. Things are quiet, until another creak of the bedsprings. Either one of them is up now, or they are both lying down. Judging by the silence, I think the latter. If only I could see them … I lean into the corner, try to peer down through the hole, but it is too close to the wall and I can't squeeze my head into the space to get the right angle. I know what I need to do. I realise how important it is now: I need to go into the village and get a new wireless transmitter for the camera; hopefully that will be enough to boost the signal back to my device. It was never a huge issue before, when I was placing cameras in more public places – but I realise now, I want to be able to watch this room in real time. Ali is scared of something. Something or someone.

I need to know what it is.

6

Ali

'What are you doing?' Jack's voice is groggy with sleep. He pushes himself up on one elbow, watching her as she pulls on leggings and a long jumper, and shoves her feet into her long boots.

'I'm not sitting around in here until they call us. I want to have a look around.'

He sighs, rubs his face. 'Maybe we should wait here. I'm still pretty tired ... Why don't you get back in beside me. A proper cuddle might do us good. What's the rush? We could just stay in here for a bit longer and—'

'You can do what you like,' Ali says. She stands up and looks at herself in the mirror. It's slightly bevelled and her face seems to shimmer in and out of focus. She pulls her hair up into a ponytail and tilts the mirror down so she can't see her face anymore.

'What were you going on about when you got in to bed? Something about the bath...'

'Forget it,' she says. 'I wasn't making any sense. I was worn out, that's all.'

She takes her make-up bag from the holdall on the floor and lays it on the dressing table. She thinks about putting on some eyeliner and mascara, maybe some lipstick, but decides against it. Maybe later – for this party thing. She'll make more of an effort then.

The dressing table has a long, narrow drawer with a small porcelain knob. She pulls it open and finds a folder inside.

The Book of Light.

She flicks through the pages. There's an introduction – 'The Essence of Us', then a page with a list of things under the heading 'Guidance for a Bright Existence'.

Ali sighs. 'Well, I suppose there had to be something like this,' she mutters.

'What?' Jack says, muffled. She glances across and sees that he has disappeared under the blankets.

'I found the Twelve Steps.' She tosses the folder onto the bed and it lands in the approximate place where she assumes his head to be. 'Give yourself something to do while I'm out. See if you can connect to the higher power. Work out what exactly it is we've let ourselves in for.' She shakes her head, but she's smiling.

Jack pokes his face out of the covers. 'Your idea,' he says.

She's about to let the door bang, but decides it would be better to close it quietly, just in case someone is listening. Paranoid, maybe, but despite the niceties, she has the feeling they don't want her wandering off on her own. Not until she knows the rules.

She locks the door with the giant key, locking Jack inside. She definitely doesn't want him roaming around on his own. Not now, and probably not ever. She's never going to be able to relax, and wonders again if the sacrifice is worth it. She's spent so much time with Jack these last few months. She could do with a bit of time to herself, but it's hard to switch off when she's spent so much time being switched on. Looking after her patients. Looking after Jack. And for what? This life? Is it ever going to be enough?

They'll find out soon enough.

She glances left and right along the dimly lit corridor. She knows where they came from – the entrance, the main stairwell. She decides to go along the corridor in the opposite direction. See what there is to see that way. From what she knows already, there are eleven people living here, including themselves, which isn't a lot for the size of the place. She did plenty of research on the building before they agreed to come, spending hours on the internet, scrolling through websites, being taken from one thing to the next: the history of the hospital; pictures from when it was abandoned on one of those urban explorers' sites – those people who sneak into disused properties and snoop around. It's an illegal and dangerous activity, one that, she discovered, was going on long before people got the ability to share photos of their finds on social media. Quite fascinating though, she imagines. She read a book about people who did it, a crime novel written by a Scottish author, where a body was found in an old tunnel. It'd been the first time she'd heard the term 'urbexing' and she'd been vaguely interested in it since. Smeaton moved here in 1995, and prior to that the people who'd managed to find their way into this place had reported rooms left abandoned, still filled with medical equipment and files and all sorts – their posts were full of glee, at finally having places to share their information with fellow enthusiasts. Where is all of that equipment now? Presumably someone eventually came and took it all away. She'd love to come across some old paperwork, something more to read about the place. There're bound to be some interesting cases – the kind of things she used to spend her time researching. She's supposed to be leaving that all behind, but she can't quite let go of her curiosity just yet. She must visit the library. Smeaton sent her a photograph of it when she first emailed him, reassuring her that she would never run out of things to read.

She'd read up on the history of the commune, too. Decided that as far as communes went, it wasn't too hippy-ish and extreme. Hence the rules. Although seeing the list like that had given her a shudder. Made her think of cults and brainwashing and crazy ideologies. But this place was meant to be different.

She has a flashback to the welcome meeting, when she'd been half dazed, not really thinking about it all, not really taking it in when they had talked in the small sitting room about finding the light.

The light.

What did they even mean by that?

Ali walks slowly down the corridor. There are only two other doors, one on either side. Unlike her room, which has a solid door with panels, these ones have a boarded rectangular space where she assumes there was once a pane of glass. Could they have been wards? It would explain why there are only two doors, and lots of wall space. Wall space that is peppered with holes where various noticeboards must have been placed. One still remains, the cork dried and crumbling at the edges. She hesitates outside the door on her left, the one on the same side as her bedroom. She has no idea what might be in there, whether it is someone's room or not. Should she open it, have a look inside? Knock? Just in case someone is in there. She presses an ear to the door and holds her breath. She tries to listen for any sounds. Nothing. Maybe she should leave it; wait to be shown around properly. For all she knows, it might even be dangerous in there. Unsafe. She has no idea how much of the building is habitable. Don't these old places have asbestos walls? She hears a faint noise. Scratching. She pulls away from the door, fast, as if she's been burned. Is someone in there? She takes a deep breath and tries to control the panic in her chest. She turns back towards her room.

Leave it. Just go and get ready for the welcome party.

But still she stares at the door, as if expecting it to open – for someone to come out, startled by her presence. Both of them laughing at the fright they've given each other. She swallows and walks back along the corridor towards her room. The lights flicker, briefly, as they did earlier, when she was with Angela and Jack.

As she's taking her key out of her pocket, she hears that sound again.

Scratching.

She whips around, but there is no one there. Nothing. She closes her eyes. Opens them again. Glances back along the corridor once more ... And what is that? She squints in the dim light. The floor. Something is on the floor.

Footprints. Small. Wet.

Leading away from her room, down the corridor.

Disappearing in front of her eyes.

7

Angela

Assuming they are both having a sleep, I decide to leave them to it and not make any noise that might alert them to my presence above. Back in my own room, I rummage in my bedside drawer for the mobile phone and the charger, and plug it in. I have to wait a few moments for it to charge enough to be able to use it, even when plugged in. It's an old phone. Pay-as-you-go sim card on the only network that gets a decent signal around here. Mobile phones are certainly 'not advised' but they aren't outright banned. No one uses them much though. Even if I didn't keep mine hidden away for the occasional times I need to use it, even if I left it out, carried it around for all to see, what would I do with it? It doesn't connect to the internet. And I have no one to call or text.

Well, that's not quite true.

I have Mary, at the local shop in the village, who sells everything that most people need, and orders in anything that people ask her to. She lets me use the internet in the back of the shop, too – and sometimes her son, Chris, helps me find what I need. Smeaton has made it clear that the internet is definitely something that we don't need at Rosalind House, but he doesn't expressly forbid anyone using it elsewhere. Now and again. Given that I don't have a car and it's almost five miles to the shop, I don't visit the village very often, unless I can persuade someone to give me a lift. And when I do it feels like the biggest adventure. Sometimes I do miss living in the village, but I wanted to come to Rosalind House, and here I am.

It's a far cry from my old life. I grew up in one of the third-wave new towns, full of London overspill and roundabouts. I'd like to say I had a happy childhood, but it was forgettable from the start. I knew I didn't belong there. I spent my time daydreaming and trying to avoid the bullies who could smell my indifference and were intent on destroying it. They started off wanting to make me like them, then they moved on to attempting to make me miserable. Neither plan worked. I drifted through my school days quite at ease with myself, knowing that it was all temporary and that as soon as I could, I would be gone.

I was fascinated by the paranormal, folklore, the seventeenth-century witch trials. I read all about Cromwell's witchfinders, and Harry Price's search for ghosts and I knew that I had found my calling. I trained myself to read tarot, dabbled with Ouija boards, kept hoping that if I cast enough spells I would find a link to the other side. I was desperate to become a medium, but it was pretty obvious that I didn't possess a channel. I was never going to become a link to the undead. So I went back to Price and his followers, read up on parapsychology and decided to make it my life's work to prove the existence of ghosts.

My parents accepted this, having long given up trying to find another path for me. I used to joke with them that I'd become a stripper. That's where that comment to Ali had stemmed from. To be honest, I think they'd have seen that as a more viable way to live my life. They died before I had a chance to prove anything. Head-on collision with a fallen tree, on a dark and winding road. I was in the back seat, and aside from whiplash, I was completely unhurt. The police were stunned. The doctors said it was a miracle. It hadn't felt like that, as I'd sat there in the car, the radio still playing an old fifties song that my dad loved, and the hiss of the engine escaping from the crumpled bonnet. I wanted to help them but I was trapped – both by the jammed seatbelt and by something in my mind that just couldn't compute what was happening. I waited there until I saw the blue lights of the approaching ambulance, and then I started to scream. I screamed for them and I screamed for me – because I couldn't see their souls as they passed, and so what hope was there that I could prove anything at all?

I could've given up then. If I had no link to my own parents while watching them die, then what chance was there that I'd find a link to another passed soul? But I was convinced it had to be possible. There couldn't just be nothing. I needed to find evidence. I carried on trying to hone a craft that quite possibly didn't exist, but I was determined. I wasn't going to give up. I'd cheated death that day and there had to be a reason for that.

But then I saw something on TV, about the villages on the fens. About some uproar over an old hospital that should've been condemned, but was now housing a community of off-grid spiritualists. That's when I knew I wasn't alone.

I wasn't able to move there straightaway. They were asking people to go through some convoluted process, spending time on a daily basis, getting to know their ways. So I took a shop job in a nearby village, which happened to come with a room. Just temporary, the owner said, while her son was working away for a while. Mary became a surrogate mother, and the villagers became my family.

They didn't want me to move to Rosalind House; Mary and the other villagers tried to sabotage my attempts more than once. They told me that bad things had happened here, that the place had a tragic past. But none of them knew the true reason why I wanted to live here. It wasn't just the alternative-community lifestyle, although that, of course, appealed. It was because I had done plenty of research of my own. I already knew about the hospital's past, and more importantly what happened before that ... a long time before, when superstition and fear ruled the land. I knew that the old hospital was said to be haunted.

And that is exactly why I am here.

8
Ali

'So, Ali. Jack. How are you finding things so far? Probably a bit strange I imagine...'

Smeaton leans back into his high-backed leather chair. Ali and Jack sit opposite him on the other side of his desk, which looks as if it's been made from an old door. Interesting, Ali thinks. She doesn't know why but she had expected something a little more *grand*. She has no idea *why* she thinks that because this is not the kind of place that *is* grand. Was it ever? She's still confused in her head about the building; from the outside it looks like a country mansion – its crumbling brickwork bound together by ivy. But on the inside it is very much an old hospital. She'd noticed the engraved brass map on the wall when they came in, a layout of the whole hospital and grounds. She hoped they'd get a tour soon, so she could get her bearings.

Jack has said practically nothing since they left the room. He wasn't particularly interested in her story about what happened in the bathroom, making her think that she was overtired and imagined it. He was probably right. She thinks about bringing it up now to Smeaton, just to find out if anything similar has happened before. Strange occurrences might only be strange if you're a newcomer. Strange occurrences like dreaming that you're being drowned in the bath. Rationally she knows that it didn't happen.

'Well, you are right about it being strange,' she says. 'I've spent most of my adult working life in hospitals, but this place doesn't feel like one. I know it's not been used as one for a long time, but I thought that there would still be the sense of ward life, the patients. I'm probably being silly. As well as that, it's messing with my head that from the outside it looks like an old country house, the kind of place that I could only dream about going to as a kid with my parents, for a walk around the gardens and a cream tea.'

Smeaton nods and smiles. 'I know exactly what you mean, Ali. When I first heard about this place, I had the same feelings as you. I actually wondered if there might be a way that I could raise enough money to turn it into the kind of place you remember. From what I've learned of the history of the area, there *was* once a grand mansion here. But it burned down, and the land was nothing but brown fields for years. Then it was rebuilt as an asylum.' He laughs and shakes his head, but his eyes don't meet hers. 'I don't know all the details. The villagers, when you meet them, they'll be overeager to tell you many stories about this place. Don't listen to everything they say. They seem to exist on myths and legends...'

Ali twitches; she hasn't voiced any of her concerns, but it's as if Smeaton is reading her mind. He seems a little cagey too – suggesting he doesn't know all the details when maybe he does. *Stop it Ali*, she mentally chides herself, *you're letting your imagination run away with itself.*

Smeaton continues, oblivious to her distress. 'You might not know what these places are like, coming from London, but where I'm from, up in the north of Scotland, things can feel very different – it's the sheer isolated nature of existence there. So I can fully understand why these places are like they are. Unfortunately, there are no full records for the building and the details of what was here. That is unusual in itself, but from what I've been told there was a fire at some point. I believe the records room was damaged. Some of the wards too. One of the patients—'

Jack speaks at last. His voice is groggy, tired. 'I don't think we need to hear about that Smeaton, if you don't mind. We came here to get away from the bleak realities of the modern world, the nightmare job that I had to deal with, all the stresses that I brought home.' He glances across at Ali and she looks away. He continues: 'We just need a simple life here. Doing manual things maybe. Things that I didn't used to do in my old job, in my old life.'

'Of course! Please accept my apologies. This is a peaceful place and people are happy here. I just get a little carried away sometimes, when I start talking about its history,' Smeaton says. 'And you know, if you ever want to talk ... You don't need to tell me anything right now. You don't need to tell me anything ever. But if you want to, I'm here. Others are, too.' He looks at each of them in turn, trying to be inclusive, drawing them both into his gaze. 'I imagine you've seen the book in your dressing table by now: *The Book of Light*?'

Ali feels a brief flutter of irritation. *Yes*, she thinks. *I've seen your book. This is the deal, Ali, you're going to have to grin and bear it.* She gives him a small smile of encouragement, and he carries on.

'As I explained to you before, I am not a religious man. This is not a religious commune. But over my years I have opened up a path of spirituality that I would like to share. The beliefs are fundamental, particularly the belief that we should all live in happiness and in light. That may sound idealistic, especially to two people with the jobs that you had, living in a city like you did, experiencing the life that you have. Of course the opposing element to light is the dark. I don't really want to say that I believe in evil, but I think that that is the fundamental nature of what I'm saying. Ali – you mentioned to me before that you're interested in psychology? Or was it psychiatry? That perhaps if you stayed working as a nurse, you may have moved into this area?'

Ali nods. 'I've been interested in psychology *and* psychiatry for a long time, actually. I started a professional development course, with the plan to take my studies further, perhaps retrain as a psychotherapist. I'm fascinated by the human mind and what it can do. I'm fascinated by certain aspects of group behaviour, you know – such as herd mentality. I'm interested in things such as coercion, the impact of controlling behaviours. Your thoughts about evil – I'm not sure I fully agree with you. I do think that we are all capable of being bad. I think we all have a shadow side. What interests me is what makes that side reveal itself. What prompts people to do the things they do, when they do the most awful things?'

She feels Jack's gaze boring into her cheek but she refuses to turn and look at him. The energy, the heat coming from him, is a physical thing. *Please Jack*, she thinks, *please don't say anything. Not now.* She takes a breath. She has got carried away, that's all. This place has an extraordinary history and it already seems to be feeding her mind. Stimulating her too much. She needs to calm down – after all, they have come here to remove stress from their lives. Make a new start.

'Well,' Smeaton says. 'This has all become a bit serious, hasn't it?' He laughs. 'You have a fascinating personality, Ali. I knew it the first time we spoke. I hope we get to spend plenty of time chatting about your ideas and your beliefs, and I hope that you will give me a chance to talk about mine. But for now, we will celebrate your arrival. I would like you to meet with the others. Have some drinks, have some food...'

'A party?' Jack says. 'That sounds good.'

Ali glares at him, but Smeaton doesn't seem to notice.

'Wonderful,' Smeaton says, clapping his hands, grinning at them both. 'Oh...' he continues, his face becoming serious once more. 'There was one thing I wanted to mention: people sometimes report having very vivid dreams when they first arrive. I think it's because of the absolute blackness when night falls, and the process of fully unwinding your mind when you are used to much more stimulation. The subconscious takes over for a while ... does that make sense?'

'Absolutely,' Ali says. Relieved. She did dream it, then. The bath. As for the footprints in the corridor – a trick of the light. The flickering bulbs and the dinginess would account for that. She forces herself to smile. 'So, this party. Is there anything you need us to do?'

'Not this time. This time you two are the guests of honour. The others have been working tirelessly to make this party special for you, and all they want from you is a chance to get to know you just a little – not too much. Maybe mention what you might be interested in doing here, and the right people will find you. For example, Jack – you mentioned doing manual things. One of our longest-serving Family members, Ford, has become a skilled craftsman since he came here. I think you'd be very interested to meet him. Ali – I'm not sure what you would like to get from this place, but I do think that starting out with the vegetable gardens and the kitchen, as much as it seems like it's hard work, is a good way to get a feeling for the day-to-day running of the place. Plus, I just know that you will love Fergus, our chef.'

Smeaton stands, raises his hands palms upward. They both stand. Ali feels as if they've been summoned to something that she doesn't fully understand. But she doesn't completely dislike it.

'Come then,' Smeaton says. 'Let's go to this party.'

Dr Henry Baldock's Journal – 30th March 1955

Today I spent several hours with the schizophrenic patients, observing their status. For some time it has been common practice to place the most severe of these patients into an insulin coma for days, sometimes weeks. I have, of course, observed this treatment before, in my last hospital, but after seeing mixed results I have become wary of this method. The specialist unit here seems to be well managed, and I was able to chat to some of the more lucid patients today. They seemed in good spirits, and were pleased with the care they were receiving. The nurses are instructed to keep the patients occupied on their days off from the injections, and today they were collecting wild flowers in the grounds, then sitting together to press them. They seemed docile, for the most part, apart from one: Joe Gleeson. I later discovered that he has only been receiving this treatment for a short while and is perhaps yet to see the benefits. He told me some unsettling stories, before Nurse Claymore calmed him down and gave him an extra dose of his usual sedative.

The most extreme patients receive ECT as well as insulin shock therapy and the two must be finely balanced in order to keep the patient functioning reasonably. Gleeson tried to grab hold of me as I left the room, muttering again about curious things; I could not discern whether they were truth or the product of his confused mind. I don't think he knew either. This is the challenge we face with patients with this condition. I am keen to learn more, and plan to attend a conference in Cambridge, on new methods to treat this disease. The problem is that I don't quite know what to make of Joe's tales. If I link them with some of the other things I have heard about in here, though, they do make some sort of sense. As a rational man, however, I have to believe that the things he has seen are a result of hallucinations, both visual and aural. This is not uncommon, but I feel as if I must convince myself. Perhaps I need some fresh air. Some time in the gardens to reflect. As I heard the nurses trying to soothe Joe after another of his outbursts – the things he claims to have seen and heard in the corridors – I had to remind myself that there are no such things as ghosts.

9
Angela

Of course I got into trouble with Fergus for being late. I was due back in the kitchen at three; he said we had a lot to do to prepare for the party. The party that is about to start. I know that Ali and Jack had a meeting with Smeaton this afternoon, but other than that it seems that since we met this morning, they have spent most of the time in their room. Now they are here, looking tired and anxious, not knowing what to expect from our gathering. It's quite a different type of party from what they're probably used to, with this hotchpotch of different people, some more eccentric than others. Those being my favourites, of course.

I know that Fergus isn't happy that things haven't been done on time. He is a very organised person, and he has rebuilt his life here. He doesn't need people like me messing things up for him. Not when he's put in such a lot of effort.

He is still constructing some sort of canapés: what I think are miniature oatcakes with some kind of hummus topping, and berries piled on top of that. Blueberries, this time. I think that is his favourite berry. I think he would make us live on blueberries if he could. Blueberries and mooli – the strange white radish that he loves so much. I walk across to him and throw my arms around his waist, gripping him from behind, hugging him. 'Please forgive me, Fergus. I was on an important mission. You know I'd never let you down.'

His body shakes gently under my arms and I know he is laughing, although he makes no sound. 'You know I always forgive you, my little fairy Angela. But today I am tired, and today I have very special guests. Today I feel like I have to impress people.'

'You always impress people, Fergus. Everyone is stunned by what you do with the foods that we get from the garden, the recipes that you come up with. We all love you. The new people will love you too. But I don't think that they are special. They are just like us. We are all here for the same reason, aren't we?'

'You know I don't think that's true, Angela. I think there *is* something different about these people. It's why Smeaton has brought them here.'

'You're sounding almost as paranoid as me, Fergus.' I laugh uneasily. Fergus does like to indulge me. I hadn't realised that he was worried about the new people too. I wonder if any of the others are. Smeaton didn't really explain things very well, but we know that money was involved, and we also know that this never happens. 'Fergus, do you think you can ask Smeaton about this? I don't think I can ... We both know he thinks I'm a silly little girl.'

'Angela, you are twenty-eight. You are far from a little girl. And far from silly. Although, you do like to come up with a lot of nonsense. Now, help me put these on plates. Although I am not sure we have any plates left, so we may have to be inventive.'

'How about we cover one of those plastic trays with foil, and then I spread lots of berries around the edges and in between, it *will* look pretty.'

'Well done, darling, thank you.' Fergus turns around and I let go. He takes both of my hands squeezes them. I close my eyes. And feel the release. 'Embrace the light.' We both say it at the same time. We synchronise so easily.

Rose bustles into the kitchen, her face red. She has a tea towel over one shoulder. 'Is there anything else to go out, Fergus?' she says. 'Everyone is here now.' Rose smiles at me, but the smile doesn't quite reach her eyes. I know she thinks I'm a fool – doesn't buy any of my theories about the afterlife. One day I'll show her that she's wrong.

'Let me take out the last tray; the *special* tray.' I wink at Fergus. 'Rose, why don't you go and get ready, join the party?' I beam at her, and she has no choice but to smile back, more genuinely this time.

She takes off her little hat and her apron, and throws them into a bucket in the corner of the kitchen. Then she goes through to the store cupboard, and I hear the sounds of her pulling her hair out of its elastic, brushing it down. I pull one of the plastic trays out from under the central table and pick up a roll of foil. I cover the tray, fold over the edges, then I start to arrange Fergus's hummus and blueberry oatcakes.

The doors open into the dining room, and I can hear chatter. Excited chatter. Glasses clinking. I wonder if Smeaton will be bringing out any of his elderberry wine tonight; I imagine this is the kind of night for it. Although we have these parties fairly regularly, we don't have wine very often.

Some people here can't handle their drink very well.

IIIII

Cyril and Ford are playing old folk songs on guitars, Cyril's voice echoing off the walls: the room is too large for our small group. Julie is hitting a tambourine on her knees at random intervals, grinning when she catches anyone's eye. Rose is standing in the corner, arms folded, but the smallest of smiles on her face. Fergus is popping his blueberry oatcake creations into his mouth one after the other, with barely time to chew, like a puppy catching treats.

Ali is sitting in the corner next to Smeaton, who is beaming with pride, and a happiness that is infectious. He's managed to convince everyone to come to the party – even Lucy, who is the least sociable of everyone here, tending to spend most of her time cleaning the corridors and reading books in her room. She was the newest member of Our Family, until me, a few months after her ... and after that came Annie and Lawrence. The shortest-serving members to date.

But I don't want to think about them now, their brooding darkness and their unkind ways. I want to focus my energies on the light and the goodness and the happy place that we are in tonight.

'Not bad, this stuff.' Jack has managed to somehow sidle up to me without my noticing, I was so engrossed with taking in the room. He's holding a wine glass, and he's grinning. He blinks a couple of times and sways gently. I hold up my own glass, tipping it towards him.

'I tend to stick to the cordial. Lemon and cucumber, this one. Maybe you should have some? I think that batch of wine has been fermenting longer than usual. We haven't had a party in a while.'

'I can handle myself, love. You need to lighten up a bit.'

He sneers at me, and he laughs and I don't like the way it sounds. I don't like the look in his eyes. I don't like being around drunk people, and I'm not entirely surprised that it's him rather than her who would be the one to show their true colours so soon. Does he think I didn't notice him staring at me earlier? Does he think I haven't already noticed Ali's skittishness, the way she keeps glancing at him as if waiting for him to do something wrong? I could be way off the mark, but if their reason for coming here isn't something to do with him drinking and womanising, I'll be surprised. *Womanising*. What does that even mean? He's a drunken lech, that's all. I give him a small smile, and I walk away, catching Ali's eye as I pass her and head for the food.

'Are you alright, darling?' Fergus is still shovelling in his canapes. He offers me a plate. 'You need to eat more. I keep telling you. One day you will fall through a crack in the concrete and we'll never see you again.' He laughs his big booming laugh and I jam two oatcakes into my mouth at once, just to shut him up.

He's still laughing when I realise my mistake. The oatcakes are too heavy and dry, the topping making them thick and sticky. I can't chew them like this. My mouth seems to be glued together, and I take a breath, making another mistake. Something lodges in my throat. A blueberry? Or some of the mushed-up oats and hummus? I can't tell and I don't care, because I realise very quickly that I am struggling to breathe.

My hand flies to my throat. I cough and spray out food in front of me, and I panic. I am panicking. And there is still something in my throat. The air around me grows warmer, thicker. My face burns, my throat contracts. I fall to my knees and the music stops, and I can hear Fergus's voice, coming from far away, muffled and distorted as if he is calling my name from under water ... and then there are hands around my waist, small hands, a woman's hands – and then a pressure on my chest, the pain barely noticeable as my head swims and swirls and my vision darkens...

And then a rush of air, and I am pulled back to my feet – and I can breathe once more, although my throat feels ragged and my head thumps as if I have been punched hard.

'Angela ... talk to me Angela.' The voice is full of concern. 'Step back from her. Give her some air. Can someone get a glass of water, please?'

Ali. It is Ali who has saved me. She is sitting beside me on a chair, holding my hands in hers. I don't know how I got on this chair. I remember almost falling to the floor, and then I could breathe again, and now I am here. I am alive.

'I'm OK now. Thank you,' I say, my voice barely a croak.

Everyone swirls and gathers around me, congratulating Ali, making sure I am OK. Fergus is upset. He panicked too, and didn't act quickly enough. Thank goodness for Ali, people say.

I just want to go to bed now, a heavy tiredness has landed on me like a blanket.

'Quite the fucking heroine, aren't you my dear?' Jack's face is puce. He is swaying more obviously now, the wine having a much greater effect since I first noticed.

'Jack...' Ali's voice is low, a warning.

'Don't fucking Jack, me,' Jack says. And he throws his glass at the wall.

Pale liquid runs down and disappears into the gap where the skirtings should be.

Silence.

I take a breath, and it hurts.

Jack's breathing is loud in the still air. Ali squeezes my hands then lets go, stands up and faces her husband. Her back is straight, her head held high. She looks defiant, and I can tell she has dealt with this before.

'We should go to bed,' she says. 'We've had a long day.' She lays a hand on Jack's arm, and he throws it off.

'Don't touch me,' he spits.

'Jack...' she says again.

'Everything OK here?' Ford has been observing for a while and has clearly decided he needs to intervene.

'Just that wine, I think ... and we're so tired,' Ali says. Making excuses for him.

I feel sorry for her. Everyone feels sorry for her. Jack and Ford stare at each other, and then something changes. Jack's face crumples, and he seems to deflate. He looks around, as if unsure of where he is, and of what he's done.

'Ali?' he says, his voice is slurred but the confusion is unmistakeable.

Ali takes him by the elbow and this time he doesn't object. We all watch as she guides him out of the room, and I take in a long, slow breath through my nose, noticing the subtle change in scent as the door closes behind them. Smoke and fire, to smouldering ashes.

10

Ali

Ali splashes her face with cold water. There is no mirror above the sink in the bathroom, and she is glad. The cold water has refreshed her, brought the evening's events into sharp focus. She and Jack must present a united front in this place. She doesn't want anyone's pity.

What the hell was in that wine? She only had a couple of glasses, but it was enough to make her a bit giddy – although the feeling passed quickly enough when she saw Angela in distress. She didn't hesitate, and she was glad she'd been able to dislodge the food. It doesn't always happen so simply. She's treated people with brain injuries that were the result of choking-related hypoxia.

Jack. Bloody Jack. He never has been good with wine, and clearly homemade stuff is even worse for him. She can't remember the last time she's seen him like that, but she can't let it happen again. If they're here to stay, she can't let anyone know what brought them. What Jack has done can never be shared with the others.

No one can help her with this, and she must find a way to deal with it better. This isn't the start she hoped for. She splashes her face again then uses a flannel to scrub off the remains of her make-up. She fills a glass with water from the cold tap, and drinks it fast. Her head screams. She refills the glass and takes it through to the bedroom with her. She lies down, hoping that once the water starts to rehydrate her, she will feel better and that she will manage to sleep, although right now it seems unlikely. Jack is already in bed, lying on his side, facing away from her, towards the wardrobe. She feels another stab of resentment. She refuses to accept responsibility for this. For them being forced to come and live in a place like this.

Jack is the one who screwed everything up. Jack is the one who made the wrong choices, and yet he is somehow coping with it better than she is. She's always been the one who's looked after him, kept him on an even keel, but she has slipped up, letting him drink. It won't happen again. She lies in bed, staring up at the ceiling, and then switches off the bedside lamp. The room is dark, so dark that she can't even see her own hand in front of her face. This is something that she will have to get used to in the fenlands. How thickly dark the place is, with no ambient light from any nearby towns or cities. Nothing to break up the end-lessly flat, lightless landscape. The complete opposite of London, the place that literally never sleeps. She tries to train her ears to the sounds of the countryside, but the place is in silence.

She tries to sleep, but it won't come.

A dream, or something she has conjured up? A woman's face, swim-ming into her vision. She closes her eyes tighter. And then she hears the scratching again, and she pulls the pillow out from underneath her and puts it over her head. Eventually, sleep takes her.

In the bright of the morning, the room seems different; her heart feels different. Her head has cleared. Jack is already out of bed, she can hear him splashing about in the bathroom, the occasional groan and sign. She throws back the covers and slides out of bed, stretch-ing, trying to wake herself up and enthuse herself about the day ahead. When they are both ready, they head down to the foyer outside Smea-ton's office to wait for him to take them on the tour. A brief flutter of nerves skitters across her stomach. Will Smeaton be cross about what happened at the party?

'Aren't we having some breakfast first, before this tour?' Jack snaps at her.

She frowns, looks away. 'I'm not hungry.'

'Well I'm starving and my head is banging. Have we got any paracetamol?'

She ignores him, glad that he's suffering physically from his behav-iour last night; he clearly has no memory of embarrassing her and humiliating himself.

The door to the office opens and Smeaton appears in front of them.

He's holding a lumpy beige muffin in each hand and is grinning like the Cheshire cat.

'Morning, morning,' he says. 'How are we both today? Things got a little lively last night, didn't they? I hope you're both OK. And please don't worry, everyone here knows how difficult it is at first – getting used to this place.' He stretches out his hands, offering them each a muffin. Jack accepts his gratefully and immediately takes a huge bite from it. Ali takes hers out of politeness, but she's really not sure she wants to eat it. Everything she's eaten here so far has tasted strange and different. Not that she thinks there is anything wrong with it, it's just not what she's used to. She knows she will have to get over that somehow, otherwise she'll starve. For now, though, she can do without this muffin of unidentifiable origins.

Smeaton guides them out of the front door. 'I thought we'd start over at the north wing, just so you can see it. But you might have heard already from the others, we don't really spend much time over there. There was a fire in there, years back – and more recently, a flood. We've turned the water supply off in there now, of course. But the floorboards are rotten, so we've abandoned those rooms. It's connected to this building by a beautiful glass walkway. Most of the panes are smashed now, but it would have been quite pretty once.'

'You going to eat that?' Jack whispers. Ali hands him the muffin, with a tight smile. She knows she needs to make an effort with him, with everyone. She should give herself a shake, start living her new life. If Jack can do it, then she can. They follow Smeaton around the edge of the main building, to the open area at the back, which seems to be full of overgrown weedy patches, some tumbledown sheds and stacks of evenly sized logs. Rusting iron railings lead down to a small door. Further on and to the right is the glass connecting tunnel. Smeaton leads them past boarded-up windows, unlocks the door and ushers them inside. Ali wrinkles her nose. The corridor smells stale, as if the same old air has been trapped inside for fifty years.

'I keep it locked, because we have had the occasional visitor here – explorers from outside.'

'You mean urbexers,' Ali says. 'I read a bit about them online. They like to poke around in abandoned buildings, right?'

'Why would anyone want to do that?' Jack says. He wipes his mouth with the back of his hand, scrunches up the two muffin wrappers into a small ball, and slips it into his pocket.

Ali takes a deep breath, and feels herself relax a little. It's the first thing he's said since they arrived, and at least he's showing some interest now – acting like a normal person.

'Well, I suppose they must find it interesting. I mean, places like this ... there's a lot to poke around. Unless they're actually looking for things that they can take. Things that they can sell? But then I suppose they wouldn't be true urbexers then, would they? They'd be looters.'

Smeaton doesn't respond, clearly as uninterested in the urban explorers as Jack is. He closes the door behind them and locks it. As they walk through the tunnel, Ali notices an odd distortion in the remaining glass, making the light look strange, milky – like under a veil. It unsettles her, but like the other odd feelings she's had since she arrived, she dismisses it. At the other end of the tunnel they enter a long corridor with many rooms on both sides. They have heavy doors with small shelves and shuttered windows. They remind Ali of a place that she visited with Jack several years before: an old prison in Berlin that was used by the Stasi during the Cold War, where they tortured and interrogated dissidents. A shiver runs down her spine. People were snatched from the streets, put into tiny cells and forced to stand for hours on end, not allowed to sit or lie down, not allowed to sleep. No one knew they were there. The Stasi kept them locked up like that for as long as they could, trying to break them, only offering leniency if they confessed to opposing the regime. The place was chilling, and she had a similar sensation now. 'Are these...' she began.

'Yes,' Smeaton says, 'these are the secure cells. For patients who couldn't be kept in an open ward. They were often dangerous, but not always. Some people shouldn't have been here at all, and became more ill by being kept away from their families and their day-to-day lives. In the fifties, there'd been so many reports of ill-treatment and neglect, a doctor was sent in to investigate, to see if anything bad was actually happening. But that's a story for another day ... if you're interested in the history of the place.'

Ali glances at Jack and he raises his eyebrows. She can tell that he's thinking the same as her. What's the real story here? What happened all those years ago?

'What about upstairs,' Jack says.

'More of the same,' Smeaton says. 'Plus a couple of the open wards. Nothing much in those now except dust balls and rats. It's up there that most of the boards have rotted. Safer not to go there at all.'

They walk to the end of the corridor and it leads them back outside. Smeaton locks the door behind him and Ali's jaw drops at the huge expanse of grass in front of them: a beautiful, well-kept lawn. Not what she expected at all. Over to one side is an ornamental pond, and next to it, a sundial. It's idyllic and it warms her, after the cold, neglected wing they've just visited. 'Well ... it's absolutely beautiful here.'

'Yes, it is.' Smeaton looks pleased. 'This garden would be where they used to host picnics, parties, fairs, fêtes – the lot. They would invite all the villagers, all the patients' families. They were grand affairs. We've been working on the lawn over the last year, trying to restore it to its former glory, hoping that we can make a feature of it. Maybe, in time, we might invite the locals back again.'

Ali nods. 'You mentioned them before – that they don't like to come here. That they're wary of the place?'

'Oh yes, they're wary indeed,' he says. The smile slides from his face, and a more cautious expression settles there. 'But it's a strange village, Ali. Full of superstitions and gossip. You'll find out more about that soon enough.'

11

Angela

As I arrive at the shop, my eye is drawn to the little black sticker in the window, the silhouette of a witch on a broomstick. I love that the village has adopted this emblem – even the schoolchildren have it on their blazers and sweatshirts. Apparently it caused quite an uproar with some of the more religious residents, but it's part of the village's heritage, and it was that history that convinced the local council to agree to it. I have one of the stickers on my bedroom window. It makes me feel part of the community.

A little bell tinkles as I open the door, and the woman behind the counter lifts her head and smiles. 'Morning, Angela. What a beautiful day it is.'

'It is, Mary.' I slide around the side of the counter to give her a hug. I love hugging Mary, my own bony frame sinks comfortably into the soft folds of the older woman.

'Apparently you have some new guests, eh? Anything I need to know?'

I step back around to the front of the counter and pick an apple from a basket, rubbing it on my skirt. I take a bite. 'I'm trying to get to know them, but it's tricky. They're definitely keeping their cards close to their chests. I know they both come from the city; that she was a nurse and he was a policeman. I think they're having some problems. In their relationship, I mean. I asked Smeaton but he told me to stop being so nosey.'

Mary sighs. 'Don't you worry about getting to know these people, Angela. They could be anyone. Didn't you tell me that they had bypassed all the usual procedures to get them in there? None of those daily trials and getting to know the group like you had to do?'

I nod. 'Smeaton did say that. He says that we need the money, and that they offered to fix the boiler and some other stuff.' I take another bite of the apple and juice dribbles down my chin into the neck of my dress.

'But surely this goes against everything he's built up there? You know what I think about that place, Angela. But at least Smeaton has always had integrity. He's always tried to run it the right way. You know we've all discussed it here in the village. We're in agreement that we're not fans of Smeaton's spiritual teachings. We wondered if he was genuine. But then who are we to judge, what, with our history? It just surprises me that he's changed his attitude and his ways for the sake of a few quid.'

'I know what you mean,' I say, rubbing at my chest, trying to wipe the juice off. 'It *is* unusual. But he has his reasons, and it's not for us to question him. To be honest, I'm not too concerned. I trust Smeaton. But there's something about this couple that I'm not sure about. I get a feeling from them. They're hiding something. I just know it. She seems spooked by the house already—'

'What do you mean *spooked*?' Mary says. 'Maybe she's just stressed. You said yourself, you don't know much about them, or what's brought them here.'

I shrug. 'Oh, you know. Just one of my feelings.'

'You and your *feelings*,' Mary says, a peal of laughter in her voice.

I feel my face fall, and Mary leans over and squeezes my shoulder. 'I'm teasing, Angela. You know me...'

'Well,' I continue, emboldened again, 'I have set up some of my equipment in their room. Well, not *in* their room. I'm not allowed to do that, Smeaton says. I've sneaked my little camera down a hole from the room above. I know I'm not meant to. I just want to keep an eye on that room. You know it's always made me feel a bit funny. The Palmerstons didn't like it in there, that's for sure. Anyway, it's not just about them, is it? It's about what I'm trying to do in that house. It's about all the other stories...'

'I wish you wouldn't get so hung up on all that, Angela. I've told you before, most of those legends are cobbled together. Don't shake your head at me, love. I know things *did* happen there – all our parents and grandparents told us the stories. It's not *just* an old hospital. I suppose it depends how you feel, what you want to believe. You're still new here. You know our villagers are full of old tales of witches and ghosts and all sorts of stuff.'

'But there *were* witches...'

'There was a *trial*, Angela. What happened before that is speculation. Those bratty sisters accusing their kindly old neighbour of bewitching them? There's the official record, but the true story is unofficial. You know my thoughts on this: it was ergot poisoning – from the rye in the fields. All five of those girls suffered the same affliction – hallucinations, convulsions. You can't buy a rye loaf around here now for love nor money...'

I sigh. 'I know that. I know all that witch stuff. I know that none of it was how it seemed back then. But the other things ... the things that happened in the fifties...'

Mary shakes her head. 'It wasn't just here that bad things happened. It was asylums all over. Right from the Victorians up to the 1970s and, you know, I'm sure it's not that much better nowadays. Stuff gets covered up. There's always an exposé at some point. People being mistreated. Someone blows the whistle.'

Maybe she's right. Maybe I'm reading too much into things. I finger the rose quartz stone that hangs around my neck. I see a glint of light on my hematite ring. Mary gave me these things. A conductor and a transducer. She's a sceptic herself, but she says they might help me connect to the spirit world. I know that she finds it all very amusing that I'm trying to be a ghost hunter and that so far I haven't seen or felt a single thing. Of course I have absolutely no idea whether any of the villagers' ghostly stories are true. It doesn't stop me from wanting to find out if there is something else beyond the realm we live in. I'm not *going* to stop. Because I am convinced that there is something there, that there is something in the old hospital. Furthermore, I am certain that these new arrivals are going to help me uncover it, whether they believe in it or not.

12
Ali

Ali follows Richard down a well-trodden dirt path bordered by a neat hedgerow. The old man is light on his feet, walking quickly across the packed mud towards a pretty wooden gate with a heart carved into its centre.

'Ford made the gate,' Richard says, as if reading her mind. 'Didn't know one end of a saw from the other when he first arrived here, but you should see what he's learned since. Garden furniture, tables and chairs, a new desk for Smeaton, you name it. If you need anything for your room that you can't find elsewhere, let him know and he'll make something for you. Made me a lovely long table from a load of old floorboards from one of the rooms in the north wing. Rest of the place is rotting, mind. You probably want to stay away from there. Anyway, here we are. Our humble vegetable patch.'

Richard beams at her and she can see the pride in his eyes. It's impressive, and much, much bigger than the small cottage garden, or maybe a few raised beds and some fruit trees she'd imagined. This is like a whole set of allotments with rows of greens – cabbages, lettuce, some other straggly-looking stuff that she doesn't recognise. Frames have been set up, with strings laced with CDs, spinning in the wind. Beneath them are canes and nets.

'Need to keep the birds away from the soft fruits,' Richard says, following her gaze. 'The sun glinting off the silver distracts them. Picked up a load of these in a charity shop up in the village—'

'So you do go up to the village? The impression I got from Smeaton was that most people barely leave the grounds. Isn't going to the village on the list of things that are *not advised*?'

Richard doesn't look at her. He crouches down and starts pulling at some of the straggling plants that she couldn't identify. 'Mooli,' he says, 'enough to last for about a thousand years. Luckily Fergus is inventive in the kitchen.'

She crouches down beside him, and her knees crack. She's not in the best shape and she knows she needs to do something about it. 'The village?' she tries again. 'Is it OK to go there or not?'

'Sure, sure,' he mutters. 'Smeaton's right though – best to acclimatise a bit first, get used to *not* being in the real world for a while. That's why you're here, isn't it? To get away?' he looks at her now, eyes slightly narrowed.

She doesn't want to sound like she's desperate for something more like her old life but she's already feeling claustrophobic, and she needs to find a way to deal with that. Richard is right, of course. She did come here to get away.

He's more right than he could possibly know.

'Right, then,' he says. 'Let's have a go at this, shall we? This stuff needs thinning out. Do you need me to show you the tools and whatnot?' He nods towards a shed at the end of the patch.

'Did Ford make that too?'

'Yes, he did. We brought most of the tools with us. Cobbled together a few things where we didn't have them. Trying to use whatever we can from the place, you know.'

She nods and he walks off towards one of the further patches, where Ali can just make out a couple of bent figures and the bright yellow of a plastic bucket. Someone in a hat pulling carrots. She can't recognise them from this distance.

She heads down to the shed, where the door is already open. Inside, the walls are lined with tools, canes, and a shelf with string, pegs and all sorts. Two wheelbarrows are stacked in the corner.

She thinks about Jack, and tries to imagine him here, wellies on, spade in hand. But she can't. Smeaton has taken him somewhere today, didn't tell her where. Jack looked pleased. Excited even. The most alert she's seen him for a long time, and certainly the most enthusiastic he's been since they arrived last week.

She's on her way back out of the shed, hoe at the ready. There's a loud crack in the air, and she starts. Flinches. She wants to think it's just the sound of a car backfiring, but she knows it isn't. She recognises the sound of a gunshot. A shotgun, most likely, in a place like this. She hadn't really thought about it before, she was so intent on getting away from the city. But of course they would have firearms here. She thinks again of Jack, wonders if it's a good idea for him to be around guns. Wonders if Smeaton knows what he's doing. Is she being irresponsible, not telling Smeaton more about their past – about what Jack is capable of?

No. She needs to try and bring a sense of normality to their lives, their *new* lives. She doesn't want Smeaton to act differently around him, and he would, if he knew. It won't help Jack anyway. She's the only one who can help Jack, and even then…

She thrusts the hoe into the thicket of gnarly leaves and tries to put him out of her mind.

13

Angela

It's a surprise, at first, when I first see the reading on the EMF meter. After all this time, I was starting to think I was never going to get a proper result. But the reading is on there for all to see, even if I might be the only one who understands what it means.

There is something in this room. Something that is not meant to be here.

Of course I haven't told anyone that I have a master key; I don't know if Smeaton has even noticed that it's gone missing, but I've had it in my pocket for months now, trying to work up the courage to investigate every single room in the place. I haven't got very far. Surprisingly, there's not been a hint of anything unusual across in the north wing, because that place scares me the most. So I'm focusing here – in this room – where I have long been convinced that something isn't right.

Smeaton intended to put the new couple in one of the rooms at the side of the building. In the same corridor as me and Fergus. But I convinced him that this room was the best one, with its two huge windows overlooking the pretty front courtyard and that lovely deep bath, in the side-room that has been turned into an en suite. I imagine it looks like a room in a quirky boutique hotel, certainly not something in an old hospital – with the metal bed, the shabby-chic dressing table, and the makeshift curtains that I helped Julie put up. I hope they like it. I hope they appreciate having the best room in the house.

I hope they like the whole house – as it is a house to me, not a crumbling asylum. It is full of dark corners and hidden treasures. Things that will never see the light of day again, and things that are waiting to be uncovered at some point in time, by people who might find a use for them. Smeaton doesn't encourage exploring, but it doesn't mean that we don't do it.

I can tell that Ali is curious about the house – she's the one who is likely to start poking around, finding things that she is not meant to. But I will tell her only what she needs to know, until I'm sure I can trust her at least.

I let myself into their room, and close the door softly behind me. Ali is in the vegetable garden; I saw her walk off with Richard. If she is with him she will be gone for hours. And I know that Smeaton has taken Jack away to the far fields where the rabbits like to run.

He took the guns.

I don't like him shooting rabbits, but this is his place and I can hardly tell him that he can't. I'm sure we can all survive quite easily on the vegetables that Richard and Julie grow, and the eggs from our happy hens, Alice and Agnes, plus milk, of course from Mr Patterson the goat. Do we really need to shoot rabbits? I don't particularly care for their stringy, grey flesh. But Smeaton told me that it's not just about eating the meat; there's the thrill of the hunt. I don't understand this, as he is a peaceful man. But I suppose everyone has their vices. Mine, of course, is an inherent curiosity, especially for other-worldly things. Yes, OK, worldly things, too. I did used to enjoy reading the trashy magazines in Mary's shop, while I was supposed to be tidying the shelves. Personally, I think that anyone who isn't a little bit nosey about other people's lives must have a very dull one themselves.

They seem to have put all of their belongings away, and the room appears quite neat. This pleases me, as it is how I like to keep my own. Ali has lined up various tubes and jars on the dressing table; her beautifying potions – some fancy brands that I wouldn't have expected, and I notice that the mirror is tilted downwards. This interests me, and I suspect that despite all her creams and make-ups, she is unhappy with herself. She does not want to stare into her own eyes, and wonder why it is that she has ended up here. Or perhaps there's another reason that she doesn't want to look in the mirror. *This* mirror, in particular. I tilt it upwards, and I sit there for a moment, facing myself, but my eyes fixed on the room behind me, and the bathroom door to my left. Watching, waiting – just in case something chooses to reveal itself. At last I sigh and tilt the mirror back to the angle in which she left it. Maybe she just doesn't like her own face. Maybe she's just a bit of an oddball, like the rest of us.

Because, however you want to look at it, this place is full of misfits. This place is for people who don't feel like they belong in 'normal' society. Why would you be here if you're normal, if you're happy, if you have a good, stable life? You would be out there in the real world with your family and your job and your nice house and your friends. You wouldn't be here in this draughty old mansion with this mishmash of people from all walks of life who have decided that the real world doesn't work for them anymore. Strangely, though, there has been a large volume of enquiries over the last year or so, from people interested in how we live. It appears that the world has gone entirely to hell, and those who remain relatively sane are looking for ways to escape. Not because there's anything massively wrong with their day-to-day lives, but more that they can no longer bear to see what is happening around them. They can't control it, they can't fix it, and they are unhealthily obsessed with the downward spiral that society has taken. When I think of the world outside Rosalind House, outside the village, and the fens, I remember an old poem that I learned at school, about returning to the land, the old ways of life. It's a post-apocalyptic tale: Edwin Muir's *The Horses*. One line always repeats in my head: *'That old bad world that swallowed its children quick.'* We are the children. We created this technological world, and it will destroy us. At least here, in Rosalind House, we can try our hardest to pretend that the real world doesn't exist. Maybe Smeaton's dream of self-sufficiency *can* work, but I can't carry out my mission without my devices.

The bed is neatly made. The covers pulled tight, equal tucks on all sides, pillows plumped. This tells me something about Ali, because I doubt very much that it was Jack who made this bed. People who make their beds in such a way tend to have neat lives and organised minds. But, then, she was a nurse. She is used to making beds. She's been trained to be fast and efficient. I move to the wardrobe, open the doors. I think they must have brought some coat hangers with them, because there weren't many in here – only a few of the old wire ones. None of Our Family has many clothes. None of us brought much from our old lives, because we simply don't need them anymore. Here we need practical clothes, clothes for all weathers. Maybe one nice thing for the occasional party that we have. And even then, just being washed and having your hair brushed is as fancy as it needs to be here.

This is a good place to be to avoid vanity, but there is a difference between being tidy and clean and being dirty and dishevelled. People maintain good standards here; it's just the way that we are. We aren't the smelly hippies that some like to think we are.

I riffle through some of the hanging garments, and I don't see anything particularly flashy. Jeans, plain shirts. A navy dress with daisies appliqued around the neckline. I imagine, like most people, they've already sold most of the things that they owned before they came here. Or perhaps they have put them in storage. Who knows what level of commitment they've made. Time will tell if they are here to stay.

I hesitate for a moment, wondering if I should leave. They should be out for the day, but what if they come back?

Hurriedly, I pull out the drawer beneath the dressing table and see that the *Book of Light* is still in there. We all have one; we all follow the rules. Such as they are. I flick through the pages, run my finger down the names of Our Family, with Ali and Jack there at the bottom. I updated this sheet for them, the night before they arrived, Smeaton letting me use the typewriter in the library. I wanted to make sure that their names were already included – I wanted them to feel that they were already part of Our Family. I hope they were pleased that we'd made the effort to keep things up to date.

I know I should leave now. Stop nosing around. But now that I've started I can't seem to stop myself. My heart is beating faster, telling me to move on. On the other side of the room there is a small bookcase.

There are a few books there, some that I know were here already, some that they must have brought with them. A mixture of things, some non-fiction, some fiction. Classics. I wonder if they've read all of these books. Sometimes people have a favourite book but they have never actually read it. My favourite book is *Wuthering Heights*, although I don't know why, because if I have read it I have no memory of it. I like the title, and I like the concept. I like the idea of the bleak, ghostly moors. That's enough for me.

As well as books, there are a couple of small boxes on the shelves. I imagine they must contain a few trinkets that they have decided to keep, things that they don't need but can't be parted from. I pick up the first one: red velvet with a gold clasp. A jewellery box, I assume. I open it, half expecting to be mildly surprised by a spinning ballerina and a creepy, tinny tune, but there is no ballerina. There are two pairs of earrings, one silver drop chain with diamonds, and the other red studs. One pair of cufflinks, engraved with the initials J.G.

I put the box back, disappointed.

Underneath there is a bigger box, approximately the size of a shoebox. It is made of wood, I think, or perhaps just very thick paper with a coating, I can't be sure. It's bigger than A4 size and I imagine that possibly it contains paperwork. Probably nothing of interest for me in there, and yet, I can't stop myself.

I reach for the box, and as I do, I hear the unmistakable sound of a floorboard creaking outside. I whip round, my eyes on the door – expecting the key to turn any minute. My heart thumps, and I hold my breath, waiting.

Then nothing.

I wait another moment for my breathing to return to normal, and then I open the box.

As I suspected, it contains piles of papers, some in clear plastic folders, some bound together with elastic bands or paperclips. Bank statements, other things. What else? Nothing of interest, yet. I'm sure I have lifted out all of the papers, and I'm about to put them back in when I realise something strange about the box. The papers I have in my hand form a small pile. But they filled the box to the top. I look at the box, and it becomes clear that the papers were only in the *top* part. There is a hidden section beneath. I feel my breath catch. A buzz of excitement runs through me like a jolt of electricity. Why is there a secret compartment? What could be so important? I stare inside. My skin prickles. I have no idea what I might find in here.

I take a deep breath, sucking in courage from the fizzing air around me. I don't know why, but I think what is in this box is important. I prize a nail around the edge of the divider, flicking upwards so that I can gain purchase. Then I carefully remove it. Underneath is a thick pile of newspaper clippings. Neatly cut, some larger articles folded in half, some small ones. I flick through. Lots of different newspapers, lots of different pictures, lots of different headlines.

But they make no sense.

I read the first one: 'Missing Backpacker Found on Side of M6'. Bradley Hay, twenty-four, from Australia, was found dead in a ditch. It's thought that he was hitchhiking around the UK and that he was hit by a truck on the motorway. Hit-and-run or an accident? No leads. I pick up another: 'Girl Found at Side of Motorway Identified'. Charlotte (Charlie) Lawrence, twenty-two, from Leeds. Went missing after she left a party on a housing estate near the slip road at junction twelve of the M1; police think she may have tried to hitch a lift home and was hit by a vehicle. No further details at present.

I read another, then another. All similar. Different roads, different suggestions about what might have happened. Hitchhikers, or people who'd found themselves on the motorway late at night. Different times of the year, over a period of several years.

Nothing to link them in any way.

Jack was in the police, wasn't he? I don't know what he did, what he worked on. Was this part of it? I flick more quickly now through the documents, keeping my ears trained on the door, listening for voices … wondering where I could hide, if I had to. I pause to read one of the articles in more detail. A couple of the hitchhikers weren't even identified. Could they be homeless? Runaways? Did the stress of it lead him to a breakdown? *Get out of here, Angela* – the voice in my head insists. But I am transfixed, my heart thumping hard now.

I scan through more of the clippings, searching for Jack's name. Anything to suggest that this was something related to his job. But there is nothing to indicate that he had any official role to play in investigating these deaths. So why, then, does he have all the clippings? And more importantly – why are they hidden?

Dr Henry Baldock's Journal – 17th April 1955

My hands are still shaking after today's events, and I fear that this entry might be quite illegible when I come to read it later on. Earlier, I supervised some of the rounds. I was interested to see the patients as they carried out their daily activities, and the nurses as they facilitated this. Usually when I walk around, the patients are in their beds. Some of them are in shared, open wards – the ones who are safe to be looked after in this way. They can be noisy places, with lots of voices. But ultimately they are safe. But there are also lots of private rooms, secure rooms, of various levels. Some for patients who are placed there because they are a danger to themselves and others, although some are only a danger to themselves. Each corridor has a large bathroom area with several baths available, separated by screens. If patients are capable, they will be allowed to bathe themselves, although there will always be a nurse or an orderly in the room with them. For the patients who are not safe or capable of being on their own, they will be helped to bathe by the nurses.

I found out today that there are no patients here who are completely bedbound; this hospital does not have the facilities for those. Although I believe it did at one time. In the first open ward, patients were having lunch. They sat at a long communal table in the middle, and things seemed to be carrying on without incident. I nodded towards the nurse in charge of the room and made my leave. I had no need to be in that room, there was nothing here that had to be recorded as a concern. I walked further down the corridor and I had a quick look into a couple of the secure rooms; the doors have a small gap into which I can peer, almost like prison cells. I do not like these rooms, but I know they are necessary. I lifted the latch on the first room and saw a man lying in bed. He seemed to be staring straight at me, and yet he didn't see me. Catatonia is one of the things that is most difficult to treat. Sometimes we try medication, insulin shock therapy and often ECT. I have mixed feelings about these methods, but it's not my job to decide the treatments here. My job is to investigate the allegations of abuse.

Further down the corridor, I heard the sound of running water. Splashes. Voices coming from the bathroom. I hurried along. The bathroom door was closed, but I could clearly hear the noises coming from within. Exaggerated whispers, trying to disguise their raised voices. My chest tightened and I sensed that all was not well. I opened the door and observed that all the partition curtains were drawn. Underneath the first I could see two sets of feet. The white leather-soled shoes that the nurses wear. I don't think they heard me coming in, because the noises continued.

When I pulled back the curtain, I was met with a scene of horror.

A female patient, was being held under water, and a nurse was pressing on her shoulders. At the other end, another nurse was operating the taps. At the sound of the curtain, the nurse holding the patient's shoulders sprung back, and the woman's face burst from beneath the surface. Water flew everywhere, spraying on my face, and I shuddered in absolute shock – because the water was ice cold.

'Just what is going on here?' I demanded, attempting to sound authoritative, despite feeling a tremble deep in my chest.

'Help me,' the woman croaked, coughing. Spluttering out water. 'Help me...'

The nurse at the tap end spoke without a hint of fear in her voice. 'This is not what it looks like, Dr Baldock. There's no need to be alarmed...'

The other nurse, clearly the more junior of the two, was drying her arms with a towel. She threw her colleague a nervous look and butted in, 'The patient was hysterical, doctor. We've been using this treatment for years—'

'Get this woman dried off and warmed up. Get her a hot drink, and a tot of whisky. Get her into bed, with plenty of blankets. Then we'll talk.'

I turned quickly and stormed out of the room, slamming the door behind me.

I did not want them to see that I was shaking.

Just as I am now.

14
Ali

'So, where do you want me?' Ali lifts an apron from a peg near the door, slips it over her head and ties the straps behind her back. 'Any hats?' she continues, before anyone has the chance to answer.

'Good morning, Ali.' Fergus gives her a wide grin, revealing his gap-toothed smile, and hands her a box of checked cotton hats. 'You've worked in a kitchen before?'

She positions the hat as best she can over her neat bun. It's one thing she has been able to bring from her old job, at least: the ability to spin her hair into an immovable bun with three hairpins in the minimum amount of time. 'Not since before I trained as a nurse. I helped out in a pub kitchen a bit when I was a teenager. I know my way around a potato peeler.'

Fergus laughs, a low growl that she can almost feel in her own chest. She's been intrigued by Fergus since meeting him at the welcoming party last week. He's a large but quiet man, with the most beautifully smooth skin she has ever seen. He's told her he was a former addict, and an embarrassment to his middle-class Jamaican family. Clearly Rosalind House and the fresh air of the fens has had a nourishing effect on his health. As well as the kitchen, he works with Richard and Julie in the gardens, deciding on the best seasonal crops to plant and helping to tend them. Apparently he'd learned to run a kitchen in a homeless hostel, so he is the perfect person to cook for a crowd in here.

'Well, you're in luck,' he says, picking up a huge blue bucket and dropping it on the counter. 'Plenty of potatoes for you to do.'

He must've picked up the look of horror on her face, because he laughs again, and points to a big steel contraption next to one of the sinks.

'Rumbler, isn't it? No potato peelings for you, dear.'

Ali breathes a sigh of relief. 'Got it.'

'After that, a big box of lettuce will need washing. Then maybe you can slice me some mooli. You like mooli?'

Another voice interrupts them. 'It's like radish but milder. Tastes a bit earthy but you'll get used to it. You'll need to. We seem to have a never-ending supply of the stuff in here. Tomatoes, boss.'

Ali turns towards the newcomer: a tiny woman with a bird's nest of blonde hair somehow contained with an elastic band and a small checked cap.

'Rose,' she says, offering a skeletal hand. 'Sorry I didn't get to chat to you at the welcoming party, I left early with a migraine.'

A brief look passes between Fergus and Rose. Clearly Rose has been briefed on how the party ended. Ali decides to ignore it.

'Thank you, darling,' Fergus pats Rose on the shoulder. Then he takes the tomatoes and places them next to the box of lettuce. 'OK, first things first. Lucy – are you ready? Time for the blessing.'

A small, pale woman appears from behind the door of a tall steel fridge. They have a well-equipped kitchen, Ali realises. Nicer than any hospital kitchen she's been in. She makes a mental note to ask about that later. It must've cost them a bit to refit it. She is curious about how people pay for things here, how they earn money.

She blinks out of her daze, realising that the others are standing in a circle, holding hands. Waiting for her. Lucy and Rose have left a gap for her between them. For a moment she is confused.

'We do the blessing of light now, Ali. It is good bonding. Makes us work well. Helps us cook good food.'

Ali suddenly feels nervous. She is not used to this sort of thing. It's as far away from her comfort zone as something could possibly be. She'd always enjoyed chatting to her colleagues in break times, but there is a closeness here that she isn't prepared for. She's used to idle chat and easy silences. Time away from the ward to gather her thoughts and help her through the rest of the day. On the surface, she'd been friendly, involved in the lives of others. But it was a front. She blinks away the image. The old life. The old Ali. Lonely in a room full of strangers, even those she'd known throughout a fifteen-year career. *Embrace this change*, she thinks. *It's the only way to forget.*

She takes hold of the other women's hands. Everyone closes their eyes. She keeps hers open. She needs to see.

Lucy speaks. Her voice is soft, and her accent is pure West Country. 'We gather in the circle of light and we hope that today will be a good day. We hope that our hands will make good food. We hope that our meal will make happy mouths. Embrace the light and be thankful.'

'Embrace the light and be thankful.' The group repeats the last line together, then they open their eyes and smile. They raise their hands, just a tiny bit, and Ali feels her hands being squeezed, firm, fast. She is momentarily startled, but before she can squeeze back, the other women let go of her.

'It helps us to focus on the task in hand,' Rose says. 'You'll get used to it.'

Ali smiles, not sure what to say.

She walks over to the rumbler and throws in several handfuls of potatoes, until the drum is full. She switches on the machine and stands, mesmerised, while the potatoes rattle and roll, sliding down into the tray when they are smooth and skinned. Scraped clean, ready to be sliced. Afterwards, she washes her hands and goes in search of coffee.

'Is there a kettle in here?' she says, glancing around, surprised that it isn't obvious.

'We have a break in thirty minutes,' Rose says, frowning, 'but if you really need a hot drink now, just go and get one from the sitting room. We don't keep the tea and coffee things in here.'

'Right,' Ali says, feeling chastised. She's not used to being unable to get a hot drink when she wants one. Even when the wards were at their busiest, there was always someone around to make a brew. She's not too keen on Rose's tone, but she can let that slide for now. She has to try and keep her irritation in check with people, especially when they haven't actually done anything wrong. Recently, she's noticed more and more that people seem to get her back up for no real reason. She hopes that coming here might alleviate her stress, eventually.

She nips through to the sitting room and makes herself a coffee. It feels like she's bunking off school, doing something naughty. She takes a few long, deep breaths while she waits for the kettle to boil, and by the time she's stirred in the milk she is feeling a lot calmer. She takes the drink back through to the kitchen, and finds the place deserted. She feels a flicker of worry. Where are they? Have they gone off somewhere to talk about her? There is a cool breeze trickling through the long room, and she realises the back door has been left open. Perhaps they've gone out to the gardens. Maybe they've gone to pick even more lettuce for her to wash. She pulls the door part-closed, not fully, in case it doesn't open from the outside – she's never come in that way, so she doesn't know. Doesn't want them to be stuck out there, when they come back from wherever it is that they've gone. She turns and frowns: there are small puddles of water on the floor. They definitely were not there before. Her first instinct is to glances upwards, looking for a leak in the ceiling. What is it with this place and its random wet patches? First in the corridor outside her room, now here. But there is no obvious drip. When she drops her head back down, she has to blink to make sure she has not imagined it.

She takes a step back.

A small boy is standing in front of her. He can't be more than six years old. His hair is plastered over his face and he is dripping wet, leaving small puddles on the floor by his side. He is looking down at the floor, and a sudden icy finger of dread shoots up Ali's back. She doesn't want to see his face. She doesn't want him to look up. Something is wrong with this boy. Something...

She comes to her senses. 'My God, you must be freezing. What happened to you? Where are your parents?' She leaves him standing there, and quickly goes to the shelves full of cloths and towels. She grabs handfuls of whatever she can, and shakes them out, trying to find the largest of them, trying to find something to wrap him in. She spins around, arms outstretched, 'Here, let me...'

The words die in her mouth.

The boy is gone.

Ali stares at the puddles on the floor, watching as they slowly disappear, knowing that the kitchen is not hot enough for them to evaporate so quickly, especially with the breeze that seems to be reaching out to her with its long, icy fingers. Then she turns, and runs from the kitchen, ignoring the cries from Fergus and Rose as they call her name, asking her what on earth is going on.

15

Angela

I definitely need to get to know Ali better now. Fergus has told me that she freaked out in the kitchen, that she was in there alone while he and Rose were out collecting herbs, and that something had happened. She rushed out red-faced, in tears. Fergus ran after her but she had gone. Back to her room? I don't know, but I'm going to have a look. I run upstairs. I don't know where Jack is. I think Ali is on her own. I have to know what it was that scared her so much in the kitchen. I press my ear to her door and I think I can hear her sobbing, but perhaps that's just what I want to hear. Something in me wants her to be scared here. Why do I feel like this? I don't remember anyone else eliciting such a reaction. I take a breath and knock gently. No answer. I wait a moment then try again.

'Ali? Are you in there?'

'Please go away.'

'Ali, it's Angela. Fergus said you were upset. I just want to make sure that you're OK. You can talk to me, you know.'

I wonder what she would think if she knew that I have been sneaking around in her room. That I've opened that box and found those newspaper clippings. I feel like I need to ask her about them, but I don't know how to bring it up without making it obvious where I got the information from. Smeaton hasn't told me any details about Jack's old job. I'm not sure he knows any more than I do. I might have it all wrong. There might be another reason for those clippings. Research, maybe. One of them might be writing something about missing persons, or hitchhikers or I don't know what. It's not actually any of my business.

I stand quietly, hoping that she'll let me in. After what seems like forever, I hear the sound of the key turning in the lock. I step back, and the door swings open gently. She walks away from me and sits down on the chair next to the dressing table. She has the *Book of Light* open at the page of things we aren't supposed to do. She looks at me, her face a mixture of confusion and fear. She is giving off a sharp scent; something has definitely spooked her. Humans, just like animals, give off a smell when they're scared. When adrenaline spikes, it swims around in your blood and leaks out of your pores. She smells like a wounded animal, looks small and scared.

'I just don't know what to make of this place, Angela,' she blurts out. 'I'm worried that we've made a huge mistake coming here. It's not for everyone, right? Living in a freaky old ruin with a bunch of hippies. We've given it more than a week and I'm really not sure ... Maybe it's time for us to move on, find another way...'

'What happened in the kitchen, Ali?'

She shakes her head. 'I don't want to talk about that.'

'Has anything else unusual happened since you've been here?' I probe.

She shakes her head again, but she won't look at me. I'm dying to know what's got her jitters up. Maybe she's a conduit. I'm excited by the prospect, but I try to keep it in check. I don't want to scare her any further right now.

'I've got a good idea. Let me take you somewhere. Somewhere I'm sure you haven't been taken on Smeaton's official tour. Come on. You'll like it, I promise. And I'll tell you some stories too. About this place. About anything you like. I'd love us to be friends, Ali. You can trust me. I promise.' I extend a hand towards her, expecting her to take it. It's a friendly gesture, I think. Although I wouldn't be surprised if I got it wrong. She takes my hand and stands up, but then she drops my hand as if it has burned her. She doesn't give me time to squeeze, to tell her to *embrace the light*.

I wonder if maybe that's what has scared her, it would have happened in the kitchen before her shift – the blessing of the light. Maybe she's not used to this kind of intimacy from strangers. I will ask about it later.

She is already dressed with her boots still on, so she picks up a coat that she has left on the bed and follows me out of the door. She locks the room behind her, and pockets the key. Most people here don't lock their rooms. There is no need to; no one has anything that anyone else wants. I think about the box again, the clippings. Hidden. They aren't meant to be there. She doesn't want people to know she has them. She doesn't want to explain what they are.

'I've been wondering...' she says, as we walk along towards the stairs, 'I've noticed various bits and bobs of equipment in some of the corridors.' She points up at the corner of the ceiling and one of my cameras winks as we pass.

I hesitate. This will go one of two ways. Most people tolerate it with a shrug, but I do get the occasional person who gets annoyed, angry even. Thinks I'm mad. I take a sharp breath and blow it out slowly. 'Well, I suppose now is as good a time as any to tell you. It might help you understand this place a little more. It's all to do with my investigations, you see.'

'Your investigations? What kind of investigations? Are you watching people here? Is it some sort of CCTV?' I can hear the tension in her voice.

'Not quite. It's not really *people* that I'm watching, although they do get caught on camera from time to time. I'm kind of watching...' I pause, I feel nervous, suddenly. Should I just blurt it out? Will she laugh? Some people do. 'I'm monitoring the entire building.' I pause again. 'For ghosts.'

We continue walking, down the stairs, along the bottom corridor, and then we're outside. She hasn't replied. I steal a glance at her, and I can almost hear her brain whirling away, wondering. Deciding how to play it.

'Ghosts? You're not serious?'

Her voice sounds slightly strained, but she hasn't laughed. That's a good start. It also confirms something for me. She's seen something already, or felt it. Because if she hadn't, she'd have had more of a reaction, I think. She'd be immediately questioning my sanity. As it is, I think she might be questioning her own. This is my chance to convince her.

'We can't just fade away, Ali. You can bury the body or burn it to smithereens, but you can't tell me that's all there is. There has to be something else out there – something for afterwards, for all the people whose souls couldn't cope with this life. If there isn't that, then what's the point of all this? What is the point of now?

'Ghosts are the ones who've lost their way. We need to make contact and help them find it. But I think that these spiritual imprints are only left behind when their body has been wronged. And, my theory is that only wrongdoers can see them.' I pause, sensing Ali flinch beside me. 'And if that's the case, then it doesn't matter what I want. It doesn't matter if I want to help. I'm never going to see one, or feel one. Because I've never *made* one, do you understand? I think you can only see ghosts if you're responsible for taking a life. I *know* they exist. I'm certain of it.' I turn to face her, put my hand on her shoulder. 'I think you do, too, Ali. What I don't understand is – what did you do to make them exist in your realm? What have you seen?'

Ali shrugs my hand away, and a cloud passes over her face.

'There's something, I know it. I wonder if it's someone who died under your care, when you were a nurse – I'm sure it wasn't your fault...' Ali bristles beside me, from the corner of my eye I can see her clenching her hands into fists. I'm getting too carried away... 'When I said wrong-doer, I meant in the sense that you were involved. When someone lost their life. People die in hospital all the time. Maybe there was something traumatic, something that's latched on to you. Am I right? Or perhaps Jack – he was in the police, wasn't he? Maybe he...'

I let my sentence tail off. She's shaking her head. She stops walking. 'Why?'

'Why what?' I don't understand.

'Why do you think I've seen ghosts? I've dealt with dead people, sure. It was part of my job. Jack's too. Are you saying...?' She stops. She doesn't want to continue, because she knows what I am implying.

I'm suggesting that, yes, she has brought something in here with her. Some sort of link to the dead. Some sort of soulful energy that has caused a reaction in this house.

We keep walking, in silence now. I need to let it sink in, for both of us. I'm not sure she believes me, but I know she is thinking about it now.

We crunch through the woods, across the mulchy floor. Light zigzags through the trees. The tyre swing is turning gently in the breeze. I run towards it and jump on, circling my legs around the back, crossing them. I swing gently, but it's not enough.

'Push me.'

She thrusts her hands into my back, a little too hard. Then she steps away.

'Tell me these stories, then,' she says.

She grabs my feet, sends me into a spin. I don't really like spinning fast, I feel a wave of nausea hit me, but I swallow it back. I lean back, trying to stop the spin, to make it swing. She senses my discomfort, grabs my legs and stops me spinning.

'Please?' she says.

I have to decide what to tell her. I can't tell her everything, because I need to be able to test her. I don't want to suggest things. I'd rather she opened up by herself. If I tell her what I think is here, she might simply agree, and then how will I know if she's telling the truth? I'm still not sure if I trust her. I didn't tell her the full details of my theory. That it wasn't just people around the dead who could carry their souls. I wanted her to believe that, because I'm still not sure if it's her or Jack that I should be wary of. For now, it's both of them.

'OK, well there are two things I'll tell you to start with. First, the witches – but that was back in the fifteen hundreds and you might even know that story because it's famous, much further afield than just here, although this is witchfinder country—'

'Maybe the other one first? Those witches' tales always end the same way. We all know there weren't really any witches.'

I shrug. She's wrong, but the other story I have in mind for her is a better one anyway. More relevant, I think. After all, I'm not investigating witches. 'There was a doctor here, a psychiatrist. Back in the early days, when it first became an asylum. 1898, I think.' I take a breath. 'He was said to like the female patients. A little too much, if you get what I mean? Back then women didn't make such a fuss. They were too scared to tell the truth. Especially if they were in here as a patient – so-called mentally ill – and the person who was doing things was a well-respected doctor. Anyway, one of them did decide to speak out. She told her husband when he visited. Next day, they found the doctor ... upside down in a rain barrel, face white and bloated like a jellyfish. They said it was an accident, but the women knew better. He comes back, after a night of heavy rain. You'll see his pale face, reflected back in your bath water.' I jump off the swing. 'So the story goes, anyway.'

Ali laughs, then. A proper belly laugh, that's too loud for this sheltered place. I hear the skittering of small animals running away. The flap of wings, the sharp caw of departing birds.

I kick the head off a fat toadstool and it puffs into the air, releasing angry spores. I glare at her and stomp back through the woods, keeping my distance from her as I run back towards the house.

16
Ali

Ali makes her way slowly back to the house. What was that all about? There's something off about that girl. Living in her own little world. All that nonsense about ghosts. Although she has to admit, the house does feel strange. But it's all explainable, isn't it? It has to be. She's fully trained in all of the sciences, and she certainly understands how the mind works. She's tired, that's all. She feels like she has just woken from a strange dream; one of those dreams that you only have when you go to bed with all your clothes on, during the day. When you overheat, and you're not quite asleep, not quite awake in that strange twilight place where you are almost lucid dreaming. Where you can drive your own fate. That weird nowhere place, where you fantasise about how different your life could be.

In fact, this is the state she has been in since she arrived here.

She knows that she has to sit down with Jack and have a proper talk about what they do next – how they cope in here. She's ready for it now. It's going to be difficult for her to accept Angela's friendship. A friendship that would never feel natural outside of this house. The problem of coming to a place like this is that you end up spending time with people that you would never choose. It's the difference between real friends versus people who you meet through work, or the ones you meet through shared interests. Finding friends, *choosing* friends, is difficult. But not as difficult as being forced into a situation with people with whom you feel uncomfortable, having to modify yourself to fit in. She'd thought she could do it, thought she could adapt easily – but it's harder than she imagined.

Because Ali has never been someone willing to modify herself. Quite the opposite, in fact. Ali has made it her goal in life to attempt to modify others – to help them change their ways. Take Jack, for example. He is not the man that she met ten years ago. She saw something in him from the moment they met, something intriguing, and she knew she had to delve further into what made him tick. Does that make her bad? Perhaps it does. But not as bad as him. If she were to tell people in this place what Jack had done, they would cast him out without a second thought. But none of them would question *her* motives. Of course they wouldn't. She's the one who stood by him as he crumbled. What Jack has done was inevitable. It was always in him, bubbling under the surface. If she is guilty of anything at all, it's of showing him what he's capable of.

Maybe Angela isn't quite right for her, but she does knows that she needs to make some friends in here. Richard, as lovely as he is, is a bit too fatherly for her. Julie, however, seems like someone that she could get along with, and although the woman is quiet, Ali suspects that she has just been waiting for someone to come into this place and wake it up a little. Someone that might just be the kind of person that she could be friends with. Could that be her? She can certainly try.

Jack has been spending quite a bit of time with Smeaton, doing various things out in the grounds, a bit of shooting, which she understands, even though she doesn't really agree with it. They're in the countryside now, and this kind of thing happens. As long as it's not near the house; as long as Jack doesn't get any strange ideas about guns. If she was to tell Smeaton about Jack's past, she's sure he wouldn't want him anywhere near the firearms.

She walks around the side of the building, towards the back of the north wing, a place that she knows she can't access unless she breaks in, but after how she felt when she was in there with Smeaton last week, it's not a place she's really keen to return to, not right now anyway. Although she *is* still curious about what happened in there. She still has memories from her childhood, from places like this. Both of her parents were in and out of such hospitals, while she was passed between various 'aunties' while 'mummy has a rest'. As much as she tries to push it away, she can't deny that her strange childhood has made her who she is.

She noticed the other day that in the space between the dilapidated wing and the newly manicured lawn, that there were several working sheds. At least that's what they looked like. She heads there now, her feet crunching on the loose gravel. She can hear the sound of what might be circular saw – a band saw. Is that what they're called? The kind of things you see in horror films where someone accidentally cuts off their hand. She giggles at the thought. The fake blood; the prosthetic hand. This place would certainly be a good setting for a horror film. Maybe it's already been used for something like that, back when it was completely abandoned. After the trust closed the hospital down. Before Smeaton moved in and tried to bring back its *light*.

As she gets closer to the sheds she can see that one of them has its door wide open, and the noise of the saw is louder. Someone is working inside.

'Hello?' she calls out loudly, not sure if she'll be heard. The last thing she wants to do is give someone a fright. She thinks again of the horror movie she conjured up, but this time it doesn't seem so funny. She tries again. 'Hello? It's Ali. Hope you don't mind me coming out here...'

She is at the door of the shed now, and inside she sees the handsome, rough-featured man that stood up for her at the party, when Jack was acting up. Ford, his name is. She remembers it because it's unusual, but also because he made quite an impression. He is someone who looks like they know how to make things, build things. Someone who knows how to deal with difficult situations. She watches him as he slides a thin plank of wood along the workbench, woodchips spitting as the teeth of the saw grip and cut. He is clearly a natural. He is wearing ear defenders, and his face is marked with concentration. She's not sure if he has heard her or not, but eventually he must sense her, and he looks up, confused for a moment. Then he smiles and turns off the saw. Ali is glad when the harsh whine ceases. He takes off the ear defenders and hooks them around his neck.

'Well, hello,' he says. Is that a smirk on his face, or just his usual smile? She can't tell, and she is trying not to be paranoid. She's worried about what he might've thought about her at the party, wondering if he thought her weak. It doesn't matter now anyway, because she won't be drinking any of that homemade wine again in a hurry and Jack most definitely won't.

Ford picks up a cloth from a workbench behind him and rubs at his hands. 'Good timing. I was just about to have a cup of tea.' He gestures behind him, where he has a kettle and a random selection of mugs. 'Care to join me?'

'Love to,' Ali says. 'But only if I'm not interrupting.'

He shakes his head. 'Ford,' he says, holds a hand out towards her. He is definitely smirking now. But she takes it as it's intended. Just a little joke, right? She shakes his hand; it is firm and dry. A strong hand-shake. Her hand feels so tiny in his. She imagines that he might crush it like the head of the flower, if he was so inclined. He turns away from her, flicks on the kettle and drops teabags into two mugs. 'Just normal tea in here; hope that's OK. I know you think that we're all a bunch of hippies, but we actually aren't. I can just about take their almost completely veggie diet, but I'm not giving up my breakfast blend for a bunch of boiled flowers that smell like something that's been lying at the bottom of an unflushed toilet.' He laughs.

Ali immediately feels at ease. She was right to do this. Not everyone is as strange and quirky as Angela. Misfits like Angela are everywhere. They're *everywhere* because they don't fit *anywhere*.

Maybe she can find some kindred spirits here after all. If things don't get back on track with Jack, who says there won't be a possibility for something else – *someone* else – in the future? She hasn't asked Smeaton about such things. She knows that the couples here already came in together, but have any others formed here? In the past? Surely there are no rules against that? She thinks about Jack, thinks about the feel of his body as he tried to hug her in bed that first day, how she flinched from his touch. But now she has an urge to be with him, wants to be close to him. She tries to imagine herself with Ford. Just watching him as he stirs the tea, she can tell that he is a different kind of man to Jack. She shakes her head as if trying to dislodge her thoughts. Her disloyal thoughts. After everything they've been through, the least that she can do is try to see Jack as her husband again, not just someone she has to look after, trying to mop up his mess and stop him from making more mistakes.

Ford walks around the other side of the saw, mugs in hands. She takes hers; its warmth is comforting, and the smell of the normal tea relaxes her more than any of the herbal ones she's had in here so far.

'So how are you settling in?' Ford asks. He doesn't wait for an answer. He wanders out of the shed into the grounds and she follows. He takes them over the grass to the pond. 'Looking good, don't you think? We've only just managed to keep it filled; the water kept draining back out into the earth, ended up having to brick most of it, and then cover it all with lots of plastic sheeting and waterproof tape. Kind of a makeshift tarp. Just hoping now that the pressure of the water keeps it in. I never imagined it would be so difficult to refill a pond.'

'You mean it was empty before? Why? I didn't think a pond would just dry up completely. Wasn't it deep? Or is it because there is no fresh water to flow into it?'

'Amazing what you have to teach yourself. What you have to do with these things when there's no one to do them for you or help you,' he says. 'It was deep, alright. The pond was part of the garden for years, but they drained it back in the fifties. Someone drowned. They decided it was too dangerous after that.'

'Oh, that's awful. A patient, you mean? At the hospital?'

'You'd need to ask Smeaton about that; he doesn't really like us talking about it.'

Ali is confused. 'But why? What's the big secret? It must be on public record...'

Ford shakes his head. 'I don't know, Ali. What you've got to realise is that there are many strange things in and around this house. It's better just to leave things be. Same with the village. I saw you chatting to

Angela, earlier. I'm sure she's been filling your head with stories. You probably think that she's making them up. But she's not, you know.'

He pauses, sensing Ali's alarm.

'You've no need to worry. She's completely harmless, she just wants to fit in. She's just fascinated by the history of this place. She knows more about it than anyone.

'Is she from around here?' Ali kicks a pebble and it bounces twice before plopping into the pond.

'No, but she lived in the village for nearly a year before she came to the house. She's well in with the locals, especially Mary – she's the one who owns the shop. I'm sure you'll be there soon enough, browsing all the things that you've no need for but still want to buy. Anyway, don't worry. Angela's a good kid.' He downs the rest of his tea and holds out a hand to take her mug. Then he heads back towards the shed. 'I need to get this finished today. You're welcome to stay and watch. But there's probably not much you can do to help today, not with this stuff. I don't want you cutting your fingers off before we've got to know each other properly.'

She smiles. 'No problem, I just wanted to pop round and say hello. It was nice to meet you properly. Thanks for the tea, and thanks for … you know. The other night.'

He shrugs. 'Nothing to thank me for. Jack's alright, you know. He's just a bit lost. I've been chatting to him a bit. He's going to start helping me out here. It'll be good for him. The two of you'll be fine. It's a big adjustment coming here. Just give it time.'

He's right, of course, and she's glad he's taken Jack under his wing. As long as Jack doesn't confide in Ford *too* much, everything will be fine.

She walks back past the lawn, past the pond. She pauses briefly at the side, trying to imagine how it all would have looked back in its heyday, imagining people drinking tea and eating dainty cakes, children running around, laughing. She closes her eyes. A gentle breeze drifts past, blowing her hair into her face. She feels at peace.

Then she hears a noise: a gentle splash. Another sound. Faint. Someone crying out?

She opens her eyes and stares at the pond, but the surface is like glass. There is no breeze. A trickle of sweat runs down her spine, and she thinks again about the boy in the kitchen. And suddenly she feels cold, so cold. Scared.

She turns away from the pond. Wants to get away from there, back to the other side of the building. As she hurries past the back of the kitchen, she stumbles. Someone is standing there, watching her. Rose.

'You want to be a bit careful, Ali,' she says. 'Don't listen to all that stuff Angela says. Ford neither. Best you keep your head down. Try to get used to the place a bit before you start trying to disrupt things, eh? This house has been here a long time, and there were things going on here long before even that. Best to leave it be, I think.'

Ali stares at her, taken aback. Doesn't know what to think, what to say. What has she done, other than be curious about the house? What has she done to make an enemy of Rose so quickly? She's still cold, still scared. She opens her mouth to speak, but before she can say a word, the other woman walks back into the kitchen and closes the door firmly behind her.

17

Angela

They've been here almost a month now, but I don't think Ali is going to be my friend. That's a shame. I thought that maybe when I tried to explain to her about the ghosts, about what I'm trying to do here, she might have understood. I wanted to hear about her time as a nurse, I'm sure she must have dealt with death plenty of times. And with grieving families, scared patients. Surely she doesn't just tell them, *Death is death. That's the end.* She must have some way of explaining it to them gently, giving them hope; she can't be heartless. I think she's scared here and I don't know why ... yet. I know that she has experienced something that she can't explain. I can sense it, even if she won't admit it to me. As a nurse, I suppose she has a scientific mind; she deals in facts. Unexplained feelings might be entirely out of her comfort zone.

But what I want to know is *why* it is happening.

This hasn't happened to anyone else since I've been here. Most people who come here feel peaceful in this house, but she appears to be feeling the opposite. Her presence is definitely causing some sort of disruption here ... Or is it Jack's? What happened at the party was worrying and although we've tried not to gossip, there has been talk. All of my equipment, which usually barely registers a thing, has started to play up. I'm not stupid, I know that most of the incidents my devices register are probably just due the atmosphere, new energies in the air. But isn't that exactly what I'm trying to prove? That there *are* energies, that there are things happening that we can't necessarily explain.

I'm disappointed.

But I'm also intrigued. Did she think that I wouldn't be interested in her experiences? Doesn't she realise that most of the time we are living here amongst ourselves? Smeaton discourages people from spending much time in the village, but because I lived there before, he lets me maintain those links. After all, I'm not even trying to deny that I'm different from the others. I will never be like them. But one thing I also know is that I love this place. And I don't want anything bad to happen to it or to any of the people here. This has become a place of love and hope. People who have been in very dark places have come here and found light. But there has been a shift now, and whatever the cause, some darkness has definitely crept in.

I need to identify it, and I need to find a way to stop it before it goes too far – before it tangles itself in our lives and makes something bad happen here. I take a deep breath in through my nose, letting the aromas in the air mingle and take shape. There's still that hint of something dark and smoky, like the aftermath of a fire. It's starting to cancel out all the other smells that I'm used to here, and I don't like it at all.

I knock on Smeaton's door, then walk in before he calls me. He's always happy to talk to me about my findings, few as they might be. Perhaps it's indulgence on his part, but we do have some fascinating conversations. He's had such an interesting life.

He's sitting at his desk, reading a heavy book with a faded cover – gold lettering that has flaked off, no dust jacket. It's impossible to tell the name of the book from how it looks, but I know that he is reading a first-edition copy of *Great Expectations*, because it's his favourite book and I know that he rereads it at least once a year. He smiles and lays the book on the table.

'Angela, how are you today? Anything exciting happening that I should know about?' He smiles and his eyes twinkle. He asks me the same question every single day, and every single day I tell him the same thing.

'Not yet, but there's always later. And there's always tomorrow.' I grin, and feel myself blush.

He leans forwards to stare at me. 'I feel like you've come here to tell me something proper this time,' he says. 'Am I right?'

I sit down in the leather chair opposite his desk. I love sitting in this chair, the leather is smooth and the padding beneath is still firm, so you only just sink into it. So you keep your back straight. It is the perfect chair for a visitor, as it gives the person sitting in it the immediate belief that they are important, and that they will be able to tell the story – whatever that story might be. I blurt mine out.

'It's about Ali and Jack,' I say. 'I think Ali's scared about something, I haven't had much of a chance to speak to Jack yet. He's been quiet since the party. Subdued. Do you think they're OK? I've tried to get Ali to open up, but she seems reluctant. Maybe you've had more luck with Jack?'

'Well, that's a shame about Ali. I felt that I had got to know her a little before she came here – from our email exchanges, setting everything up. I felt that she was quite open with me, but since she arrived, I agree with you, she seems closed, wary. I'm not doubting my decision to let them come here, but I do think that there is something that needs to be explored. As you know, this place is not for everyone.'

He is referring to the last couple who came here, Annie and Lawrence Palmerston. They left after two weeks. Not what they expected, Smeaton said – that was the official line. But I saw the old black book in her suitcase, with the strange symbols on the front. They were occultists, Mary reckons. She says the whole village knew about them. Wherever they are now, I'm sure they're not doing anything kind. I have to commend Smeaton for getting rid of them so quickly, but it's a worry that they seemed to be so nice and normal on all their assessment visits. I guess people like that are skilled manipulators. They know how to present themselves. They know how to infiltrate. They know how to pick on the vulnerable.

I shake my head, as if trying to dislodge the memory of them. Bring myself back to the present. 'And Jack?' I ask. 'You've been spending some time with him, haven't you? How's that going?'

Smeaton nods. 'Surprisingly well, actually. When he first arrived he seemed a bit spaced-out. I thought he might be on drugs, antidepressants maybe, something sedative.'

'Especially with what happened at the party,' I cut in, 'I'm not sure that elderflower wine mixes well with medication.'

'Quite. Well, I did ask, but he said no. But they've been here a few weeks now, and he seems much clearer of mind. So maybe it was just stress, his previous life—'

'Do you think there's something wrong with Jack?' I interrupt.

He shrugs. 'I don't know. Everyone needs a bit of help sometimes. But Jack almost seems to be helping himself by being here. And,' he pauses, steeples his hands, 'I'm probably speaking out of turn, but being with *me* a lot of the time, and not with Ali might be helping him. I get the feeling their relationship was very intense. I hate to use the term codependent ... And they were both working in stressful jobs.'

'He was a policeman, wasn't he?'

'Yes. He worked in child protection. He was part of a team of social workers and medical staff who reviewed children at risk, investigated their parents, new partners, all that sort of thing. His team was linked to something high profile, something that went wrong. It was a big deal, but of course none of us would have known about it. The only person who has any real, regular contact with the outside world, is you, Angela. And if you don't know, no one here does.'

'You know I never pick up the papers when I'm in Mary's shop,' I say, hoping he doesn't catch the lie. 'I want to avoid the real world as much as anyone else does. I certainly don't want to be reading about abused children.' I pause, glancing away. I don't want to seem too keen, too probing. 'Do you know any more about what went wrong?'

Smeaton shakes his head. 'He didn't tell me the full details. But he ended up having to leave the force due to stress. It pushed him over the edge, he said. He has huge periods where he can't even remember where he was or what he was doing.'

'Some kind of breakdown?' *Am I pushing too hard?*

'Perhaps. He told me he would wake up in strange places, with people thinking that he was drunk or on drugs, whole days of amnesia where he had had no idea that he'd even been to work. In the end his superiors said it wasn't safe for him to be on the case. They sent him for tests, and they said it was burnout. He took retirement, and Ali looked after him at home, giving up her own job to do it...' He pauses, takes a sip of tea.

This explains a lot, I think. About their dynamics. I'd assumed, as we all did, after the incident at the party, that he had hurt Ali in the past. Seems we weren't quite right about that. 'How stressful for them both.'

'Indeed. They lived like this for several months, and I think this time might have been too much for both of them. Two of them together in a small flat, him suffering from some sort of psychotic breakdown that no one seemed to be able to diagnose; Ali unsure whether she was his wife or his carer. You can imagine why she might be traumatised herself.'

'I had no idea.' I say, quietly.

My mind is whirring as I process this. He worked in child protection. Nothing to do with unexplained deaths on motorways or unidentified victims. I think about the newspaper clippings. Wonder again, what his interest was in these. Could it be because of his breakdown? Maybe he got confused, maybe he can't even remember cutting out the articles at all. Maybe he doesn't even know that he has them.

It's at times like this I'm glad I'm in the country, in this house, in this community.

Safe.

We have to be safe here. It's all that we have.

18
Ali

After breakfast Ali says, 'Do you fancy walking into the village with me today? We've been here a month.' She gives Jack a grin. 'We must be settled in enough now to risk being corrupted by the locals.'

Jack shakes his head. 'I don't think so. There's some stuff I want to do here. I've been helping Ford build a new area for the chickens. He thinks there are foxes getting in; we lost another one last night. I'd like to get started on that now, if that's OK? You go, though. I'm sure someone will go with you. Or it might be good to have some time to yourself?' He picks up his cereal bowl and his mug and carries it through to the washing area. Then he disappears outside. Ali is left at the table by herself, Jack's words bristling. He knows she doesn't like to be by herself. Everyone else is already off doing their jobs. She doesn't seem to have found a regular job yet – still helps out with many things. That suits her just fine for the moment; variety was always a thing she liked about nursing. She was always the one who was called on to deal with the more unusual cases – the things that disturbed the other nurses. Plus, she's hoping to spend some time in the library that Smeaton mentioned. If he ever tells her where it is.

She takes her own breakfast things through to the kitchen and offers to help wash up, but Rose shakes her head. 'Don't worry about it; you know I like doing it.'

Ali smiles and leaves through the back exit into the gardens. She doesn't say anything else to Rose. The woman has had a go at her several times when they've worked a kitchen shift together, telling her quite aggressively that she'd had to re-wash all of the pots that Ali had done, because she hadn't done them properly. Hot rinse, soak, scrub, cold rinse, drain, dry. Apparently Ali's pots were still greasy, not enough rinsing, not enough scrubbing. Ali couldn't be bothered to argue with her then, and she can't be bothered to argue today. Besides, she's still not sure what she meant by that comment outside the kitchen a few weeks ago, about not stirring things up. Who does Rose think she is? Clearly not someone who takes kindly to newcomers.

She walks out onto the lawn and decides that she will walk down to the other end where she hasn't been yet, maybe try and find the natural perimeter, walk all the way round. She was keen to go to the village, but now she isn't so sure. Jack is already different. He seems to be happy to make more of his own decisions, happy to spend time without her. She isn't used to it.

She walks round the edge of the lawn, listens to the gentle chirping of birds in the trees; there isn't much else to listen to. Her mind drifts, and she thinks about Jack. About what he was like when they met. About the night they met. When it all started.

It was July 2008. They met at the *Blue Light Ball*. A regular night in one of the shiny late-night bars at the end of Clapham High Street. It was a monthly thing, meant to be for all the services. So generally the place was full of police, firemen, nurses, and anyone else who'd heard about it, and fancied themselves a bit of something in uniform. There were plenty there, and it wasn't just the men who liked to pretend they were something that they weren't. Uniforms usually elicit two key reactions: there are those who despise them, and the authority they represent; and there are those who are inexplicably attracted to them, no matter what the person wearing it might look like. For the ladies, firemen, always come out on top. Think the Baldwins in *Backdraft*. For the boys: nurses – the more Barbara Windsor in *Carry on Doctor*, the better. The police usually came somewhere after that, for both males and females. There was an extra-special thrill when the gender norms were reversed, female fire officer, male nurse.

It was easy enough to tell the fakes. They talked about things that they'd seen on TV shows as if they were real. Ali would often select one of the fakes, just to wind them up. Simpering, and laughing at all their jokes, before delivering a caustic blow and walking away. She feels a little guilty now – maybe it wasn't a very nice thing to do, but it was just banter. No different from the blokes who thought it was smart to pretend to be something they weren't. She remembers Jack being one of the quietest of his crowd, but not at all shy. He had the right balance: not pushy, but when it was clear that you were keen, he was interesting to talk to, engaging. Not just one of those typical bolshie lads trying to impress. It wasn't just lads who did that obviously, there were plenty of girls who'd try to use their positions of power to ensnare men. Many people who wear uniforms have the propensity to play power games, but those people never come out on top in the end.

Jack had stared at her with big puppy-dog eyes, and although he had been chatting easily to two of the other girls in her group, when it came to Ali he seemed tongue-tied, stumbling over his words. Ali prided herself on being funny, good with a perfectly timed putdown, knowing how to back it all up with a nice compliment. She liked to have fun. One of Jack's friends, one of the bolshie types, tried the full-on charm offensive with her, but it didn't work. He was far too much of a Flash Harry for her, and despite what he thought of himself, not actually very good looking. Appearance was never actually the first thing that Ali went for, but there was something about Jack that attracted her immediately. He had a certain look, especially those eyes. Especially the way that he looked at her, like she was some kind of goddess. Ali took care of herself; she knew that she looked good, but she wasn't vain. She had never been short of men, though, always having her pick, usually having brief flings, short-term relationships. Just enough to make sure she wasn't on her own too much, but she still had her freedom. She probably did like the idea of control just a little too much. The occasional bossing around of the juniors on the ward, maybe. She was fascinated by this element of behaviour – often observing the senior doctors and how it all worked so effortlessly for them. But she'd never really known what it was like to truly control someone. Didn't even know that she could.

Until she met Jack.

She remembered sitting in the dark corner of the bar, her and Jack deep in conversation, two champagne flutes in front of them that someone kept topping up from the bottle of cheapo two-for-one Prosecco that sat in an ice bucket on the table. They drank a lot, talked a lot. They were all words and hands and deep, longing looks. She was desperate to get him home, but not just because she wanted to sleep with him.

There was a connection there. That way he looked at her ... it was something special. Something important. She remembered when his bolshie friend came over to them at the end of the night, worse for wear, trying to persuade them to go back to a party with a bunch of the others. There were stage-whispered mentions of orgies and swinging. Not Ali's scene. Yeah, she had tried a few things. And she didn't mind what other people got up to, but she much preferred one man at a time. Preferably the one that she had chosen. Jack had told his mate that no, they weren't going to come. He'd suggested to Ali already that they went to a late-night café. Have some coffee, something to eat. More time to chat.

His mate had laughed, shaking his head, and said to Jack, 'Christ, man, you've only just met her. Think about it, you don't want her wrapping you around her little finger, not straightaway anyway.' He laughed. Ali had been a little bemused by this, wondering what he meant. He must have sensed her confusion, because he continued: 'He's got a bit of a *thing*.' He made air quotes with his fingers and laughed. 'When he likes someone, he gets a bit obsessed. Play your cards right, love, and he will do absolutely *anything* you ask him to. Anything.' He winked, and slapped Jack on the shoulder, before disappearing off with a girl on each arm. Ali looked at Jack, and saw he was gazing at her intently. A smile on his face as if he had drifted off somewhere, but taking her with him.

He would do anything for me, would he?

Ali wondered about this. Wondered if this lovely, sweet man might just be the little pet project she'd been looking for. She wasn't going to tell anyone that bit, of course. And she felt a little bad even thinking it. But it wasn't just about fun, coming to these nights? She'd had a bit of an agenda all along. She had an idea for an academic thesis, and she needed a subject. It had been tricky to recruit, because the subject had to adore her ... and most importantly, the subject had to have no idea that he was part of an experiment.

And of course the subject had to have certain propensities...

Oh Jack, she'd thought. *What were the chances of finding you tonight?*

She is back at Rosalind House before she knows it. She barely remembers the walk at all, but she's enjoying the sun on her cheeks. Most of all, she's enjoying remembering what Jack was like in the beginning, how it all started. The fun they used to have. She said jump, he said how high? It was a game that they'd both enjoyed.

Now she just needs to make sure he plays by her rules.

Dr Henry Baldock's Journal – 20th April 1955

I think after what I have seen so far, some changes will have to be implemented sooner rather than later. I was unsure about coming here under the guise of a new doctor, when in fact I was sent here by the authorities to check on procedures and report back – the whistle-blower had told us some worrying things and it seemed that this was the correct way to approach matters, to observe rather than accuse. It was also thought that my presence here might be enough to deter anything untoward. But it did backfire somewhat. I reacted too passionately to the scene in the bathroom, and perhaps should have appeared less shocked – especially as it was one of the things I'd been warned to look out for. Cold-bath therapy is one of the worst forms of quackery, and one that has no place in a modern medical facility. However, I worry now that the trust I had started to build with the staff has been lost – but maybe it's not over yet.

They still don't know who I am. They only suspect, and I think if I can get them back onside I can find a way to deal with this without causing further distress. I think perhaps going back to some of the older methods will help. They used to organise many things here, tea dances, family fêtes; all of these things giving the patients something to focus on and contribute to. I know that many of the women were keen bakers before they were admitted here. With supervision, they can be allowed to enjoy some of these pleasures again. And getting some of the men involved in prettying up the gardens again; mowing the lawns is done, of course, but perhaps planting some flowers will be therapeutic.

Perhaps, in time, we can persuade them to be involved in putting on a show – in the past, some of these patient-led shows have been a great success – the creativity of performance and preparing the sets a great therapy. But perhaps something simpler, first, a garden party – with all the patients' families invited. The staff's families, too. Something to bring them all back onto an even keel, appreciate what they have here – in this beautiful setting, and there is good being done here. I am certain that something like this will help mend the frosty atmosphere, make this a happy place once more.

I don't know where the deep sadness has come from, but I know that I do not care for it one bit.

19

Ali

Ali knows that only she can make things better for them both. She waits until Jack has had breakfast and gone outside to his usual job, which now seems to be helping Ford – collecting wood, chopping wood. Ford is teaching him how to make things, and Jack has seemed a lot happier these last few weeks. If Jack can forget about what he's done, then maybe she can too. As long as she stays out of Angela's way, things will be better. As long as she accepts that Jack has changed now, things will be better.

She finds him in the woodshed, alone. 'Hey,' she says. 'You're on your own? Where's Ford?' She walks over to be closer to him. 'What you doing?'

Jack picks up a rag and wipes his hands. 'He's gone to the tip to get some stuff for the gazebo. I'm not sure what. I wanted to go with him but he said it be better if I stayed here and got on with this. He's asked me to prep these planks for some decking. It's to go outside the back doors into the garden. One of his ideas to spruce this place up. He's got all these plans – have you seen them?'

'No, I haven't but that sounds great,' Ali says. 'Can I have a look, then?'

She is still impressed by how easily Jack seems to have adapted. She needs to take a leaf out of his book and try to relax. She follows him over to the other side of the woodshed and watches as he unfolds a large sheet of paper. He lays it out flat, then puts a few different objects on the corners to keep it that way: two stones, a piece of brick and a large chunk of glass.

'This is the lawn, as you can see.' Jack runs a finger across the paper. 'And the pond. Still having trouble with that, trying to make sure it's sealed up properly. Ford is pretty sure that he's got it right this time. From what he says, the only way it will leak now will be very gradually, through the groundwater path, into the soil. We've got markers in there so we can measure the water level, see if it's draining away or staying put. There is a natural drainage pipe, obviously, to stop it flooding out when it rains.' He points to another section on the plan. 'This bit over here ... he wants to turn this part into some sort of games area, a croquet lawn, I think. This is the kind of thing that Smeaton asked him to do. He wants to recreate what it was like back in the olden days. When they had garden parties here. It's a nice thing for the community, and beyond – he hopes.'

Ali is impressed. She likes the vision, likes the effort that has been put into this. 'So Ford is doing this all by himself?'

'Well, he has me now,' Jack laughs.

She smiles. 'Jack saves the day.'

'I'm joking ... of course he's got other help. Lots of people are doing things for the new garden. It's just at the moment, there is not much for the others to do. We need to make the decking boards first. Then he'll probably get some help to lay them, and we'll need to level the land. Richard will bring various tools round from the shed, I imagine.'

'I'm proud of you,' Ali says. 'I didn't know how things were going to pan out here, but it seems like they're going well. For you, anyway.' She pauses, but Jack doesn't reply. 'Look, I know we haven't spoken much lately,' she continues. 'Ships in the night, and all that – you always seem to be off out doing things and I'm still feeling a bit lost. So, I just want to say I'm sorry if I've been a bit tetchy, I'm still finding it a bit difficult. I haven't found my people yet. And I've had a bit of bother with Angela, but nothing to worry about...'

'Bother? What do you mean?' Jack says, a note of worry in his voice.

Ali shakes her head. 'Sorry. *Bother* isn't the right word. I just found her a bit clingy, maybe. She's a bit of an odd one, but I'm sure she's harmless – that's what everyone keeps telling me. I don't know though.

I felt like she was pushing me for information. Not sure if it's just natural curiosity or if—'

'If what? She can't know anything, can she? About us?'

Ali shrugs. 'I'm not so sure. She goes into the village. She knows people – she used to live there. She might have looked us up.'

'So what if she has? All she's going to find is what we used to do, our jobs. That's all there is. You're worrying about nothing. There's nothing else online that can harm us, is there?'

Ali hopes that Jack is right, but she's not sure. She's been careful, tried to keep it all under control. But has she been careful enough?

She thinks back to that first thing they did – the first time they played 'the game' ... she'd dared him to steal as much as he could from the newsagents at the corner of their street. He'd come back with two bars of chocolate, hidden inside a rolled newspaper. She'd laughed at how pathetic it was, but he'd been so pleased with himself – that he'd done what she asked. That had been the start of it, and they'd got away with it – and much more. She kept waiting for a knock at the door. The police saying they'd been caught on CCTV. But they never were.

Who could've known how far Jack would let them take it?

She gives Jack a little wave and walks back towards the house, pausing for a moment at the pond.

She crouches down and dips a hand into the water, swirling it gently. A thin string of pondweed slithers to the surface, wrapping itself around her finger – slimy, cold and wet. She tries to flick it off with her other hand, but it won't budge – the tendril pulls tighter. She grabs hold of it, yanking and tugging, feeling her heart start to beat faster ... faster. She pulls back sharply, her body landing on the grass with a bump.

The weed slips back under the surface, as if pulled from beneath.

After a moment, the water stops moving, and everything is calm once more. She stares down at her hand, and sees a sliver of a cut, a single droplet of blood.

She swallows back a hard lump of breath, and slowly gets to her feet. Blood trickles down her finger and she wipes it on her jeans. Her heart is still beating faster than it should, as her mind tries its hardest to tell her that nothing strange has just occurred.

Nothing strange at all.

20
Angela

Ali is halfway into the kitchen when, instinctively, I grab her by the arm and pull her back. 'I know you've been avoiding me,' I say.

She whirls around. 'Hey,' she says. 'Don't grab at me like that.' She shrugs herself away from me and I notice a smear of something on her jeans. *Is that blood?*

'Oh God, I'm sorry, Ali. I'm sorry. I didn't mean to grab you. Are you OK? Did you cut yourself?'

She shakes her head. 'It's nothing.'

'It's just that I've been looking for you, the last few days. Wherever I go, someone tells me you've just been there. Starting to get a complex here. Have I done something wrong?' I smile, and I'm trying to make my voice sound light, like I'm not really bothered, that it really was just a mistake that I kept missing her. But I can tell that there is no mistake. I can tell that she's been staying out of my way. Ever since I took her to the swing in the woods, told her my theories about ghosts. Asked her what she'd seen.

I get it. I'm not stupid. Maybe I went in too soon, but it was just a conversation. She doesn't have to believe me. She doesn't have to be interested. But she can still talk to me, can't she? Not treat me like a leper. She looks uncomfortable now, biting her lip. She looks like she wants to be as far away from me as possible. To be honest I haven't really experienced this level of dislike from someone before; people tend to take me or leave me. Some think I'm a joke and some don't. I know who my friends are most of the time. But Ali ... I just can't read her at all. Apart from the fact that I *know* she's hiding something. I know she's felt something here.

I've done this all wrong. It was Jack I should have targeted. From what Smeaton says, he seems much more open. Much more keen to embrace this new life. I wonder if he'd be interested in what I'm doing here. Maybe I should be offering *him* a tour of the *real* parts of the building. Not just the official ones. Not just the bits of the story that Smeaton tells, to keep everyone appeased. I know the truth about this place. I know more than most people know. But not because Smeaton told me, but because I knew before I came. I'm not even sure that Smeaton knows the full extent of what happened here. But the villagers do. Because the villagers have been here for a very long time.

'Look, Ali, we seem to have got off to a bad start here. Can we try again? How about I take you and Jack out for a walk, show you some more of the hidden sights. I know you've been around most of the place with Smeaton, and with some of the others too. But I can tell you lots of stories. All about the history of the place. Nothing to do with ghosts, I promise.' I grin.

She frowns. 'I don't know, Angela. To be honest, I'm more about looking to the future, not the past. Jack and I came here to start new lives, to learn new things. To become different people. I know you're keen on all this stuff. But it's not for me. I don't really want to know about the creepy history of this place.'

I am thrown by this. Who doesn't want to know the history of the place where they are living? She's lying. She doesn't want me to tell her about the ghosts, which is fair enough. But why wouldn't she want to know about the rest of it? She's a nurse. This is a hospital, and there are so many stories to be told. I truly thought she'd be interested in hearing them. What happened to the Samuels, tried for witchcraft in 1593; what happened to their descendants just fifty years ago – the taunting ... the drowning...

I don't like that she is pushing me away like this. It makes me feel nervous. I try to push the doubts out of my mind, stop thinking about what Mary said in the shop. That we don't know them; we don't know what they've done. Maybe they've done nothing. Maybe we are being harsh – not giving them some space just to settle in at their own pace.

'OK, Ali. I just need to ask you about one thing, and then I'll leave you to get on with whatever it is you want to do.'

Ali shrugs. The fight seems to have left her; I can almost read her mind. *Anything for a quiet life.* That's what she's thinking.

'Right then, let's go and get a tea or something, shall we; I know I don't need to be in here right now. I'm sure it's all under control.' I glance into the kitchen and see that they are all busy preparing lunch. If any of them have noticed us they haven't said anything. People here are good at that, when they want to be. Of course they will have heard the full exchange. But whether they mention it or not is a different thing.

We walk through to the small sitting room and pour ourselves hot water. I drop a raspberry and nettle bag into my mug. Ali frowns before choosing something else. Lemon, I think. I curl onto the sofa, cross-ing my legs. I hold the mug in both hands, finding it warming and comforting. Ali sits on an armchair, completely upright. She holds her mug by the handle, the other hand underneath gently supporting it. She is not relaxed. I wonder if maybe I shouldn't do this now. I am slightly worried about how she will react, but it will be my last attempt at trying to rattle something out of her, before I leave her alone and go back to observing her from afar.

'Smeaton told me that Jack worked on a horrible child-protection case. That he had to retire due to stress.'

Ali looks down into her mug; her shoulders slump. 'Actually, he had a complete breakdown. He was forced to take medical retirement. Anyone would've, with all the stress he was under. It nearly killed him. I looked after him myself, nursed him through it. But it was difficult, even with my training. When you turn from wife to carer things are never the same.' She looks up at me, 'I don't know why I'm telling you all this,' she says, 'but it kind of feels good just to say it.'

I ponder this. Then make a rash decision. 'Don't be mad Ali—' I say. I let the sentence hang in the air unfinished.

Ali sits up straight again and puts her mug down on the side table. She's staring at me now, her eyes wide and bright. 'Don't be mad about *what* Angela. What have you done?'

Her tone is fierce, but there is something else in there. She smells sharp, something bitter coming off her, like grapes that have shrivelled and soured. Why would she immediately assume that I had done anything? Her reaction puzzles me, as most of her reactions do. She's calm one minute, then flies off the handle the next. She doesn't seem to know who to talk to, or how much of herself to give away. She's confused, that's for sure; but she's right. I have done something. Something I shouldn't have done, that has sent my imagination into overdrive. I'm just going to have to tell her, and deal with it.

I swallow a lump of air. 'I know it was wrong, I know I shouldn't have done it, but I was just trying to get to know who you are. Most people when they come here, they don't bring much. We've nothing to go on, we need to learn about them. All we have is what people say, but you barely say anything. I've no idea who you are. You seem to be a closed book on every level.'

She leans forwards in the chair. 'What did you do Angela? Please … just spit it out.'

'I didn't mean to.' I pause, take a sip of my tea, grip the mug tighter. 'I was telling you about my equipment, about the rooms I have to put things in, I was trying to tell you before – your room, there was always lots of activity. But Smeaton told me I couldn't put anything in there. But I already had, so I just had to go into pick something up so I could set it up elsewhere. I promise you, I didn't mean to snoop—'

'What do you mean snoop? Did you go through my things?'

'Not really, no, that's not what I mean. OK yes, I did go into your room. Looked at your dressing table, in your wardrobe. Looked in your bookcase.'

'You had no right. That's our private stuff. I should speak to Smeaton about this. You had no right to be in my room. No bloody right!'

'I know that. I'm sorry.' I look away. 'It's just, I don't know … I guess I was curious. I opened the box—'

'Box? What box?'

'The box on the bookcase, the one full of papers. Clippings. Articles cut out from newspapers … You know what I mean.' I start to cry then.

I don't mean to. I didn't think I would. I thought I was strong enough for this conversation, but now I know I'm not. I don't like being in trouble. I'm scared. Her expression scares me. As for Jack – I don't even know what he might do when he finds out. He hasn't said much to me before, but he does stare at me quite intently. I haven't really thought about it too much before, but now I realise that something about him really unnerves me.

'You had no right to go in that box, Angela. Those are private papers. Not even *my* private papers. Jack's. Jack's work things. You shouldn't have been in there, Angela.'

Hang on ... she is lying. Those clippings aren't related to Jack's work. I know they aren't. They don't fit. It doesn't make any sense. I don't know what else to say to her now. I don't know if she will go to Smeaton, but I think she will. But I expect that she'll go to Jack first, and I won't have heard the end of this. I'm such an idiot. Yes, it was wrong of me to look at her things. But that's not my biggest mistake. I should have kept my mouth shut, just continued to monitor her, started to try to get to know Jack, to see what I could learn there. Because there is a secret hidden in that box.

I think back to their arrival. The strange smell in the air, the silence. The horrible, heavy feeling of dread that draped itself onto me. That's why I couldn't stay to meet them. I had to get away, but I didn't know why. I didn't know then, that the feeling of dread that I'd felt was all related to them.

What did he do, I wonder? What did Jack do that Ali is trying her best to keep hidden?

Ali stands up, and I can see that she is shaking, she's trying to control it, but it's definitely there. I sit where I am, frozen. Speechless.

'This was a mistake, Angela. You really shouldn't have snooped in our stuff,' she says. 'Jack...' She stops herself, shakes her head. She has gone deathly pale, looks like she might throw up. She's terrified ... and now, so am I.

21
Ali

She needs space. Feels like the walls are closing in on her. Angela is getting too close and she doesn't know what to do. Could that strange girl have taken anything from that box? She wouldn't put it past her.

Right, she decides, shaking herself and squaring her shoulders. Time to do some snooping of her own.

She heads upstairs and along to the far end of the building, where she knows some of the bedrooms are located. Fergus told her where his was in the kitchen one day; he said she was welcome to visit him any time, if she wanted to talk – why is everyone so nosey in this place? What he *did* mention, though, and what's useful to her now, is that his room is in the same corridor as Angela's.

She turns the corner, and is faced with a long passageway. It's the same as all the others: chipped lino floors and peeling paint; a musty smell of mould with an underlying hint of chemicals. The doors are all closed, but there is a shimmer of light coming from one of the doors at the end. Fergus's, maybe? She knows that Angela is not in her room right now...

She stops walking, and tries to decide what to do. Any of these doors could be Angela's, but maybe they're locked, like she locks her own. And if someone is in that room at the end, she doesn't want to disturb them – and more importantly, she doesn't want them disturbing her.

This is a stupid idea, she decides. She shakes her head, turns around and walks, quickly and quietly, back around the corner towards the stairs.

It's then that she sees the figure.

She hangs back against the wall, trying to pull herself in tight, make herself invisible. She doesn't recognise who it is that is standing by the door to the room down the end of the corridor – the room that she knows is above hers. That room is empty, her mind tells her. She knows this. She's seen it for herself. *This is ridiculous*, she thinks. She has every right to be here, does she not? Besides, they must've seen her now ... She opens her mouth to speak; but then something stops her.

She doesn't recognise the woman in the corridor. Has never seen anyone dressed like this in the house before. An old-fashioned grey dress, long dark hair pulled up into a bun. Ali takes a step back, trying to disappear around the corner again, but the floor gives her away – just the faintest creak...

The woman in the grey dress turns around. Her face is twisted in anger. 'You,' she says, walking towards Ali, her arm outstretched, pointing, accusing, 'You,' she says again, louder this time.

Ali is frozen. She can't move, can't scream. She closes her eyes tight, willing the woman to go away. This mad woman, pointing at her, shouting at her ... who is she?

A door slams somewhere close by, and Ali opens her eyes.

There is no one there.

Was there ever anyone there? Or was this just another of these tricks that her mind has been playing on her?

She waits until her breathing returns to normal, and then she makes her way down the stairs, trying all the while to convince herself that nothing untoward has happened.

IIIII

Ali feels subdued at dinner. She eats but doesn't want to speak. She's still trying to process the strange things that have been happening, trying to rationalise them in her brain. What was it that Smeaton said – about the subconscious taking over? That's it. That must be it. She knows that she has to talk to Jack, and soon. While part of her still thinks that Angela's ghost stories are complete nonsense, she can't deny that she's been spooked. Even more so, knowing that

Angela has seen the news clippings and is now highly suspicious. She thought that saying they were related to Jack's job would be enough to get her to back off. But she saw the look in the younger woman's face. She was terrified. Ali didn't react well; she realises that now, letting her own fear rise to the surface like that. But it had been a shock. She'd thought that Angela was going to tell her something else about the room, that it was bugged or something. Not that she'd been poking about in her things. It hadn't crossed her mind that anyone here would do that, which was stupid of her. Why should people be any less nosey just because they live in a place like this? It's obvious now, in hindsight, that everyone here is probably gossiping and speculating about them both, and she's made it all worse by closing herself off so much.

She glances across at Jack, who is shovelling huge mouthfuls of spicy couscous into his mouth, oblivious to her distress. A bubble of anger pops in her throat, forcing her to cough, clear her throat. This is not how it was meant to be. Except that it is *exactly* how it was meant to be – she's the one who can't seem to let go of the past. Every day that Jack grows stronger, Ali feels weaker inside.

'Do you mind if we just go back to our room after this,' she asks. Jack grins through a mouthful of aubergine stew. He has adapted to the semi-vegetarian diet here a lot quicker than she has. OK, so they do have rabbit now and again, but she doesn't like having to pick the shot out of the damn stuff.

'Whatever you want, love. I'm quite tired actually. It was a pretty full-on day, in the end.'

They both decide against dessert, Ali because she is still struggling with the food and some of the strange ingredients, and Jack, she assumes, because the couscous has continued to expand in his stomach and he physically can't fit anything else in. Having made their excuses, they walk back along the corridors instead of joining the others in the sitting room for tea and games. Jack takes her hand. Her first instinct is always to pull away. But maybe it would make more sense to appease him right now; she needs to keep him on an even keel, for what she's about to say. She's not fully convinced by his mental normality, despite the way he appears.

It's like he's read her mind. 'I feel like a new person here, Ali,' he says. 'I never thought I would. But this life, away from it all ... I feel so different. All that stuff that happened before...' He pauses. She can't look at him. 'All that stuff, that I did ... I just don't feel like that person anymore. I feel like it all happened to someone else, another Jack.'

She says nothing.

Back in the room, she locks the door and leaves the key in the keyhole. Jack, as always, immediately goes and lies on the bed, throws his hands behind his head. Gets himself comfortable. She pushes back another burst of anger. Or is it frustration? She wonders if she will always feel this way. It feels so unfair. Why is it that *he* thinks that he can just move on, acting like nothing ever happened? He can't have forgotten all of it. She is sure of that. And yet *she* still has to live with it every day. She has to accept what he did, and keep it locked up inside her, where it festers. Driving her further and further away from the person she wants to be. She is suspicious and paranoid, and this was never who she was meant to be. If she was doing what she was meant to, she would be writing all of this down. These would be her follow-up findings, after the initial experiment – the project that she was working on. But it's abandoned, now. It's not as if she could publish it anyway. Not under her real name, at least. Not with any mention of her relationship to the subject – but then what would be the point? Her relationship to the subject *was* the whole point.

'I'm getting worried about Angela,' she says. 'She's too nosey. She keeps telling me stuff, and I have no idea if any of it's true. But...' She pauses.

'What?' Jack says. 'She's a nice kid. She's been nothing but welcoming. Her offers of stories, tours ... She's excitable, excited. She clearly likes having some new people here. If she's a bit exuberant, is that not a good thing? You don't have to be so negative all the time, Ali,' he says.

Ali balls her hands into fists. 'Jesus, they've got their hooks into you, haven't they? All this positivity bullshit? *Embrace the light*, eh?'

Jack sighs. 'I really can't be arsed with an argument tonight, Ali. I meant it when I said I was exhausted. And you're getting yourself stressed when there's nothing to be stressed about. Isn't that why we've come here? All it's been since we got here is silences and arguments...'

'You can't just run away from your past, Jack. We moved away, but that's a physical thing. It's going to take a lot longer to change things mentally, for me at least. Have you genuinely forgotten what you did? Have you forgotten how much I've helped you get over it all? As for your precious Angela, she's no bloody angel. Fairy Fucking Angela. You know she was snooping in here don't you? You know she's found your box of fucking shit?'

Jack sits bolt upright; his eyes widen in surprise. '*My* box?'

Ali stomps over to the bookcase, pulls out the grey box and upends it on the bed, spilling out the contents. 'Yes. Your box. She's found the clippings. The clippings I told you *not* to bring. Why the hell didn't you get rid of them all when I told you to? Why would you keep a damn *record*?'

Jack stares at the papers. Picks them up and starts to rip them into pieces. Then he starts to laugh. A horrible cackling laugh that she hasn't heard for a very long time. It gives her an instant chill. He shakes his head, still smiling, and throws the ripped fragments into the air.

'Fuck's sake, Ali, they're just clippings. To be honest I had completely forgotten they were in there. I thought that box was full of bank statements.' He climbs out of bed and walks across to the wardrobe, opens it wide. At the back, in one corner, there is a stack of shoeboxes. He lifts a couple of them up, slides out one from nearer the bottom and brings it back over to the bed. Ali is trembling now. She recognises this box. She didn't know that it was in there. She thought they'd got rid of it, that day when they went to the landfill site and buried so many things.

'So ... she didn't find *this* box,' Jack says. He takes off the lid and tips the contents onto the middle of the bed. It's full of small Ziploc bags, each one labelled with a sticker. The name – if they knew it, the date, the road where they picked them up. Ali looks away. She can't look at the stuff. She doesn't need to look at it, to know what's in there. A belt.

A necklace. A notebook. A wallet. Trinkets, from people who were too desperate, too trusting.

'Why have you still got these?' Ali says, quietly. She feels tears pricking at her eyes. They can never escape this, can they? He might be able to pretend that it's all in the past, but she can't. Their faces come to her, every night as she's on the brink of sleep. Purple and bloated. Their eyes popping. The fear and shock. Then nothing, as their lights are snuffed out. And every time, she replays it, she says never again – but it is a sickness … *his* sickness – and all she can do is try to treat him as best she can.

'I couldn't bury all this. It was never going to be safe anywhere, except with me. Besides, you say I'm trying to forget about what I did? I won't let myself. I know you've tried to help me forget, but I don't want that. I need to remember. Every day, I feel like memories are coming back to me. And you know what? I'm not scared. I am repulsed. But keeping this stuff reminds me what I'm capable of. Keeping this stuff makes me feel strong. It keeps me on track. To make sure I never do it again.'

A tear runs down Ali's cheek and she wipes it angrily away. *Is that right?* She thinks. *You're never going to do it again?* The steely resolve that she'd felt before comes back to her like a hard slap to the face. *Are you sure about that, Jack?*

22

Angela

Rustling and scratching sounds wake me first, before I realise that the screen on my phone has lit up. Something has activated the camera in Ali and Jack's bedroom. I sit up in bed, and peer at the screen. I sigh, and watch. It's only Ali. She's out of bed, pulling on a coat over her pyjamas. What is she doing? The sound isn't great through the phone, hence the rustling and scratching. But I'm curious to find out what she's up to. I pull on some clothes myself, and a pair of boots.

I tiptoe out of my room, trying not to make any of the floorboards creak. There is one particular board in between my room and Fergus's, which always has to be avoided when sneaking around late at night. I'm still watching the screen, and see that Ali is no longer in the bedroom. The time on the screen says 1:25 a.m.

I need to know what she's doing.

As I turn the corner and walk towards the front of the house, I hear the unmistakable sound of a gunshot. I stop, startled for a moment, and then I understand. I walk faster, dropping the phone into my pocket. There's no point watching her room now. Then I stop, trying to force my ears to hear something, to hear her creeping around.

I move on. I'm in her corridor now. I pass the room next to hers and pause again briefly, listening. But there is no noise. I take the staircase up to the next floor, and tiptoe into the room above Ali's. The window here is similar to the one in her room, facing to the front. I position myself at the edge of the window so that I can see out as best as I can, without anyone being able to see me – and then I wait.

After a moment, I see what wakened Ali. It's exactly what I thought it would be. Their flat-bed truck is parked in the driveway. In the moonlight, I can just make out their silhouettes. One of them is sitting on the back of the truck, something in his hand. It's not switched on, but I know that this is his torch. The lampers are here. I don't know why they've come up to the house like this. Usually shining the lamp at Smeaton's bedroom window is all they need to do. They're just making him aware that they're out there. A courtesy that they have always offered. Although we are all used to them by now, and they rarely wake me up.

I can't hear what's happening outside, but I see the light go on at the front door, and I know that Ali is going to appear there. I slide the sash window up a couple of inches. I've had to unstick this window before. It sometimes gets jammed, and it can often get very hot in here, and sometimes very cold. It's one of the places where I have tested things. I've checked the floors, running a marble across the room to measure the incline, and I've checked the temperature often and found it to be extremely variable. I crouch down and put my face to the gap, breathing in the cool, still air. I catch a faint whiff of gun smoke, which might be real or might just be my imagination; either way the smell exists for me.

Ali is standing with her arms crossed. She shouts first. 'What the hell do you think you're doing? It's the middle of the bloody night!'

'Sorry to disturb you,' the man holding the big torch jumps off the back of the van and walks towards Ali. 'Didn't expect any of you to be awake this time of night.' His face is clearly lit now by the heavy, hanging moon, and I recognise him: he's a friend of Mary's son, Chris. I'm pretty sure his name is Robert. The other three men climb out of the truck, and walk around to join him. One of them is chewing gum, snapping it in his mouth. I swear that I can smell the mint – that it's spearmint, not peppermint.

Robert takes a couple more steps towards Ali. The man to his right, who is holding a shotgun and whose name I don't know, joins him. I glance back at Ali. Her arms are no longer crossed, and I see that she's holding something. I'm not sure what is. A long piece of wood? I squint, and as she moves forwards I work out what it is. It's a cricket bat. The one that hangs on the wall inside the foyer. Some famous cricketer donated it. It's an ornament, and I'm shocked to see Ali wielding it like that. I don't think Smeaton will be pleased if he finds out that she is brandishing this antique like a weapon.

I can feel a prickle of electricity in the air now; excitement and fear radiating from the men standing by the truck. Adrenaline pulsing from Ali, as she tries to defend herself against what she perceives to be a threat. I should call out. I should tell her that it's nothing to worry about. That the lampers come here every so often, shooting foxes. Getting rid of the vermin. They attack their sheep and chickens, and never just take one to satisfy their hunger. Foxes are the serial killers of the animal world. They kill for sport, as much as food. It's hardly surprising that the farmers and their helpers do the same to them. I'm not sure I agree with it, but it's nothing to do with me. They shine their bright torches into the foxes' faces, and it stuns them. The animals don't see the light as a threat. It's to do with their eyes – with them being nocturnal. While the foxes stare, the men get an easy shot. The agreement with Smeaton is that when they drive by the house, they come a little way up the driveway and shine their light towards the house, just to let us know that they're here. So that we don't panic when we hear the gunshots.

This is the countryside ... gunshots are not unusual. But when it's the middle of the night, it's a simple courtesy. We don't have much to do with the villagers, but we do coexist on the land.

Ali holds the bat out in front of herself as if she is waiting for someone to bowl. 'Yeah, well you did scare me, as it happens. I don't sleep well. I heard the guns, then I heard your truck. Saw the light shining inside – I've come from the city, where this kind of shit in the middle of the night usually involves a robbery.'

The men laugh.

'Last thing we'd be doing around here is trying to rob the place,' Robert says.

Ali snorts. 'You trying to tell me there's nothing here of interest, are you?'

I can almost feel her bristling. Despite all that she's experienced in the city, she's not used to this kind of behaviour. These country boys, playing with her. They have no malicious intent, but she doesn't know that. She is seeing what she wants to see. What she expects to see. I hold my breath. I know I should call out. I should call on Robert, tell him to stop. To back off. He'll recognise me. He'll listen. Or I could run downstairs to Ali, go out and join her. Put this to an end. But something stops me. Call it a morbid fascination, but I want to see what she's going to do next.

I want to see what *they* are going to do next.

Robert and the man with the shotgun take a few more steps towards Ali and she stretches out her hand, waving the bat at them menacingly. 'You need to go now ... go back to your beds, little boys. You shouldn't be here.'

'Oh, the newcomer is a bit of a feisty one, is she? Seems like she might've fitted in here, back in the day – with all the other mad bitches. Or is that witches?' Robert glances around towards the others and they all laugh again. 'Maybe you just don't know what us country boys are like, eh? Maybe you just need to get to know us better.'

A shiver runs through me. It's not like Robert to be so nasty, especially mentioning the witches like that. The family accused of bewitching the Throckmortons were pardoned. The villagers are usually much more respectful about the past. Ali has riled him, that's for sure.

Robert takes one more step towards her. He is almost close enough to touch the bat, now. He's still holding the torch. 'How about we take you for a little ride and show you around the place properly? I think you'd like that, darlin', wouldn't you?' He glances around at his boys again. 'I know that *we'd* like it. We'd all like it very much.' Laughter again, but it sounds different now and I'm not sure that *I* like it.

In fact, I don't like what's happening here at all. I'm pretty sure that the boys are just winding her up, but I've never seen them do this before. I think they're sensing something off her, just as I have. They don't trust her. They don't like her. Do I like her? I don't know yet. But this ... this is all quite disturbing. I can see her face, teeth bared. Eyes shining. She looks like she wants to hurt someone. Is this how women have to live in the cities now – in a constant state of fear from a man's words?

'Get the fuck away from me,' Ali hisses. 'I'll scream. I'll get the others down here, because that's the right thing to do. But I'm not scared to deal with you myself, you little bastards.'

The other men walk forwards until they are all in line with Robert. They are all staring at Ali, and their expressions are confused. Robert drops his torch and holds up his hands in surrender. 'We're only messing with you, missus. We'll be off now, OK?' he smirks, and then he bends down to pick up the torch. Before I can make the decision to shout something out of the window, he flicks the switch and directs the beam straight into Ali's face, dazzling her. She stumbles backwards, bat still in her hand.

She's screeching now: 'You little fucker...' She regains her stance, but the men have moved back towards the truck. They're laughing, pointing at her, ridiculing her. One of them makes a circling gesture with his hand, pointing at his head. 'Madwoman,' he mouths, silently. Robert turns to say something to one of the others and just at that moment, Ali swings the bat.

It connects with the side of his face, making a horrible cracking sound against his cheekbone.

'Jesus Christ,' Robert drops the torch again and clutches his face. I think he is OK. I don't think that Ali swung as hard as she could've ... Luckily she was dazzled by the light, and Robert wasn't as close to her as he was before. But still – she has attacked him. The men retreat. As I had thought right in the beginning, they are not here to fight.

She's the only one who's fighting.

They climb back into the truck, all except Robert, who is still holding his face. 'You're crazy, missus,' he says. 'Crazy. You know what they used to do to crazy bitches round here...' He shakes his head, before jumping onto the back of the truck.

They used to dunk them in ice cold baths, amongst other things, I think. That's what they used to do to the 'crazy bitches' round here.

I watch as they drive away, too fast. Robert sitting on the flat-bed with his back to the cab, watching the house the whole time. Holding his cheek with one hand, swinging the torch beam at Ali with the other. Back to the village. Where they will no doubt pass on the story to everyone who will listen.

That will not be the end of this.

23
Ali

'Jack, are you awake?' She pushes his shoulder, shakes him. He doesn't stir. How can he be asleep, with all that racket outside? The window is open. How can he not have heard the noise, the gunshots, the shouting? The truck, almost outside the window. She pushes him further and he flops onto his back, and for a moment she is alarmed. Wonders if he might be dead. Has she given him too much this time? She leans her head close to his chest, then to his face, feels the breath against her cheek. He's alive, but he's in a deep sleep. Ali sighs. She remembers, now, what it was like before. Afterwards, when she had to calm him down.

What just happened outside has rattled her. Those *men* have rattled her, taunting her like that – calling her a madwoman. A bitch ... and what was that about witches? She wishes now that she let Angela tell her some of her stories. She's starting to wonder if there might be something in them after all.

She shakes her head. *Stop it. You need to stop this.* Is she heading for some sort of breakdown? Is she going to end up like Jack?

After tonight's little episode, his manic rage, throwing all those things on the bed, she'd had no choice but to give him something to make him sleep. All those things that he shouldn't still have. Ali rubs her face; this is a nightmare. How could she have thought it would be OK? The stuff in the box is an issue. Their car is an issue. Angela is now an issue, too.

She has to get rid of all of it. Jack will have to get rid of all of it.

She walks through to the bathroom, picks up a glass and fills it with icy cold water from the tap. Then comes back through to the bedroom and stares down at Jack; he is still breathing deeply, completely out of it. She hesitates. And then she makes up her mind. Flicks the glass and splashes the cold water in his face.

He sits up fast, something between a shout and scream comes out of him, and he flails around on the bed, not quite sure what happened, not sure where he is. He rubs water off his face, blinks, then he sees her. Realises what has happened.

'What the hell are you doing?' His voice is slightly slurred, groggy. As if he has been drinking, but she knows he hasn't. She emptied one of the capsules into the glass of water beside his bed earlier, watched him drink it. He'd screwed up his face a little, then continued to drink. The water tastes funny here anyway, she's still getting used to it herself after a lifetime of filtered water in the city. He's been asleep since. She had forgotten what he looked like when he was out cold.

'I can't believe you slept through all that. Those men outside, they would have attacked me, you know. It was self-defence.'

'What was self-defence? What've you done?' He is wide awake now, his voice almost back to normal, but he still has that slightly confused look on his face. Like he's not sure why he was asleep. And he has absolutely no idea what's going on.

'Those men in the truck, shining lamps, shooting foxes. I don't know what they were doing driving up the way they did, but they were up to no good, I'm sure of it. They tried to tell me that Smeaton said it was fine for them to do this, but I don't get it, the lamp thing. They wouldn't explain, so it was clearly dodgy.'

'You really haven't spent any time in the country have you, Ali,' Jack says. 'Lamping is a pretty normal thing to do around here, Ford told me. They shine the light at the animal to stun it, so it gets kind of mesmerised. Then they can get close, and shoot it. That's what they were doing. Did they have dogs? Or just guns?'

'For Christ's sake! I don't know,' Ali is annoyed now and feels slightly stupid. She wonders if they actually weren't doing anything wrong, and now she's the bad one here. She attacked one of them with a cricket bat. She wonders what they'll do about it, if they'll come back. If they'll tell Smeaton. She can explain it away, surely? A vulnerable woman out here, a bunch of rowdy men. Middle of the night. She was wound up tight after what happened with Jack earlier. It's not her fault if she overreacted. They were taunting her, calling her names ... there was more than a hint of menace in their voices. She comes from a place where late-night visits from strangers are never a good situation.

'Well anyway, it's not just that. I realised I was being watched. Angela...'

Jack sighs and climbs out of bed. His T-shirt is soaked. He pulls it off over his head, and she notices that his muscles are more defined than before, all the hard work paying off. 'Angela again. What's she done now?'

'I just told you, she was watching me. From the window above this. I don't know what she was doing in that room, I don't think it's her bedroom. I thought we were the only ones with a bedroom facing the front? She said something to me before about that room, about some of her ghost-hunting equipment. Have you ever heard the like? The girl's head is in the clouds. But I'm still worried. What was she watching me for? What's she up to? I told you already, Jack, I think she knows something – just a bit. And I think she's going to keep pushing until she works out the rest.'

'She can't know anything, Ali. No one can. Only us. Right?'

'You need to do something about her. Talk to her. Get her off our case. Please?'

Jack doesn't reply. He climbs back into bed, and Ali unlocks the bedroom door.

'Where're you going now?' he asks. She ignores him.

She'll never manage to sleep now. No point even trying. Not while he's awake, tossing and turning, muttering in his sleep. She can't give him any more drugs tonight, not without him realising. Not without risking an overdose. She locks the door behind her. She always locks him in.

She walks downstairs and along draughty corridors. The dark is heavy, like velvet. Just the occasional chink of moonlight through a window making the place bright enough to navigate. She could switch on lights but she knows that half of them don't work, and the other half buzz and flicker. Besides, she doesn't want to risk anyone else waking up. Not now. She walks out through the kitchen, knowing that the door won't be locked, knowing that she can get back in. Out in the garden, moonlight shines on the new lawn, but the trees at the bottom are in darkness, standing straight and still, watching her. She walks across to the woodshed, the doors are locked; no one is around. It's too late.

She has to try hard to hear any sounds at all. Without the moon, she would be blind. These flat, bleak fields – so different to where she has come from, so difficult to adapt to. The darkness smothers the land like a thick blanket. She concentrates hard, hoping to isolate sounds. Maybe an animal rustling around somewhere, the leaves of the trees. An owl's hoot. But there is nothing, not even a breeze. It is a sad, eerie place.

But she needs the air, and she sucks in great lungfuls of it, trying to calm herself down. The house is smothering her, her own thoughts are trying to bring her down, convince her of things that aren't real. Could Angela have been right? Have they brought something to this house? Awakened something that's lain dormant here for all this time?

She knows she should go back inside, get back into bed and try to sleep. But her mind is racing now, worrying. About Angela. About Jack. About everything. No one knows anything. Rationally, she knows that they can't. If they did, why wouldn't they come to her? Or go to the police? If anyone knew the truth, they wouldn't be able to keep it to themselves. Not for long anyway. She walks carefully along the edge of the lawn towards the pond. The pond that they have had so much trouble keeping full of water until now, since Ford fixed the waterproofing once and for all. 'Fully filled and fully foolproof,' he said at dinner, laughing. 'No way that thing is draining away again unless someone comes and empties it with a bucket while I'm asleep'. She crouched by it earlier that day, marvelling, for a brief moment, at the picture-perfect reflection of the house on the water. The water as smooth as glass; the house with its harsh lines and strange lurching shadows ... until she freaked herself out getting her hand trapped in the reeds. She's wary of it now. Doesn't want to get too close, and yet it seems to summon her, somehow, and she finds herself walking towards it once more.

She is halfway between the kitchen and the edge of the water before she realises that there is something very wrong.

She lurches forwards, reaches the edge of where the water should be. But there is nothing. The water has gone; the pond is empty. Her heart flutters in her chest. No ... it can't be. It's only been hours since she was here. Ford was adamant that it couldn't drain away again. She turns back, runs to the building, yanks open the door and closes it tight behind her. It doesn't make sense. Why is it empty? She hurries through the kitchen, and then she sees it. On the floor, something that wasn't there before. Definitely wasn't there on her way out. She would have remembered. It would have stopped her in her tracks, just like it has now.

Small wet footprints.

Her eyes trace their path. They're coming in from outside, into the kitchen, heading off into the main house. She is cold, suddenly. Freezing. She hugs her arms around herself. Her jaw set, trying to stop her teeth from chattering. She stares at them, transfixed, as they slowly disappear.

Slowly, slowly. One by one. Until they are gone ... and she blinks. Wonders if she even saw them at all.

Dr Henry Baldock's Journal – 29th May 1955

The saddest of days, and although there will be a full, official report to be sent to the authorities, I feel I must also document it here for completeness – and in some way as a therapy for myself to try to understand what has happened today.

The idea I had for a hospital fête was well received, and plans quickly put in place. I had hoped for this kind of response, and was in fact far more positive than I had dared imagine. The staff were immediately buoyed by this new task – they had a sense of purpose for something more than their daily tasks – those repetitive, laborious, often stressful duties, and trying to cope with all that might be thrown at them, both mentally and physically. The patients, too, were excited. It was as if everyone here had felt that same black cloud hanging over the place as I had, and they were just happy that someone had recognised it and come up with a solution.

It's incredible how quickly things can be put together when people set their minds to it.

After witnessing Jessie Samuel's mistreatment, I was wary of having her in reach of the nurses who had seen fit to administer the barbaric cold-bathing treatment that was one of the things I was sent here to report back on. But with the prospect of seeing her husband and son again – the pair having been too distressed to visit when Jessie had been all but catatonic for the last few weeks – she had perked up. This, of course, supports my theory that the treatments offered to women suffering her sorts of condition have been woefully inadequate. I believe she had been struggling with a delayed depression that was the result of giving birth to her son; she had been coping but not coping, until she could no longer fight it and her GP suggested she come here for a short stay. But isolation and shock treatments were not what she needed. What she needed was love and hope; but it seems that here I can't say such things out loud for fear of being called a quack.

For the fête she had helped bake cakes and scones and had assisted with the decoration of the tables out on the lawn. I saw her, when her boy ran up to her – that beaming smile on her face. I was hopeful then that she was curable, as long as she was looked after, and no other stresses were placed on her. I was talking to her husband about it all, and he seemed to grow younger in front of me as we discussed the good news of Jessie's recovery.

None of us realised that the boy had run off, until it was far, far too late.

Oh, how I wish that there had been time to dredge the duck pond before the party. To remove the reeds that were clustered under the surface like thousands of soft, winding shackles. Perhaps then, he mightn't have been trapped beneath the surface. It haunts me, still – why it was that no one heard his cries for help.

Or if they did, why they didn't do anything to help him.

24
Angela

I think I have enough now to go to Smeaton. He's a rational man, despite his spiritual beliefs – in fact, maybe because of them. He doesn't believe in God and Heaven and Hell, but I know he believes that there is something bigger at play in this world, and that we are here to shape it. For years I felt like I didn't fit in with the world I'd been placed in, but coming here changed that. Some people might be afraid to embrace the light, to hope for the goodness of the life to come if we choose to make it so. But it felt to me like a light, *the light*, had been switched on. Of course, I had always believed there was a dark. A true dark that manifests itself in the simplest of ways.

I am getting closer to finding out the truth.

Ali tried to palm me off with some stories about Jack's old job. I know he was a detective. I know he dealt with horrific crimes ... that they plagued him, made him ill – forced him to take early retirement from his job.

But what bothers me is that I've only heard this second hand.

And now, the stuff that I found in that box – the news clippings, the scribbled notes underneath. I know it's only part of the story. None of this is enough for me to convince Smeaton to question the pair of them further, though. Besides, what am I actually accusing them of? Am I being ridiculous? Is my imagination running away with me?

Julie told me last week that Ali was talking to her about hearing strange scratching sounds outside her door, that she'd seen wet footprints seemingly vanishing before her eyes. She says she has felt as if someone has tried to drown her in the bath. There are so many stories about this place. I haven't even told Ali them, but she might've heard them elsewhere. She knows that I am desperate to prove the existence of ghosts. Is she playing me? But if so, why?

I'm in my room, putting on my shoes when I spot the envelope poking out from beneath the door. My chest flutters. I unseal it carefully and pull out the single sheet of paper inside.

I know you have questions. Meet me by the tyre swing at noon.

I peer at the writing. It slopes slightly to the right, not that I have any idea what this might mean about the person who might have written it. I look at its looping script and rounded lettering and try to decide if they were male or female. But I can't tell. I've no idea who's put this envelope under my door. Ali or Jack, maybe? Or maybe it's someone else – someone else knows what they are hiding and they want to tell me on my own, so we can join forces, decide what to do. Could it be Julie? Ali seems to have confided in her. I'm not sure I have ever seen her handwriting before. It could even be Rose. She's been acting weirder than usual lately and I've no idea why. I know I should go straight to Smeaton. He will know what to do. But I fear, as usual, that my curiosity is going to get the better of me.

It's always been my downfall.

I take my shoes off again and pull on my winter boots instead, because I know that the ground is still mulchy after last night's rain. The fields of the fenlands don't ever fully drain.

I pick up my bag. Then decide against it. I want to be able to walk across the fields unencumbered. Besides, what do I need? I'm only going for a chat in the woods. I'll find out who invited me soon enough. It's actually quite exciting. I walk briskly down the corridor, glance up into the corner at my new motion-detecting camera. The one that Smeaton told me I wasn't allowed to put there. He doesn't understand; it's not just about getting a clear photograph of something. It's about capturing changes in the air, like mists auras and orbs. All those sorts of things. They might show up in the pictures, mightn't they? This corridor seems to be the most active one in the building – well, in this wing, anyway. I try to keep away from the north wing, with its locked doors and crumbling floors. Even I don't want to hang around that place. I did try, initially, with some of the basics, but I got no sense that there was anything around. Whatever happened in this place, it has left its imprint in this wing. The nicest wing. The one where we're living.

I'm almost at the staircase when I hear a noise behind me. A faint creak, perhaps a door being pulled shut.

'Hello?' I call out, 'who's there?'

But there is no answer, and although I stand there, unmoving, for what seems like an age, I don't hear another sound. I sniff the air, hoping I might sense someone that way, but there is nothing except the usual smells of stale air and peeling paint. Deciding that my mind is playing tricks on me, I hurry down the stairs.

I don't pass anyone on the way out. I can't remember if there is something happening right now, something that maybe I'm supposed to be at. Perhaps everyone has gathered for something, something important. I think Smeaton is trying to encourage people to attend more of the communal activities. People seemed to have drifted into their own lives a bit too much recently. Maybe that's because the others have also started to think that something isn't right here. Maybe they *are* listening to me after all. But I doubt it. Maybe I'm just getting a bit desperate to find my purpose here.

Outside, the grounds are quiet and there is barely the hint of a breeze. I inhale a long breath through my nose and find that there is nothing unusual in the air. I'm safe then, I think. Nothing to suggest otherwise. There's no olfactory warning. I glance back at the house once, twice, as I head off down the driveway. Still no one around, but I glance back once more before I cut through the hedge and into the fields towards the woods. Most people here like to walk in the woods, but I don't think any of them come to the swing. I don't know who it was who strung the tyre on a rope and tied it to a tree – but it has been here for at least as long as I have, and I love to swing on it, with my eyes closed, listening to the creak of the rope against the branch and letting myself drift away.

I wish I hadn't brought Ali here. I thought it would be nice, something to bond us, but now all I feel is that she has soiled the one special place that I had for myself. Maybe I will talk to Ford, ask him to move the swing for me. Into a new part of the woods, where no one else goes.

A strong feeling of unease washes over me as I hike across the sodden field, everything is silent, nothing moves. My watch says it's five to twelve. Whoever is meeting me must be there already, or else they will be late. Unless they are coming the other way – along the road. Someone coming from the village, maybe? Someone who knows I've been talking to Mary about the newcomers? I pause for a moment. Turn around, and take in the house that is now far off in the distance. I turn the other way, towards the road up ahead. There is no one around, and no one knows where I am. I think about what I'm doing and suddenly I am scared. Who is scaring me? Or what? I don't even know. I realise that I don't want to be here, in this field; I'm too exposed. The lampers like this field – well, they used to. I imagine Ali has scared them off now, after her behaviour the other night. Of course, they will come back eventually. But maybe not for a while.

I head towards the thickest part of the woods. I decide that I will avoid the tyre swing, and instead I'll cut through to the road, and head into the village to see Mary. I'm out of my depth and I don't want to do this. I don't want to meet whoever it is who has left me that note. I don't know why, but I just know that something is very, very wrong. Mary will calm me down, give me tea, cake. She will tell me to go straight to Smeaton. Maybe she'll even drive me back here.

I am halfway through the thickest part of the woods, and I can see the road ahead. I can feel my heart beating hard in my chest. I don't like this silence. It doesn't feel right at all. There are no animals scurrying, not even the sound of leaves blowing gently or a twig falling from a tree. I walk faster.

I'm almost at the road, when I see the shape of a car. It isn't moving.

It is about twenty metres away. Why is it parked there? A dog walker, someone who couldn't wait until they got to a toilet? Someone having some fun with someone else? But no one comes down this road. Not often. Hardly anyone has a reason to come to Rosalind house.

Fear grabs at me, like snarling branches, and I know that I don't want to walk towards the car. It's not safe. I turn, planning to head down to the sparser part of the woods, get back onto the small dirt track that leads back to the allotment and the gardens. Someone will be there; someone is always there. I hurry, still ignoring the eerie silence of the woods. The birds have stopped singing, and I know that this is not a good sign. Perhaps a storm is on its way. That would explain the strange electricity that I can feel buzzing all around me.

Then I hear a snap.

The unmistakable sound of a branch breaking under someone's foot.

I start to run, but it's too late. A figure steps out from behind the old oaks. I can't tell who it is at first. They are dressed in dark clothing, hood pulled tight around their head, covering their hair; face angled down – the shadows obscure the rest of their features. My heart stops. I'm trapped. If I turn back, I have to go towards the car, and I've already ruled out that as a good plan. If I head back into the fields, I am too exposed, there will be nowhere to hide, I will be an easy target. I can run, but I don't know if I can outrun this person. And I don't even know if they are alone. All of these things spin through my mind, all of my options, none of them good. But while the thoughts are spinning, and my options run out, the figure is approaching me, walking slowly, no need for them to rush, because they know, as I do, that I don't have any choices left.

I stand where I am, waiting. Resigned to my fate. I should never have come here. I should have left all this alone. I could've stayed with Mary – never come to this house at all – and I would have been happy there. I would have been loved.

'What is it that you want?'

The figure in the shadows says nothing. There's no point turning around. There's nothing I can do now. There's no escape. I close my eyes because I don't want to see what's going to happen next.

'You just can't keep your nose out of people's business, can you, *Fairy Angela*?'

I know then. I recognise the voice. I would scream if I thought there was any point. But there isn't, so I don't. I keep my eyes tightly shut. 'Please,' I say. But I'm not even sure I say it out loud.

'Please—'

Part 2
THE DARK

'The murdered do haunt their murderers, I believe. I know that ghosts have wandered on earth. Be with me always – take any form – drive me mad! Only do not leave me in this abyss, where I cannot find you!'

—Emily Brontë

25

Smeaton

Smeaton unfurls his legs from the lotus position then lies flat on the floor, stretching his arms above his head, pointing his toes. He feels taller after every meditation session. That feeling of the muscles being locked and tight, then released and stretched beyond their capacity. He loves the breathing, too. The long, slow breaths. He tries to explain it to people who have never meditated before, but he finds it difficult. For all his education, travelling, his knowledge and beliefs, he still struggles to put into words how focusing his thoughts and becoming acutely aware of his mind and body feels. If pushed, he will say that it feels like having your soul moulded into every tiny corner of your body, and letting it seep outside of yourself into a cloud of contemplative peace. But even he is aware that this is a lovely description that makes no sense whatsoever to someone who doesn't know how to develop their own body into this realm.

He's tried to make things clearer in the book – his book. His roadmap for peaceful and productive community life: *The Book of Light*. If there was ever a book that explained itself in the title, this was definitely it. The residents have all had positive reactions to it. They lived it now, without thinking. The newcomers, though ... he isn't sure if they have embraced it just yet.

He's given them time, of course. As much time as they need. He has offered them both meditative coaching, and both have declined – so far. But that was to be expected. Ali and Jack are very different to the others here – the most unusual new residents they have had so far. It was a risk, letting them in. But one he thought he could bear. Especially with the offer of funding, which, he had not actually asked for. Ali had seemed very determined to get away from their current life and he had felt a longing in her, through her messages. He couldn't turn her away.

He *is* concerned though. What Angela has told him is a worry – because he has noticed the same himself. But there is little point in being concerned and doing nothing about it, which is why he has resolved to nip things in the bud right now. He needs to draw the community together, more than ever – making sure that Ali and Jack *and* Angela are part of it. He may dismiss Angela sometimes, with her talk of ghosts and spirits, but something has caused the energy to shift in the house – something that he can't rationalise, and can't explain. There's no doubt that the residents are unsettled, and it all started when Jack and Ali arrived.

He's also aware that Angela has been spending more time in the village lately, since the newcomers arrived, in fact. They've talked about that before, and he knows that it happens when Angela is feeling insecure. Mary is like a mother to her, and if it wasn't for her desire to be part of the community here, he knows she would still be lodging with Mary, above the shop.

So today, he will make a point of going to chat to everyone, get to know what's going on. Letting them all know that he's here, and he's listening. He's seen what happens when the so-called leader takes his eye off the ball, and he knows where it can end up. That's not going to happen here. It's time to become active again – make sure that everyone is on board with things.

Time to exert a little authority.

He starts by writing a note: *Guided Meditation – tonight at 7 p.m. in the lounge – this is not optional.* He draws his little dove symbol, and adds a smiley face and a heart, for good measure. He takes out his pack of white tack from his drawer and rips off a piece, separating it into two small balls. Then he sticks the note on the door to the dining room and heads outside.

The day is clear and fresh. He can hear the faint sounds of an electric saw, snaking its way around from the back of the building. Ford, most likely. Or perhaps Jack. He will go around there soon. First though, he wants to go to the herb garden. He'll find Julie there, or perhaps Rose, if she's not still in the kitchen. He adores the smell of the herbs. He thinks of Angela, then, knowing how she feels about the garden, because she enjoys nurturing the plants, but the smell is often too overpowering for her. It always amuses him when he sees her wearing a scarf wrapped around her face, trowel in hand. He wonders where she is now, realising that he hasn't seen her for a while – she wasn't at breakfast. Nor dinner last night – but that's not too unusual. She's like a little bird, seemingly existing on scraps and seeds, but still healthy. Both meals in a row is a little unlike her, but then again she was in the village and probably has a stash of snacks from Mary to get through – another of those things that she doesn't realise he knows about. He smiles, thinking how much he enjoys Angela's slightly childish innocence – always seeking something that's just out of her grasp. He hopes she never loses it. But he also hopes she can find a way to settle within herself.

Many of the residents have similar traits, but they are learning to deal with them. Finding new ways to be. He likes that he is here for them, to help them achieve that.

At the herb garden, Julie and Rose are having a discussion over which types of basil to plant.

Julie smiles when she sees him, but keeps talking. 'You know that Fergus is fussy about his herbs. He's said before that he prefers sweet to Thai, because he thinks the Thai one makes everything taste like Thai food...'

Rose shakes her head. 'That's nonsense. I say we plant both, maybe some lemon basil too. Keep him on his toes.'

'Maybe we can find some alternative to mooli, too – tell him there's been some blight that only affects that, so we can't plant any more of it. What do you reckon, Smeaton?'

Smeaton grins. He is happy that the two women are getting on. Rose can be a prickly pear, at times. 'I think you should plant whatever you want. Fergus will adapt. I love his cooking, but I wouldn't mind a bit more variety, to be honest.'

They both make shocked 'ooh' sounds, then dissolve into laughter.

'Just letting you know, I've planned a guided meditation for us tonight. Been too long since we did it. Would be nice for us to regroup. By the way, have either of you seen Angela?'

Julie shakes her head. 'Not today. Cyril said something about seeing her heading off into the woods. Said he thought she was nipping off to the village again.'

Smeaton sighs. 'That'll be it. I'll need to have a word with her again. These visits are getting all too frequent.' He winks. Then he lays a hand on Rose's shoulder, gives it a little squeeze. Wants to let her know that he's glad to see she's making an effort.

He finds Cyril and Richard at the shed near the salad greens patch. Richard is yanking lettuces, while Cyril sits on his fold-out chair. He decides not to disturb them, just calls from the end of the section, 'Guided meditation at seven, OK? No excuses.'

They both give him a little wave, and he strides off around the other side of the building to look for Ford. A cloud moves, the sun warms his back and he turns, raising his face up to it, like a sunflower.

Everything seems to be running smoothly.

He's not sure why he was so concerned.

26
Ali

Jack has slept through breakfast again. She's brought him an oat-flour roll with rosehip jam and a chicory coffee, after eating her own after the six a.m. Taizé singing class to which she's found herself strangely drawn. She expected him to be awake now, and starving, but he is still asleep.

She needs to be careful about the dosage that she's giving him.

It's working, in that the after-effects are continuing, making him more placid during the day. The burst of mania that he experienced a few days ago hasn't recurred. But she also needs to make sure that she doesn't run out. Once the capsules are gone, they're gone, and although she doesn't mind a bit of exploratory chemistry, she doesn't know how he might react after having been on them for so long. After all, there is no way to check the long-term side-effects. She did try to wean him off, but that didn't work and now she's concerned that Jack is trying to remember, that he is questioning too many things – and he is getting it muddled in his head.

She can't have that happening.

She lays his breakfast on the bedside cabinet beside him. Leans down to his face, just in case. One of these days she's sure she's going to put her ear to his mouth and not feel the breath there. But how much will she *really* care if that happens? She can pretend to others, she can even pretend to him. But she's having a tough time pretending to herself. She feels sick at what he did. At his face, after each time he did it. His glazed, empty eyes. Then the sex they had afterwards, him wild, her terrified – but excited – the fear and thrill of not really knowing what someone is capable of. And then the next day, he would wake up with no memory. And he would go to work.

And he would be confused, and out of sorts. And he would make mistakes.

She leaves him be, satisfied that he will wake up, eventually, and goes outside. Out front, there are still tyre tracks on the gravel from the truck. She wonders if anyone else has noticed, but no one mentioned it at the singing, or at breakfast afterwards, or at the guided meditation last night. There are other things to think about now. The pond, for one. Ford hasn't been around for a couple of days; she doesn't know if anyone else has noticed yet that the water has gone. Jack was confused when she told him, but he didn't have any answers. As for the footsteps in the kitchen, she's already decided that she didn't see them. That it was her overactive imagination. Just like the other time, when she saw the same boy. She's in a strange new place, and waking-dream hallucinations aren't as uncommon as you might think.

In the allotment, Julie is on her knees, attaching nets to canes, looking after the berries. Fat, juicy strawberries – Ali has an urge to pick one and pop it in her mouth. Julie turns when she hears her approach. 'Don't they smell delicious,' she says, beaming.

'They really do. And so many ... Will we ever eat all of these?'

'We can, and we will,' she says. Still smiling, she bends down to pluck several strawberries off the vine and puts them in a small wooden bowl. She hands it to Ali. 'Help yourself. We'll eat as many as we can when they're fresh and the rest of them I'll keep for jam. You might have noticed we've got plenty of jam, we're never going to run out.' She laughs.

Ali takes a strawberry and bites into. It's so ripe ... sweet pink liquid spills down her chin and onto her white T-shirt. This would have annoyed her once, but she doesn't care right now, because she has far bigger things to worry about than a stain on her T-shirt. She has Jack to look after, and she has to think of a way to deal with her own decaying mind, which has been plagued with visions of restless spirits since the moment she arrived – and no matter what she does to try and rationalise it all, she can't help but feel she is descending into an abyss. She tries to clear her thoughts. Focus on the sensation of the strawberry, the taste, the smell. The stain on her T-shirt. She feels herself snap back to normality. It's only a T-shirt. What's the use of a white T-shirt in a place like this?

Julie takes a strawberry from the bowl and pops it into her mouth. 'So how are you settling in? Everything going OK? Tiring yourself out with all this fresh air I imagine...'

'There is that. Fresh air, manual labour and all this fresh fruit and veg. It's only been a few weeks but I feel like a different person.' She feels bad, lying to Julie. The woman has been kind to her. But Ali doesn't feel like a different person at all – well, not in any good way. She's just as stressed and anxious as she was before they left the city, and now she has the added worry of Jack's medication running out. She'd hoped she wasn't going to have to give it to him, and now that she's started she's worried about taking him off it again. But she needs to keep him under control, for everyone's sake.

'Well, you know where I am if you need anything.' Julie goes back to the berries.

Ali lays the bowl on the ground, picks up two corners of the netting and helps stretch them out. Julie smiles again. She is always smiling, as if there are two invisible threads pulling her mouth into the default happy position. Ali read an article once, suggesting that the more you smile, the happier you actually become. Maybe that's what Julie is doing. Ali is not yet convinced that the residents of Rosalind House are truly living the nirvana that they project.

'I was wondering something, actually,' Ali says. 'You might not know anything about this, but Smeaton told me a story ... well a bit of a story. About something that happened on the north wing. A fire that one of the patients started? I think that's what he said.' She pauses. Wonders if the next part will get her in trouble. 'And something else, about a little boy?' She doesn't mention the pond, trying not to lead Julie into anything, but she is sure that these waking dreams, as she likes to think of them, must be connected to something awful that happened here.

She's terrified of hearing the truth, and yet she's pushing for someone to tell her. What *did* happen here? Who is the boy who plagues her? Who was the woman in the corridor, and why was she so angry? They might not be real, but something about them is real – an imprint of them from the past. Could that be something that really exists? Her mind pushes and pulls at her, casting doubt at every turn. She is loath to show any weakness, but she is struggling to cope now.

Julie looks away. 'You asked Ford about this too, didn't you? A while ago. He told me. Only Smeaton knows the full story. There are records, I think. Somewhere. I'm sure he'll tell you if you're really interested. But to be honest, none of us like to talk about that stuff much. We don't like to think about it. It was a very sad thing. A whole family destroyed, and all to do with rumours and small-minded gossip about some long-dead relatives who were accused of witchcraft. I think it's what got the hospital shut down, eventually. Maybe there was more to it than that. I can't really remember.' She waves a hand as if flapping away at a small fly. 'Like I said, best to ask Smeaton.'

'Sure,' Ali says. She doesn't push any further; Julie's reluctance is just the same as Ford's had been. No one wants to talk about this. They're not gossipy types, it seems. But Ali isn't sure if it's gossip that she wants, or if she just wants to know what actually happened. She feels that somehow she must already know the story, must've read it somewhere, or been told it long ago. Otherwise how could she keep dreaming about the boy? And why did she react so badly when the lampers called her a witch?

'I think I'll go for a walk,' she says. 'It's a lovely morning.'

'Take a basket, you'll likely come across some brambles.'

'Isn't it a bit early for them? Thought they come in autumn?'

'Ah yes sorry, not brambles. Elderberries and rosehips, though. Always things to forage around here. You don't have to if you don't want to. Just go and get yourself some fresh woodland air, stretch your legs. Don't worry about collecting things, it's not like we actually need any food. You should explore to your heart's content, It's easy to get lost, though, so be careful.'

'Maybe I'll leave a trail of breadcrumbs,' Ali says, with a grin. She walks off towards the woods, wondering about Julie's confusion with the brambles. Trying to work out if she meant anything, or if she just got confused for a moment. Maybe her smiling is a way of dealing with the fact that she can't remember things properly. Like the story about the boy. Or maybe she hasn't been in the woods for a while. Ali already knows there are no brambles there.

The woods are dark and decaying, and full of dead things.

27

Ali

Ali is in the kitchen when Smeaton comes flying in. His hair is wild and he looks stressed, or maybe worried; it's hard to tell. She has been chopping carrots for half an hour, and a large pile of orange discs sits in a box in front of her. Her next job is equally mundane; she could take a break now. The others are busy elsewhere, Fergus has gone out to collect some things from the garden. Rose has gone off to buy some more plastic containers from the shop in town, after a mildly amusing incident where *someone* placed a few of them too close to an oven.

'I think I've seen more of you today then I have the entire time I've been here,' Ali says, smiling. She dries her hands on her apron. Smeaton smiles back, but the odd expression is still on his face. 'Are you on your own, Ali?' He says. 'That's good actually. I wanted to ask you about something.'

Ali tries to keep her face neutral, doesn't want to give anything away. There are lots of things that he could be asking. This is not the time to become paranoid and appear worried. She concentrates hard on keeping her face as natural and relaxed as she can manage, and gives him what she hopes is an inquisitive smile. 'Oh yes? What can I do for you? Can I get you something to drink? Maybe I can sneak you a brownie, they're for tonight but who's going to miss one little piece?' She uncovers the tray and wafts it towards him. A warm chocolatey smell floats into the air.

'Thank you, but I think I'll wait. I'll enjoy one better if I look forward to it. Tea would be lovely though, the raspberry one is my favourite, if you have it.'

Ali busies herself making the tea, taking the water from the urn that they use for the endless boiled pasta and grains, and the teabag from the couple of boxes that she's brought in from the lounge – Rose hadn't been happy when she'd introduced this change, but then clearly Rose wasn't used to drinking tea as she worked. She keeps her face turned away, still trying to keep the worry out of her expression. Something in his voice concerns her, and she has a spike of worry that Angela has told him something about Jack's clippings. No matter what he says, she will plead ignorance – if need be, she will spin this to her favour and berate Angela for snooping. She turns back around and offers him the cup.

He raises it to his face and inhales the scent. This is probably the nicest herbal tea they have here, made from dried raspberry leaves and pulped seeds. There's another ingredient too, which is Julie's secret apparently. Ali hopes she passes on the recipe before she forgets it. She has made one for herself, too. She inhales the fragrant steam, and feels it calming her down. *He doesn't know anything*, she thinks. *You're being ridiculous.*

'I had a call earlier,' he says. 'From Mary. You know Mary?' he scratches his head. 'Or maybe you don't. You haven't been into the village yet, have you?'

Ali shakes her head. 'You recommended staying away from the village, until we were settled. It's been few weeks now, but I haven't felt any need to go there yet. Neither has Jack, as far as I'm aware.'

Smeaton nods. 'Of course. Well, Mary runs the shop, but to be honest I think she wants to run the whole village. She knows everyone and everything ... looked after Angela when she first came to the area. She told me there was a bit of an incident the other night, late. With the lampers?'

Ali breathes in her tea, pushing her face almost entirely into the cup, trying to hide her smile. If that's all it is, she can handle it. That was an honest mistake.

'I'm not sure what they told you...'

'Well, I think that Mary might have got the wrong end of the stick, but she says that you attacked one of the men with a cricket bat?

Osborne James's cricket bat from the wall in the foyer. He was a patient here at one time. Came in for a brief stint of treatment and went on to become a county legend. Anyway, I was sure that bit couldn't be true ... that the story had grown legs. I'm sure it was all just some silly misunderstanding?'

Ali sighs. Tell the truth or keep it vague? In this case, it might help her to tell the truth. Might be the best way to keep him from asking questions about anything else. 'They scared the life out of me, Smeaton. They did try to tell me that you had told them it was fine to come here, and that shining the light into the window to alert us was normal. It was silly really. I got such a fright. And, you know, where I used to live, men turning up late at night on your doorstep was generally not a good thing. The sounds of gunshots startled me initially, but when I heard the truck, the tyres on the gravel. It completely freaked me out. I thought they were coming here to rob us ... to attack us. Haven't you seen *Straw Dogs*? The original, I mean. It's a classic movie ... horrific, but...' She shakes her head, letting her sentence tail off. Of course he hasn't. 'I didn't mean to get so angry, but to be honest they were quite cocky. One in particular was trying to lead the others on. I think they thought it would be funny to wind me up, but there was bit of a clash there, I admit. They weren't expecting my reaction; I didn't *mean* to react like that. I hope he's OK. I don't think I hit him that hard. It was meant to be a deterrent more than anything else.'

Smeaton takes a mouthful of tea. Nods. 'Yes. OK. That does make sense. I suppose it's my fault really. I should have warned you that they might be around. Thing is, even with my room around the side of the building, it's so natural for me to hear them that I don't even think about it anymore. But I must have been in a deeper sleep than usual that night. I'd had some of Rose's special tea. I daren't ask her what's in it, but it does encourage a good night's sleep ... if the occasional alarming dream.'

Ali puts down her mug harder than she intended, and crosses her arms. She's not really interested in Smeaton's nightmares or Rose's special tea right now. 'Did Mary call to complain about me? Or was she just letting you know? I'm worried now that I've badly upset those men, and her. I don't want to do that. You know that Jack and I came here for a fresh start, the last thing I want is to have any trouble with the locals. Or you, for that matter.'

'Please,' he says. He takes another mouthful of tea, lays his cup down. He has almost finished it. He must have an asbestos mouth, because hers is still boiling. 'Don't think any more of it, Ali. But please do come to me in future, if you have any concerns. About anything. I mean that. I'm here for you, Ali. Please feel that you can talk to me...' He pauses, scratches his head again. 'You know that Angela is a little concerned about you too...'

Ali keeps her face blank. 'Concerned about what? I know she was a bit upset with me, when I dismissed some of her stories. Maybe I was a bit harsh. I'll talk to her...'

'She's a sensitive little soul, our Angela. But she does have a good heart. I know she'd love to be friends with you. Maybe you could give it another go? I'm sure there's common ground, one that doesn't involve talking about fenland folklore and ghosts.'

He smiles, and Ali smiles back, but she's gritting her teeth. He's telling her to toe the line: don't upset the locals; don't upset Angela. She clenches her hands into fists. She wants to get annoyed about this, but she knows that it won't do her any good in the long run. She needs to make an effort. She is here to stay, after all. She silently vows to try harder, to paint on the face that she needs to survive in here – just like the others.

He squeezes her arm, then turns to go. He takes a few steps, then stops, turns back. 'Oh, I meant to ask,' he says. 'You haven't seen Angela anywhere, have you? I've been around most of the place today, but I can't seem to find her. I meant to ask Mary but with all the lamper stuff it went clean out of my mind.'

She doesn't look him in the eye.

'No,' she says. 'I haven't seen her at all.'

28
Angela

I wake up ... and at first I am confused because I have no bedcovers, no pillow. I'm on my side and underneath me and around me are piles of packed leaves, twigs. Dirt. I sniff, and I'm more confused. Because I can't smell anything. I don't think there's ever been a time in my entire life where I could smell absolutely nothing, even when I've had a cold. My strangely acute sense of smell seemed to become enhanced as I grew older, but I don't remember a time ever when it wasn't there. I curl over further to the side and sniff at the mulchy ground, imagining the smell that I know should be there. Earthy, mouldy. Damp. Cold.

But there is nothing.

I sit up, brushing leaves and debris from my boots. I glance around. For a moment I can't remember why I'm here. I'm curled into the hollow of the old oak. Was I sheltering from the rain? Did I lie down for a nap, and lose track of time?

Then I remember.

The note.

I was heading to the tyre swing, wasn't I? I shuffle around, remembering the car. There was definitely a car, but it's gone now. I try to piece it all together. The figure walking towards me, the crunch of footsteps... I pull myself up into a standing position, still brushing dirt off myself. I lean back against the oak, and I inspect my hands; under the nails there is dirt, on my palms there is dirt. I turn my hands over and notice how pale they are. Have I got hypothermia? It's not cold enough for that, is it? I don't understand. I rub my hands together, a simple automatic action. Trying to get some heat, some colour back into them.

But then I notice something else.

I'm not cold.

I walk towards where I think the car was parked. I don't know when it was parked there. I don't know how long I have been here. Why would I be sleeping under the tree? It makes no sense. A vague memory swims to me. A figure coming closer ... but then what happened? Did I fall? Did I hit my head? I close my eyes, tightly. Ball my hands into fists, try to push the nails into my palms, but I can't feel them. I can't feel anything.

Perhaps I'm in shock. Things are coming back to me now. Someone hit me over the head. I just don't know who. Or even if I'm right. Maybe I dreamt it all. Maybe I tripped and fell.

I think about the note. Was there even a note? I shove my hands into the pockets of my jeans looking for the small piece of folded paper that I know I put in there yesterday ... At least I think it was yesterday. I've lost track of time. I have no idea now how long I've been here. And the note is not in my pocket. I sigh. Why is no one looking for me? Will they believe me? Will anyone believe that I had the note, that I came out here to meet someone, that someone hit me over the head and I've been sleeping here ever since? I must've been out cold. Maybe that's why I am numb. I must have a head injury. I need to get help. I need to be seen by a doctor. I lift my hands to my head feeling for injury, scratches. Bumps. But I feel nothing.

There is something very wrong with me. You hear about this sort of thing, after a head injury. I no longer feel like me. It's definitely shock. I need to get back. I will go to see Julie, and I know she'll listen to my story. She'll make me hot sweet tea; she'll feed me homemade lemon biscuits. She will believe me.

She will help me.

I take a few more steps towards where I think the car was, but there is no evidence there that I can see. If it was parked in the road, as I think it was, there will be nothing for me to find anyway. It's a waste of time. I turn back around and start to head back towards the house ... and then I see something lying on the ground. Right next to where I was lying. I hadn't seen it, because I had turned the other way, looking for the car. Looking for the figure. Searching for the note.

So I didn't see the small broken thing lying bundled like a pile of rags on the forest floor.

I walk slowly towards it. But I am not scared, because I understand now.

I crouch over the figure, the small broken figure. Her eyes are closed. And there is a nasty gash on the back of her head, where she has been hit with something hard. I throw my hand to my mouth and stagger backwards, unsure of what to do next.

It all makes sense now. Why I can't smell. Why I can't feel. Why I am not retching in disgust at what I have found. I place my hand on my chest, hoping for a heartbeat. Hoping, just hoping, that I am wrong. That I am hallucinating. That maybe, just maybe, I am not even here. That I'm still in bed, wrapped in my warm blankets. That I didn't find a note under the door, I didn't disappear into the woods without telling anyone. That I'm dreaming it all. Of course I am. I want to cry, but no tears fall.

This is not how it looks.

That's not my body on the ground.

I'm not dead.

Am I?

29

Ali

Ali is supposed to be in the kitchen for the rest of the day, helping prepare dinner, but she can't stay now. She leaves the box of carrots, shoves everything else under the countertop. Scribbles a quick note saying she had to leave because she had a headache. Then she throws her apron and hat into the wash bin and hurries upstairs. She throws open the door and marches into the bedroom, hoping to find Jack gone. Hoping that he is up and about, doing something useful. But there he is, still in bed. Still asleep. Can he really still be asleep?

'Have you been here all day? Do you know what time it is?' She yanks the blankets off him.

He stirs, opens his eyes. 'I've been up ... I was out in the woodshed earlier, just doing some stuff. But then I just felt so weak, I thought it was dangerous to be around those tools. I'm so tired now, Ali. I'm getting worried. Maybe I'm just getting a cold or something like that, but it feels a bit like before ... you know?'

Ali swallows. This is the last thing she needs. She needs his help now, more than ever. They can't leave things as they are. 'Jack, come on. They're starting to get suspicious. I think Angela has said something to Smeaton about us. He came and asked me questions. Said it was about those stupid bloody lampers, but I think he was sounding me out. Told me to make more of an effort with people. As if I'm going to do that. We need to go now. We need to finish this thing.'

Jack shrinks back, pulls the covers up to his neck. 'I don't think I can do it, Ali. Not again. It scares me. It scares me, because I keep having these dreams. I don't know if they're real. I think I can remember what

I did, and then you tell me what I did ... and I should be disgusted with myself, knowing the truth. But I don't feel that. I feel numb. I feel nothing. But I want to sleep forever and I don't want these dreams. Sometimes I think the people from my dreams are here with me, in this room ... and I'm groggy. I thought doing some work today would help, but I felt things around me starting to swim and I knew I had to stop. Ford is away, and I was scared I might cut my hands off. Or worse.' He pauses, looks away. 'I was scared that I would hurt myself, and that it wouldn't be an accident.'

Ali wants to scream, but she knows it won't do any good. As Jack was speaking, all she could think was that she feels that same; she's been having bad dreams; she's plagued by visions, by hauntings, by things her senses tell her are true but her rational mind – on which she's always relied – tell her can't be. Why can't she retreat into herself like Jack is doing? Because this is how it has always been. She's the one who has to take charge.

She sits on the bed, pulls out one of his hands from under the covers. Squeezes it. 'You have to get a grip, Jack. I need you to help me. I can't clean up this mess by myself. You know I can't. Please. Throw on some clothes and come with me.' He looks as if he's about to protest but she stares at him, keeps squeezing his hand. Refuses to look away. She's not doing this on her own. She physically can't. No way.

Eventually, after it seems like time has completely stopped, he gets dressed and they leave the house. Luckily, everyone else seems to be busy. There's always plenty for people to do here, which is a good thing. Especially now. Ali climbs into the driving seat and turns the key in the ignition. Hopes that they still have enough fuel to finish this. Jack gets into the passenger seat, slams his door. He slumps into the chair, drops his head into his hands. 'I'm sorry Ali, I'm just so tired.'

She closes her eyes, grips the steering wheel. He was good at this, in the beginning. A memory slides behind her eyelids. A young man's terrified eyes as he slips off the platform just as the train thunders into the station, Jack grabbing his arm, pulling him back. The young man crying, thanking Jack for saving his life. Oblivious to what had gone before … Jack moving close to the young man, waiting until just the right time, before bumping his hip into the back of him. Hard. Reaching out and grabbing him back. Screams, confusion. Jack's confused face as he looked into her eyes, 'What happened, Ali?'

She ignores him and starts the engine. They drive around the perimeter road. It's not far, and it would be quicker to go across the field. But she can hardly drive across the field. She is slightly concerned that Rose will be coming back from the village in Smeaton's van, with her stupid plastic boxes. She doesn't want anyone to see them driving out, doesn't want anyone to be asking questions later. But there's not much she can do about it. If Rose passes them, she will come up with a convincing lie. She is getting good at them. Besides, the sun is just beginning to set and they don't have much time. The first part of this really needs to be done while it's still at least partly light.

She drives them to the woods. She recognises the spot where she was pushing Angela on the tyre swing the other day.

She pulls off the road, pauses, her hand on the key, thinking. Then, pressing her foot to the pedal she drives them further in to the trees. With the car off the road they are partially obscured. There's a better chance now that if anyone does drive past on the perimeter road, that they might not see them. It's a risk, but it's worth a shot.

She should have dealt with this problem straightaway, but she couldn't. She couldn't do it herself and Jack was in no fit state. Mumbling and crying and stumbling around like a drunk at an office Christmas party. Pathetic. They get out of the car and she pops open the boot, lifting out the old rug that is kept in there. The one that has been used successfully, many times before. She walks slowly into the woods, making sure there's no one around. Jack trails behind her, making a snuffling sound, and she turns to see that he is crying.

'Pull yourself together Jack,' she snaps. 'You need to stick with me on this. We'll deal with your little problem, and then it will be done OK? If we can sort this out properly, then maybe it doesn't have to happen again. You think you can manage that?' He sniffs. Then nods. Wipes his eyes. His face is set into an expression of grim determination.

It would be easy to get disorientated in these woods. Lost. So much of it looks the same, with its equally spaced trees, all the same size. Nothing much to distinguish them. Easy to forget where you are … to turn around and walk the wrong way. But somehow, as if a homing beacon is signalling her, she knows where to go. She walks towards the one tree that is different from the others, the old oak with the hollow trunk. The tree that has been here for a very long time, before someone planted all the others. As they get closer, her heart starts to beat faster. A horrible chittering thrill runs through her. *What if it's not there*, she thinks. *Then what?*

But of course it is there.

Still covered partially with leaves … but she can see the heel of a boot poking out from the hollow. Jack makes a small whimpering sound, then he coughs.

'I'm OK,' he says. 'Sorry.'

Ali closes her eyes, opens them again. The trainer is still there. The body is still there. The chitter in her chest starts again. She crouches down and starts to pull away the blanket of leaves and twigs that have been used to try and hide her. It had been a temporary measure, until she worked out what to do.

She turns the body over, and sees that the tiny animals of the forest floor have already started to feast. A bubble of nausea pops in her throat. A chattering of voices starts in her head. She swallows, takes in a deep breath through her mouth, trying not to breathe in the stench.

Come on, Ali. You can do this. You are the strong one, remember.

She gives her shoulders a little shake. They need to get rid of it fast. Get it far away from here.

Ali unrolls the rug and lays it on the ground. Jack reaches into the hollow, alert at last. His instincts kicking in. He takes hold of the ankles and drags. Ali gets under the shoulders. For a slight girl she is incredibly heavy; but they always are. Heavier than you think. Dead weight: it's a real thing. They lift her onto the blanket, crossing her ankles and hands. Rigor mortis has started to wear off, and she's almost pliable now, ready for them to take her away.

They pause, both of them staring down at Angela's body. Ali glances at Jack, wonders what he is thinking. But she knows what he's thinking: nothing. *She* is thinking that this didn't have to happen.

Jack crouches down, and begins to slowly roll her up in the blanket.

Dr Henry Baldock's Journal – 6th June 1955

I am appalled. The police investigation has ruled the events of last week to be nothing more than a tragic accident.

I am also worried.

I did not want to provide them with my private notes, the ones where I accuse some of the staff of mistreating the patients, because if I were to reveal the things noted in this journal before I have time to complete my findings for the board, then my whole investigation will have been in vain.

Oh, the dilemma that faces me! All I can hope is that there are no repercussions to this tragedy. I must ensure that Jessie is looked after with great care – for the effects of what has recently happened as well as her original ailments. As well as the depression she's had since childbirth – she is now having to face the grief of losing her boy.

There have been many visitors since the accident. It seems that she was a well-known figure in the village. I want to say well-loved, too, but there was a certain suspicion in the manner of some of the visitors that concerned me; it was almost as if they were checking that she was still here. We must do our best for her now, and just pray that she does not blame the hospital for what has happened. Her husband, too, is in a bad way, but thankfully he's being looked after by his brother's family on one of the neighbouring farms.

I just can't help feeling that there is more to this story. Something that as an outsider, I am not privy to. I may need to question Jessie's nurses again, to see if they can shed some more light on this terrible matter.

30

Smeaton

He doesn't like to use the skeleton key. Doesn't want people to think that he is invading their privacy in any way. Despite the communal nature of this place, that's not something he would ever want to do. But he has no choice. He has been all around the house and the grounds today, he's chatted to everyone doing their work, and not one of them has seen Angela.

Before he gets himself into a state with worrying, or takes any further action, he needs to check her bedroom. It would be unlike her to be sick. He's rarely known her to be ill the entire time she's been here, and she's certainly not one to oversleep. Sometimes he wonders if she ever sleeps at all. She spends far too many nights roaming the corridors, hiding in dark rooms. Waiting for an apparition that is never going to appear.

He's sceptical, of course, like most people are, but he would not say that he is entirely a *ghost atheist*. More of an agnostic. He hasn't told Angela this, but he has looked into parapsychology a little himself. There are always stories, things that are told through the generations. There were plenty of those in his old commune, the one where he grew up. The one that was just like this, until it wasn't. People change. Things change. Mostly there's no way to avoid that.

He left it to come here to start something new, vowing that he would keep running as it was always meant to be; as his father had always wanted his own commune to be. Before he became unduly influenced by others. This is not about preaching to people, or trying to convince them of some kind of *new power*. This is about living happily together, with some shared beliefs. Angela shares his beliefs, as do the others. That's why they're here, that's why they've stayed. Everyone is free to leave, of course. Some have come here and found it not to their liking. Some people will always choose dark over light, such as the Palmerstons – but thankfully they had left before they had to be asked to, before they could taint this place with their evil ways. Some of them worry a little about Angela, concerned for her mental health. But he doesn't think there's anything wrong with her. She's just one of society's *differents*. She's just someone who wants to fit in, and she's just someone who wants to believe in something.

Something otherworldly.

And who's to say she's not right?

He turns the key, but before he pushes it open, he raps on the door. Two knocks. Calls her name, but there is no answer. He pushes open the door and walks inside. Fairy wings hang over her bed, and he smiles. Remembers her wearing them at some of the parties. He can see straightaway that her bed is neatly made, and her room is tidy and uncluttered. In fact, there is nothing to suggest that she has been here this morning at all. In which case, where is she? From what he's gathered, no one has seen her since yesterday morning. Smeaton considers himself to be a calm person by nature, he is not someone prone to manic episodes, not someone to overreact. But Angela was very agitated the last time they spoke, and he doesn't know what to think now.

He checks her bathroom and finds it is also undisturbed. He picks up a towel that is hanging over a wooden rail, and it is bone dry. He frowns, wondering what his next move should be. He knows that sometimes she goes into the north wing, although she often denies it – says the place gives her the creeps. Says she's seen strange things in there. Orbs, balls of light-energy. Things that apparently appear when spirits are trying to communicate, before they have managed to find a form to show themselves.

He's not convinced. She's also mentioned a smell. A charred, blackened smell. How a smell can have a colour; they are her words, not his. Of course, a lot of that wing *is* still blackened from the fire. Some parts of it were cleaned, various equipment and necessary things salvaged. But a lot of it was left just as it was, as if the staff didn't want to be tainted by anything that had been in there. He's never noticed anything in particular, apart from that old musty smell of a place where the windows are never opened, where still air hangs constantly, like a shroud. He knows that she has a key for the north wing, knows that she took a copy of his, and when he tells people not to go there, his reasons are honest. Some of the floors *are* still unstable, but overall it is just not a pleasant place to be.

Perhaps it's the obvious place for her to be right now. After all, she has mentioned that there has been more activity lately, readings on her various gadgets. Things happening that she hasn't seen before. Why now? He wonders. But if he is to believe the physics of it all behind the scenes; the displacement of energy, changes in the atmosphere – then there *is* something different.

The newcomers.

Two new beings walk within these walls. Surely that is all that it is? New energy, new atoms, new particles whizzing around, disturbing the peace. He doesn't believe that it's the undead causing these changes. It must be something to do with the living. Angela might believe there are restless spirits here, awakened by a shift: the family of three hung on the mill common, accused of witchcraft back in 1593; and the family of three who died in tragic circumstances, right here almost four hundred years later. The two families were distant relatives, but they were all innocents accused of the same crimes; accusations borne out of the same basic ignorance. No, what is disturbing things now is far from that. The new energy is intelligent and brave – and most definitely something to be concerned about.

There is a stack of notebooks on the small table next to her bed, next to them is a thermometer, a marble and a row of neatly lined-up pencils. He smiles, realising that this little displays sums up Angela very well. Neat, inquisitive, slightly odd. He picks up the first notebook from the pile and opens it – then he stops himself. Should he be reading her things? It could be a private diary … but then it is just lying beside her bed. Not that anyone is meant to be in here without her knowing. He bites his lip. Puts the book down. Lines it up again. He's about to walk away, and then he changes his mind. He flips it open, decides he will just read the first page. But he needn't have worried. It's nothing personal. Just a list of dates and times, mentions of red or green, temperature measurements. Notes. Thoughts. It's her ghost-hunting log. There is not a day when she hasn't recorded something, in her neat, flowing script. Most days, the notes say the same thing. *No activity to report.* He feels sad for her. Wishes that she could observe some kind of strange phenomena just to give her purpose to all her work.

Something pings inside his head as he lays the book back down. There is no entry for yesterday. He picks it up once more, flicks through again. Yesterday is the only day that has been missed ... and today, of course, but perhaps she just hasn't had time to fill it in yet. Something feels wrong, but he doesn't want to get himself worked up just yet. He's sure there's a perfectly valid reason for the missing entries...

He lays the book down then heads downstairs again, checking a few of the rooms on the way. Nothing. He needs to collect the keys for the north wing from his office; he keeps them separately from the main bunch, because he has no real need to go there regularly.

A thought comes to him, as he reaches his office. Something that makes more sense than Angela being in the north wing, waiting for ghosts. Mary had called him earlier about the lampers. Perhaps Angela has gone to see her – to tell her about Ali and Jack. Maybe she thought he wasn't listening to her concerns. He picks up the phone and dials the number for the shop. Mary answers after two rings. 'Smeaton?'

He wonders how she knows it's him, he doesn't call very often. But then she probably has a phone with caller ID on it, whereas he has an old Bakelite from the 1950s. It still works perfectly well, and it's not as if anyone needs to use it very often.

'Mary, I just wanted to let you know. I spoke to Ali earlier, and she is, of course, very sorry about what happened. She explained that she felt scared and threatened, not because of the boys in particular, but just what she's used to, you know?'

Mary blows an exasperated sigh down the phone. 'Yes, well, she's one of these city types, I suppose. She's new here, and Robert says it doesn't hurt too bad. He says he'll drop it, so long as she doesn't behave like this again.'

'Thank you. That is very kind of you. Thank you, Mary. I'll make sure, of course. Oh ... but there is just one more thing.' He tries to make his voice sound casual. 'I was wondering if you'd seen Angela today at all?'

'No. I haven't seen her for a few days actually. It's usually a Tuesday or a Thursday she comes in. So, I wouldn't necessarily be expecting her until tomorrow. Why? Have you lost her?' Mary laughs, but it sounds a little hollow.

Smeaton pauses before answering.

'That's the thing, Mary,' he says. 'I think that maybe we have.'

31
Ali

She's alarmed when she hears the metallic clang of the gong. Smeaton told her on the first day that the sound would travel far, but she hadn't really believed it until now; until it echoed through the building. Sweat breaks out on the back of her neck, and she rubs at it roughly. Jack is sleeping again now, that half-sleep, half-wake twilight that he has existed in for the last few days. She stares down at him, as he snores quietly. Her chest feels tight. She knows she needs to get him out of the bedroom again, but for now she has more important things to worry about.

She hurries down to the sitting room where she knows that everyone will be gathered. She slows her pace, wanting to rush but not wanting to arrive breathless. Clearly something bad has happened, for them to be summoned like this, but she has to keep her panic in check. She hopes that it won't seem too strange that Jack is not with her, but all she can do is tell them that he's sick and hope that no one pries further. She is the last to arrive. Except for Angela, who's not likely to show up anytime soon.

Because of course, that's what this is about.

'Is Jack not with you,' Smeaton says. He says it kindly but there's a flash of something in his eyes that worries Ali. Only slightly, but enough.

She shakes her head. 'He's been getting these terrible headaches. He keeps taking himself to bed. He used to get medication from the doctor, back home. But we didn't bring any here. Jack convinced himself that they were stress-related, and that being here in the fresh air would make them magically disappear. Stupid really. Maybe I should go into the village and get him some—'

'You can do that later if you don't mind, Ali. As I explained to you when you came here, when I sound the gong, it's because I need everyone here. Because there is a crisis of some sort.'

He glances slowly around the room, checking them all out. Ali follows his gaze and takes in the sea of nervous faces. She wonders how many of the others have something to hide. All of them, probably. But she doubts that any of them have anything as huge as she and Jack do.

'What's going on?' It's Rose, of course. The one she always seems to clash with in the kitchen. Her voice is high-pitched, ready to deal with a drama with more relish than is strictly necessary.

'It may be nothing, but I wouldn't have called you all here if it wasn't something sufficiently *unusual.*' Smeaton stops wringing his hands and drops them to his side. His voice may be calm, but he's exuding a panicked air that she has never seen from him before. His usual unflappable demeanour has been well and truly flapped. She puts on an expression of concern, hoping that it fits everyone else's.

'It appears that Angela has gone missing,' Smeaton says.

There is an audible, collective gasp.

Rose chips in first. 'What do you mean, missing? Maybe she's just gone to the village. When did you last see her?' She raises her palms, turns around the room trying to catch everyone's eye, one by one. 'Who saw her last?' Her gaze comes to rest on Ali, and everyone else's gaze follows.

'It's been a couple of days since I've seen her,' she says. 'Someone else must have seen her since then? She's probably in the village. Has anyone actually checked?'

Everyone starts to speak at once, arms gesturing, voices rising. Eventually Smeaton claps his hands, and everyone is silent again. As if a telepathic message has been passed to them all at once, they silently form a circle and everyone looks down at the floor, holds their hands to their sides, grasping for each other.

Ali takes the two hands offered to her, Ford on her left, Julie on her right. She feels them squeeze, and stares down at the floor, and after a moment of silence and nothing, she glances up, wondering what's going on. Rose is staring directly at her. Before she can react in any way, Smeaton makes a small sound in his throat, and then she feels the squeeze again, and this time she squeezes back. They all release their hands, letting the invisible cloud of worry pass into the air, as is their way here. She tries not to sigh, tries to stay focused.

Smeaton is talking now, but she is not taking it all in. She's worrying now about Rose, about why she was staring. Wondering why it is that Rose seems to have been on her case right from the start. She hasn't taken her for a friend of Angela's. She seems like someone who finds fault with everyone and has to try very hard to keep her thoughts to herself. Ali silently chides herself for not making more of an effort with Rose, for not trying to find out what it is that makes her tick.

'Have you got that, Ali? You know where you're going, yes?' She blinks and realises that Smeaton has been talking to her, but she has no idea what he said. 'You're to go with Rose and check the rooms in the south wing. Rose knows the places Angela might've been, or might be. Although, if she is still in this house, I'd be surprised. She'd hardly ignore the gong.' He claps his hands again. Chattering ceases.

'I'll be on my own,' he says. 'Everyone knows where they're going, yes? See you all back here in one hour. We'll regroup and decide what to do next.'

Ali holds back. Stays in the room until only she and Rose remain. 'I hope she's OK,' Ali says.

'As if you care,' Rose huffs. 'I think Smeaton wants me to be with you so that I can keep an eye on you. You know that, right? Everyone's been talking about you, Ali. Jack too. His up-and-down moods ... and after a few weeks of work with Ford, he's taken to bed, you say?' She barks out a dry, humourless laugh. 'There's something you two aren't telling us, isn't there? I had a feeling about you as soon as I met you. You can tell a lot about a person by observing how they wash dishes, you know.'

Ali feels herself start to sag. She follows Rose, who is still wittering on about dish-washing, out of the room and waits until she has carried on down the long corridor, then she darts down one of the corridors to the side. Fast. Praying that the door that she needs to be open is open today. She hears Rose calling her, hears her swearing under her breath. Hears her saying that she will carry on by herself, and don't worry, she'll be telling Smeaton about this.

Ali doesn't care anymore. She slips into the room and closes and locks the door behind her. She didn't expect to find anyone in here, so it's no surprise to find it cold and empty. It's not a room that's used very often. She walks over to the desk and sits down. Pulls open the drawer beneath the desk, takes out a piece of paper and feeds it into the typewriter.

She starts to type, just a few lines. Just enough. When she's done, she sits back in the chair. Closes her eyes. Breathes out long and slow.

This is all fixable. She knows it. She has dealt with far worse before.

A rattling noise makes her jump, and she opens her eyes. Someone is turning the door handle, back and forth, trying to get inside ... but she knows that she has locked the door. Her heart starts to beat just a little bit faster. She holds her breath, keeps still. She doesn't want anyone to come in and find her here, sitting at the desk. She hears a voice outside. Rose?

'I'm sure this room is meant to be left open, isn't it?' A sigh, and then the rattling stops. Ali waits a moment longer before catching her breath. She stands, making sure that the chair hasn't been moved, making sure that everything looks just as it should; then a cold prickle sweeps across the back of her neck and she turns, looks over her shoulder.

It's him again. The small boy with wet hair plastered to his face. He is dripping small puddles on the floor. It's the same boy, the one she saw in the kitchen.

He's not real; she knows that he is not real. He is a waking dream. It's a psychological reaction to stress, that's all. Just her mind playing tricks on her, in this unfamiliar room. She screws her eyes shut tight. *Go away. Go away*, she thinks, willing it to happen. For the vision to fade away and leave her alone.

There's a click, as if someone has unlocked the door. She opens her eyes, draws in a breath, expecting to find someone standing in front of her, someone real, not some ghostly figment of her imagination. But there is no one there. Relieved, she hurries towards the door, and slips out into the corridor.

'I locked this door. I know I did,' she says to herself, quietly. Then she lets herself out the fire door at the side and doesn't dare glance back, for fear of seeing those footprints again.

32

Smeaton

There is a faint breeze blowing around the corner. Smeaton heads towards the library, and notices that the fire exit at the end of the corridor has been left ajar, but only slightly, as if someone has thrown it closed from the outside and not pushed hard enough. He assumes this means that someone has already been down here, although he had explicitly told Rose that he would investigate this room himself.

This is not a room that is used regularly, and he prefers to keep it as a more private space. Although he knows the people do often find a way in now and again, and he says nothing as he has made it common knowledge that Rosalind House is everyone's house, and there are no secrets in here. Even if that is not strictly true, it's nice to have a framework for his beliefs.

He can tell straightaway that something is different. He can feel something in the air, as if it has recently been disturbed. That fizzing of energy, when someone has just left the room. He's thinking like Angela now, he realises – with his senses attuned to electromagnetic activity. *Poppycock*. The voice in his head laughs at him. But is it?

He sits down at the desk and sees the paper sticking out of the typewriter. Only one person uses the typewriter, and that's on very rare occasions. This room is supposed to be full of memories, like a museum. It contains books and notes and records that are not for others' eyes. He doesn't want to scare the residents by telling them about some of the things he's found in here. He wants to believe that this was a good hospital, and that the staff here were good people; but he knows that might not be the case. The asylums didn't always achieve what they'd set out to do, and were the scenes of many horror stories. There's no point in upsetting the Family with all this stuff, is there? That's what he'd decided when he took the place over from the local authority – who were extremely glad to be rid of it. Paying security to keep out those urban explorers and scavengers wasn't something they wanted to budget for. The locals had tried to convince him to burn the place down, but he wasn't going to do that. Not when it was such a perfect place to set up his community. And as for all the other stuff – the stories about the house that was here before they built the asylum – he decided right at the start that no one needed to know anything about that. It's unfortunate that Angela found out for herself – from Mary and the other villagers. He always hoped that Angela wouldn't spread all that talk among other members of the Family – about suspected witches being held here before their trial, but he suspects that she has.

He turns the wheel and rolls the sheet of paper out. He starts to read, and when he realises what it is, he lays it flat on the table and rests his chin on his hands. His shoulders slump, and he sighs.

Dear Everyone,

I know that you will find it strange and unlike me, that I have not said goodbye. But things have been different here for a while, and I no longer feel like Rosalind House is the right place for me. As you know, I have been to many places before I came here. I had thought that this place would be my final destination, but now I'm not so sure. I knew that if I told anyone I wanted to leave, that they would try to stop me, and I didn't want that as I knew I would be easily persuaded. I'm taking some time away to travel, to seek new places and new things. Perhaps I will be back, bearing gifts from around the world. Perhaps I won't.

To my Dearest Smeaton … thank you for everything. For understanding me. For believing in me. Please can

```
you tell Mary not to worry, because I'm fine. I am
looking for something else, more than she can give.
More than anyone can.

With all my love, and all my light,

Yours always,

Angela x
```

Damn. He wasn't expecting this. He always thought that she would tell him if she wanted to leave, and he never really believed that she would want to go anywhere other than here.

He scratches his chin. Maybe there is something else ... she's had a fight with someone, and hasn't confided in him. Things weren't going according to plan with Ali. Or perhaps it's Mary, or someone else in the village. He needs to go there, talk to them. Maybe she's said something to them that she hasn't said here. She has seemed a little on edge lately. Thinking about it, he's not sure that Angela has been fully herself for some time. And it surprises him somewhat, that she has left him a note like this. Not folded, not signed. Not left on his desk. But then again, perhaps she knew that it could only be him who would find it in here, adding an extra layer of authenticity, in case there was ever any doubt that she had typed it.

Of course she typed it. It was exactly in her style, and as far as he's aware, she was the only one who ever used the typewriter. He remembers the childlike thrill on her face when he told her she could use it occasionally, as long as she looked after it well – it is an antique, after all. He really will miss her.

A thought strikes him, then, and a rush of panic almost chokes him. Was it Angela who just left? Did she leave the fire escape open? He jumps up and hurries across to the window. He cups his hands to the glass, stares outside. But it's already getting dark, and there is no sign of anyone out there.

Besides, Ford and Richard are walking around the front grounds at the moment. They'd hardly miss her if she is out there. And if she has just left, where has she been up until now? What has she been doing? She must have heard the gong – she must've known they were all frantically looking for her.

No, it can't have been her.

He turns back to the desk. The note bothers him a little, but in many ways it does make sense. It is *very* Angela, he concedes. He knows he must tell Mary now, ask her more about their last visit, if anything odd happened.

But there's something else he wants to check first. Something that's been bothering him for a few days now. He'd thought about it after something that Ali had said, when they'd chatted in his office. And he'd forgotten the details and needs to know them now, just for his own curiosity more than anything else, while he's here.

He walks back to the door and finds that it's slightly open. He pushes it shut, locks it. He's sure he closed and locked it when he came in. He shakes his head, worries that he might be going a little bit mad himself. The door is definitely closed now, and locked. He pulls the curtains closed, just in case any of the men outside happen to come to the window and see him in there. He'd rather not let anyone else know what he's doing right now. It doesn't concern them and it has no impact on anything here, so why share it and cause worry?

No one knows anything about it, and there's no need for that to change.

He heads to the bookcase behind the desk, to the middle shelf, where a stack of books with faded blue fabric covers lie flat, flanked on either side by three thick, green fabric-covered books standing spine out. He slides the flat stack of books off the shelf and places them carefully on the desk, and a puff of dust makes him sneeze. He pushes his hand to the back of the shelf, to the small gap in the middle. He has to feel along with his fingers to find the button.

He presses it, and takes a step back, letting the bookcase swing away from him, into the short corridor behind, revealing the hidden door. He takes a small Yale key from his key ring, and steps in to open the door. He walks inside, leaving the door open, because no one can come into the library with the main door locked, so he knows he's safe. Besides, there are no windows in the small room at the back, and it is a claustrophobic space. He would hate to be locked in there by accident.

A quick glance is enough to know that Angela isn't hiding in here. Not that she would be, but he wouldn't be surprised if she had found the room and stolen his key. He knows she's taken his key to the north wing before, and made her own copy.

The room is not so much a room as a large cupboard. The walls are lined with shelves containing box-files. The patient records, from all the years that the hospital kept them. It's a metal-lined, fireproof safe room, which was locked when he first came here. He felt it was best it should stay that way. The authorities hadn't wanted the records back, it seemed. From the moment the place was closed, it was abandoned, and no one wanted any more to do with it.

He's spent many hours perusing these files, and some of them don't make for very nice reading. Especially the small journal that he keeps locked in another drawer, in the cabinet in the corner. It's the diary of Dr Henry Baldock, who came to investigate this place in the 1950s, after the authorities heard reports of patient mistreatment. His visit sparked a series of catastrophic events, and he recommended the place be shut down. He published an academic paper, later – about the use of coercion and control in a psychiatric setting. It was a chilling read – about how patients who had come in with one ailment, or in fact, no ailment at all, had been manipulated and moulded into someone else altogether. He remembers the phrase, *coercion and control*, from that meeting with Ali. From her talk about her thesis. Ali's theories on the creation of evil were something that he had wanted to learn a bit more about. There had been some familiarity there, as if she knew this theory well – Dr Henry Baldock's theory … Could she have come here on purpose, to try to find out more? It wouldn't be the first time. The Palmerstons had come here with a similar agenda.

He shakes his head. Surely not. She isn't continuing her research, is she? She came here with Jack to start afresh. His imagination is running away with itself, and he stops what he is doing, tries to breathe in a few long, slow breaths, trying to get himself back under control.

He lays the journal down and reaches into the drawer for the other thing he keeps in there. The old cardboard file that he'd found hidden with the journal. He opens it, flicking through the photocopied pages. He'd never found out who'd brought this here, but at some point, someone had wanted to tell Dr Henry Baldock something more about this place.

He flicks to the court transcript: April 1593 – the trial of the witches accused of bewitching the Throckmorton girls and murdering Lady Susan Cromwell – and the chilling statement from Alice Samuel that was to seal her fate: 'Madam, why do you use me thus? I never did you any harm as yet.'

As yet.

He's always tried to dismiss Angela's superstitions and foibles as nonsense, but he can't deny that something has unsettled the house over these last few weeks. Perhaps Angela, being so sensitive to all this – believing it as she does – couldn't cope with what she perceived to be ... an awakening?

33

Angela

The dull clang of the gong resonates across the fields. I've never heard it from so far away before; but it gets used so little that I wonder if the sound really has carried this far, or if perhaps it is only me who can hear it. It seems that I can still hear as acutely as before, all that is lacking is my sense of smell.

I rush back to the house, but I don't feel that I am hurrying at all; it's as if I am barely moving my feet yet moving faster than I ever have before.

I suppose there have to be some advantages to my situation.

I wait outside the window, knowing that everyone will be gathering in the living room, listening to Smeaton's instructions. They will all be sent looking for me ... but will they find me?

My body is not where I left it.

I couldn't go with it, when they took it away. I tried, but it was as if an invisible force prevented me from following. I watched them drive off in the car, my body wrapped in a blanket in the boot. Despite my unfortunate demise, they took care of the removal quite well. I just wish I knew where they went.

I'm not sure why I couldn't follow them. I think that maybe now that the essence of me is no longer part of my body, I cannot stay with it. Incredibly, after all the years of research and interest into this whole area, nothing is quite as I expected. But then again, I wasn't expecting to be proving my theory quite like this, and not having any way to tell the others that I was right.

I wait until they have all left the room. I see that Rose is keeping an eye on Ali, and I hope that maybe someone else will see what I have seen, hear what I have heard. Someone else will work out what to do about Ali and Jack.

I follow Smeaton. I think that he must be going to the north wing, although why he thinks I'd be in that awful place, I have no idea. I keep a good distance behind him as he walks along the corridors. He does not glance back, and I realise that my footsteps do not make any sound. So much to learn.

When we get to the door of the north wing, he rummages in his pockets, then I hear him swear. He doesn't swear often. 'Damn it, those keys,' he mutters to himself. 'Why did I take them off the main ring? Stupid.' He whirls around and he is face-to-face with me. I'm less than a metre away from him. Looking straight at his face, and he is looking straight at mine.

Yet he doesn't see me.

He blinks and the expression on his face changes for a moment and I wonder if maybe he has felt something, senses me somehow. He takes a step forwards and instinctively I step out of his way. I still have no idea if that theory about ghosts being able to pass through solid forms is true, and I know that I don't want to test it out right now. He passes by me without stopping. He walks back along the corridor, hesitates around the corner from his office then seems to change his mind. He turns the other way and marches along the bottom corridor. I try hard to force my feet to make noise on the cracked lino, but they don't. I stare up at the lights, and to my delight, they start to flicker. He pauses briefly, glances upwards. Shakes his head. He is still convinced that the lights just have an electrical fault. Maybe they do. I wonder if he will mention it to Ford again, ask him if he can have a look. He doesn't believe any of my theories about the energy in this corridor, despite me trying my hardest to make him believe it right now.

I follow him into the library. He leaves the door open just a crack, just enough for me to sneak in there behind him. Then he notices and closes and locks it. But he doesn't notice straightaway. He sees the paper sticking out of the typewriter first, and I know I didn't leave that there. I've written myself various notes on the typewriter, over the time I've been here. I'm always careful to remove the paper and take it up to my room. I'm sure Smeaton knows I've used the machine more often than strictly permitted, but he's never said anything. I replenish the pack of paper with a few sheets from Mary's shop every so often, just to keep up the pretence. He's peering at the paper, rolling it out. He frowns and lays it on the desk, so I position myself behind him so I can read it over his shoulder. I can't believe it!

Except I can.

This is exactly the kind of thing that she would do. I wonder if Smeaton will be able to tell that it's not me behind these words ... but to give her credit, she *has* made it sound like me. There was I think-ing she didn't listen to me, but she clearly did. She has picked up the rhythm of my speech perfectly, even in written form. She has even mentioned Mary, and that upsets me.

Mary will be destroyed by all this, when it comes out. When they realise what's happened to me. When they realise who Jack and Ali are. *What* they are.

Smeaton folds the paper and slides it into his pocket, then he walks over to shut and lock the door, and close the curtains. I have no idea what he's doing ... and then I see. All this time I sneakily spent in here, and I never properly explored. I thought I had taken every single book off the shelf, but clearly I was wrong.

He slides the bookcase back into a small connecting corridor, before opening the room behind, thankfully he leaves the door open, and I follow him straight in. I am amazed. Files. Hundreds, thousands of them. Things I'm sure I would love to have read. Things that he has chosen to keep hidden from us all. Then he takes out something that looks like a small journal, and he carries it with him as he goes out.

I hurry out behind him before he can lock me inside. I have no idea yet if I would be able to get out such a place. I don't know when he might come back in here.

He locks the hidden room and lets the bookcase slide back into place, then he replaces the books from the desk onto the shelf, opens the curtains and peers out of the window for a moment before shaking his head and unlocking the door. He glances around the room once more. Then he slips out into the corridor again. He pauses at the fire entrance, which has been left open slightly, and stares outside once more. There is nothing to see.

I'm not there, I whisper into his ear. But he doesn't hear me.

I follow him back to his office. There is a piece of paper stuck to his door, announcing a guided meditation session for the previous night. I missed that. I used to enjoy those, that weird feeling of drifting off while wide awake, the dull, muted clang of the gong to wake you back up. Maybe I'll go to the next one. I wonder if I can still enter a trance. He locks the small journal in his drawer. Then goes to collect the key for the north wing that I know he wanted earlier, but it is not there.

He sits down at his desk and drops his face into his hands. He's muttering something under his breath, but I can't quite hear him. Eventually he picks up the phone, dials a number that I recognise. I hear her voice and I feel the heavy weight of sadness wrapping me like a cloak.

I can hear her smiling, even down the phone. 'Smeaton, twice in one day? I'm guessing you're calling to let me know that Angela is safe and sound?'

Smeaton says nothing.

I'm here, I say. As loudly as I can. I'm standing right next to his desk. I try to pick up a pen, but it just slips through my fingers. *I'm here*, I say again. I hear the voice at the end of the phone, the smile gone now, 'Smeaton? What's going on?'

A tear rolls down Smeaton's cheek, and still he can't find any words.

I need to go to the village. I need to find out if Mary can hear me, or even better ... if she can see me.

34

Ali

'Come with me, Jack.'

He's sitting on the side of the bed, rubbing his hands on his knees. Then he lifts his hands to his face, rubs at his eyes, pulls his hair. She has not seen him this agitated for weeks.

'Come on, please. I've got the key to the north wing, let's go and have a proper walk around there. Everyone is looking for Angela. They'll just assume you're doing the same. Smeaton won't mind that I've got his key once he realises what I am doing. I took the chance to go get it during the commotion. I just get the feeling he's hiding something from us. I don't know what. I don't even know how it can help us. But I can't keep running around the rest of the building looking for Angela, knowing that no one is going to find her.'

Jack stops fidgeting and rubbing, and stares at her. 'We shouldn't have done that, Ali. She's not like the others. We shouldn't have done it. Why did we do it? I don't understand anymore.'

'I told you ... she was working things out. She was going to get us into trouble. Ruin all our plans.' She clenches her hands into fists. She wants to punch him. Why doesn't he get it?

Jack shakes his head and laughs, 'Plans? What, like our new life? It's a disaster. We can't stay here.'

'Just come with me, come on. Get out of this room for a bit. Let the others see that you're willing to help. They were getting suspicious earlier.'

He nods. Stands up. She looks at him, and what he's become. Those weeks of fresh air and exercise – all that heavy manual work. For a while they'd given him a rosy glow, brought some light back into his eyes. But it has gone again now, in the days that he has spent barely leaving his bed. His eyes are flat, dead. His skin is pale. And no matter how many times he might've cleaned himself, he still smells unwashed, different. That weird scent coming off him, like before. The way he was when he had to give up work.

She offers him a hand, and he takes it. He seems smaller, his shoulders slumped. He is shrinking in on himself somehow. She can't let him go on. Not like this. It's no good for either of them. She guides him out of the room and locks the door. They walk along the corridors, out one of the back entrances that she has seen before, and around the side to the entrance of the north wing.

It is dark now, and the air is heavy. Just the gentle *whump whump* of the wind turbines in the field nearby. She has remembered to bring a torch, just a small one that she collected from the sitting room. There's a basket of them there, for anyone to use. The kind of thing you probably need in the country, she supposes. She switches it on now and they follow the beam of light through the corridors, which seem darker and narrower than she remembers from her time here before in the daylight. She is not really sure what she's doing; she just feels an urge to visit this place now. She thinks about Angela, all her talk of spirits and ghosts. Witches in the village. Ali shakes her head; tries to shake out the creeping madness. The madness that she knows is starting to cloud her thoughts, despite what she might want to believe. The hallucinations ... the accusations. She is struggling to keep control of her own mind, let alone Jack's. There is a stale smell in the air, a faint hint of something charred and old. She grips Jack's hand tighter and he grips hers back.

'I'm not sure this is a good idea,' he says. 'Why are we even here? This place gives me the creeps.'

'I don't know yet. I just – I don't know. I felt that I had to come in here. Something to do with Angela. I don't know. Something lured me, I suppose. Besides, it's the best time. I can't see why Smeaton would come in when it's dark, and anyway, he can't because I have his key.'

She walks along the corridors, shining the torch over the various doors. Something stops her from opening the small hatches and shining the torch inside. She seems to be dragging Jack along behind her now, his feet shuffling.

Her mind flashes to how she imagines this place must have been in the past. The sounds of shuffling feet, the smell of grim hospital food wafting down the halls, the squeak of the lino. The other noises: clatters and shouts. People locked in the cells.

What happened here? she thinks. *Something happened here.*

At the end of the corridor there is a room with double doors and a white plastic plaque still firmly in place: *Electroconvulsive Therapy Room 1.* Not such a common procedure now, but it's still in use, for extreme situations. Not like in the sixties, when it was used far too much. Both of her parents had been treated with it, she'd found out. Her mother, when she was pregnant. It was said to be safe, apparently. She's not so sure about that, often wonders about the effects it might've had on her mother's unborn child. Her mother's *only* child.

She pushes the door and it swings open. Jack protests, doesn't want to go in, so she tries to drag him over the threshold, but he lets go of her hand and backs away. He seems terrified, all of a sudden, and she doesn't know why. She walks into the room and immediately the atmosphere changes. Faces seem to swim in front of her, open mouths screaming.

Shaking, shuddering. Sighs.

She blinks, and it all goes away. Her heart slows. The room is stuffed full of equipment. A reclining bed with stirrups sits in one corner, but there is stuff piled up all over the place, thrown everywhere. Discarded. Why has no one taken it away? Has it all been left here since they shut down the hospital? Surely there are uses for these things. Something that they can do with it all. Why can't they strip it down and sell it? Smeaton mentioned that they needed some sort of income stream. There are all sorts of things in here, and she's surprised that no one has thought to make use of them.

She walks over to a piece of machinery, a white box connected to various wires. She touches it, and jumps back as if she's been electrocuted. This is what she came in here for. This is what she needs to be able to deal with Jack – because if she can deal with Jack, then surely her own mind will quiet down once more and she can try to live in some sort of peace. She picks up one of the cables, careful not to touch the electrode. Will it even still work? She's about to flick the switch, when a sound from behind startles her. She turns, assuming that Jack has come in behind her, but the light is dim and she can't make out his features. There is definitely a figure by the door. 'Jack?' she says, under her breath. She shines a torch at the door and the figure disappears. She tries not to panic, convinces herself that it was only a shadow. Just a shadow. Not another vision – hallucination – not another being trying to shatter her increasingly fragile mind. She pushes the door open and walks back out into the corridor. Jack is crouched down opposite, leaning against the wall, hugging his knees.

'Please Ali ... please take us away from here. I can't stand it. I keep seeing them all – their faces – taunting me – reminding me of what I did ... I need to face up to it all. I need help! Let's just go home. Let's go to the police. Let's tell them everything. Please...'

The treatment will have to wait a little longer.

Ali finds a new resolve. No. She can't have this. She's not letting Jack go to prison. He'd never survive in there.

And there's no way she's going there herself, either.

It's time to put an end to her experiment, once and for all.

Dr Henry Baldock's Journal – 17th July 1955

I can barely believe I am writing this, but I am. The entire hospital – three hundred patients and fifty staff – was evacuated today due to a fire in the north wing. Thankfully it didn't spread far, but the signs are that it was started deliberately. The firemen told me there were smears of cooking oil found on the outside walls, and they suspect that someone took some into the wing – into Ward 3 – and set fire to it. Was it luck or accident that the patients from that ward were all in their various treatment rooms at the time of the fire? We won't know for sure. Sadly, there were three fatalities. Two being the nurses that I'd had to reprimand that day for the barbaric water treatment, and the other ... There were no other serious injuries, although many were affected by smoke in the other wards and rooms nearby. It's a miracle that all of the patients were led to safety. I wasn't aware of it until I heard the screams coming from the lawn. Some had thrown themselves into the pond and, after the recent tragedy there, it's nothing short of another miracle that none of them drowned. The pond is so deep.

No doubt we will have to drain it soon. Too many bad memories.

I knew what had happened before they told me. I knew who had started the fire, and I knew it was deliberate. I also knew there would be no way she could have survived it.

They carried the charred remains of Jessie out into the waiting ambulance, taking her to Cambridge I assume, although why it was an ambulance and not a mortuary van I'm not sure. They took the nurses away separately. I don't know why.

That poor, poor woman. Again, I can't help but feel that I failed her. That we all failed her. She should never have been able to get her hands on that cooking oil, much less a box of matches. I can't help but wonder if maybe someone helped her along. I am convinced that the poor woman was targeted for some reason – her mistreatment, her son – and now her apparent suicide. I don't for a minute think that she would have intended to hurt any of the other patients.

But I realise that I don't understand what is going on here at all, and I suspect that no one will be willing to tell me.

35

Angela

I want to see Mary, but I can't seem to pull myself away just yet. I wait with Smeaton, in his office. He seems at a complete loss as to what to do about me. I move around as much as I can, sitting near him, standing behind him – then sitting on his couch, standing by the door. I try to pick up one of the little angel cards from the bowl by his door, but I can't do it. My fingers just slip through as if they are made of air. Nothing I do seems to cause any reaction in him.

So much for my theories about electrical energies in the atmosphere.

It seems that the naysayers might be right after all. There are no such things as ghosts. But then – what am I? I know I am here, at least I think I am. I can see him; I can hear him. The only things that are missing are my abilities to smell and to touch. Plus, of course, there's the absence of my physical being.

As far as Smeaton is concerned, I am gone.

Despite the absence of physical sensations in my non-existent body, I feel sad. It manifests itself as a darkening of the scene in front of me, as if someone is slowly dimming the light. Smeaton's world shrinks into a vignette before me, the edges creeping inwards until it is just him in the middle and nothing beyond. I try to think of nice things, to make the blackness dissipate. I don't want to disappear into a nothingness. I can't believe that that is all there really is for me now. I start to wonder about that research into the consciousness of the soul and I wonder if this is all there is – if it is now up to me to decide whether I continue to exist in this limbo or disappear altogether, to accept my fate along with the realisation that there is nothing beyond.

I try to focus on happy things: the first day I came here, when Smeaton showed me to my room – the biggest bedroom I had ever had, with a huge window overlooking the bright green of the lawn behind the house. I found out soon afterwards that I had apparently hallucinated the colour of the lawn, imagining what it once was – when they told me this, I saw the reality. Soil and patches of yellowed grass. Weeds. Not now, though; now it is a lawn again. Thanks to Ford. What else? Mary. Mary has always made me happy. Giving me gifts, showing me love. Then there's learning to bake delicious carrot cake with Fergus. Discovering the Taizé chants and feeling the deep sense of grounding and warmth that they bring to the whole room. Growing my own herbs: thyme, lemon verbena and rosemary, and sprinkling them on salads and having Julie tell me how difficult it is to grow good herbs and how I was a natural.

The vignette shrinks away, and the room swims back into focus. But I realise I have been carried away with myself for a while, because Smeaton is no longer in the centre, at his desk. He is no longer in the room.

I hear the sounds of an argument outside and I am thankful that Smeaton has left the door to his office open or I'm sure I would be trapped in here. I head out, and see that there is a small congregation outside the front door. I slip out, and stand close to the building, watching. Listening.

'It's not right, Smeaton. We all know that Angela hasn't done a bunk. It's not like her at all, is it?'

I recognise Chris, Mary's son, and several of his friends. The same men who were here only a couple of weeks ago, chased away by Ali. Robert still looks furious at being smacked with the bat.

'Please, boys. We need to stay calm. What do you want me to do? She's a grown woman. If I go to the police they'll laugh me away. She left a note—'

'Anyone could've written that,' Chris says. 'And with what's been going on here, we'd have thought you might be a bit more concerned.'

'What do you mean?' Smeaton says.

'She's told my mum plenty,' Chris says, ''bout your new guests. Suspicious of them, she was. She told you too, right?'

Smeaton turns away, his eyes boring right into me. But there is no indication that he senses me there. 'I don't know what you think you've heard—'

'Don't give us that crap, Mr Dunsmore,' another of the young men says. I don't know his name. 'You know about this house ... about all the bad stuff—'

'Hang on,' Smeaton interrupts him with a wave of his hand. 'I know nothing of the sort. All these stories getting spread around – they aren't helpful, you know. We are a happy, peaceful community. To suggest otherwise...'

'No one is suggesting anything, Smeaton,' Robert says. 'This is not myth and rumour. We're from this place, remember? Our families are from here. We're not like you and your blow-ins. You were warned when you came here that this place was abandoned for a reason...'

'Enough,' Smeaton says. He is angry. He is so rarely angry, but I know that he hates all the old stories about the house. Refuses to believe them. Mary has been here many times, trying to teach him about the past, tell him about the people, about what happened here – but he refuses to accept any connection. It's just an old building, I've heard him insist, many times.

But after seeing that secret room, and knowing there's so much in there that he hasn't shared with the rest of the community, the file that he was reading as he walked out ... I'm just not sure that I believe him anymore.

Maybe I never did.

36

Smeaton

Smeaton lets out a long slow breath. He raises his hands, palms facing outwards into the crowd.

'Let's all take a minute here, shall we?' he says. 'We are all on the same page. We all love Angela, and wish that she had spoken to us before she left. But you must remember – Angela is a free spirit, as you all are.'

'Free?' says Chris. 'Is that what you think we are? Some of us have jobs to do, families to look after, we can't just up and leave when it suits us. Angela had a responsibility—'

Smeaton shakes his head. 'I'm afraid she did not, Chris. I know that you and Mary are very fond of her, having known her longer than even I have...'

'She's like a sister to me. I didn't want her to come to this place, you know. Mum took her in when she turned up in the village, and we thought she was happy. We couldn't understand why she wanted to give up her nice life with us to come and live in this...' he looks up at the building, gestures at the crumbling façade, '...this draughty old ruin. With you bunch of—'

'Bunch of what?' Smeaton says, smiling. He is not intimidated. He is used to Our Family being called any number of imaginable names. Hippies, freaks, weirdos, nutters, loonies ... He's not stupid. He knows how the outer world sees him, and Our Family. He learned from a young age that people outside tend to distrust what they don't understand. He'd like to tell these people that other people might have a list of names to call them, too. Simpletons, inbreds, *culchies*, rednecks. But

Chris wouldn't see the irony, and this is not the time for a lecture about how society views closed communities.

Someone in the crowd says something under their breath and Chris lowers his head. 'Sorry,' he mumbles. 'I'm just a bit upset.'

'We all are,' Smeaton says. 'Now listen – why don't you all go back home for now, and I'll do a bit of investigating back here. I'll ask everyone again if Angela mentioned anything about going away. I'll have a look in her room to see if there's anything that might help. She must've got the idea from somewhere. Chris, maybe you can ask Mary again; was she perhaps looking at any travel magazines or anything like that? You know, she might drop us a line soon, from wherever she is. I'm sure she's no idea that she's caused all this fuss.'

There is more mumbling from the crowd, but eventually they seem to be placated. Chris's friend Robert says, 'OK ... but if you could let us know if you hear anything?'

Smeaton nods. 'Likewise,' he says. 'Now you all go and enjoy your evenings.' There are a few muttered 'goodbyes' and a few raised hands. As they trail off down the driveway, Smeaton calls behind them, 'Embrace the light!' and one of them turns around, shakes his head.

'Oh well,' Smeaton says, turning to Cyril, who has joined him on the front step. 'Can't expect them to believe in what we do, just like that.'

'Right enough,' Cyril says. 'I'll put the kettle on, shall I? I think I need a sit down.'

Smeaton waits until Cyril has gone inside before he looks up at the window above. He saw movement there a moment ago. Felt that someone was watching. Ali or Jack? He wasn't sure which one. He hasn't seen Jack for a while. He's not sure the man is adjusting as well as he'd originally hoped. He's been sick for quite a few days now and, although Ali has assured him that it's all in hand, perhaps there's more to it, and a doctor should be called.

But he can't worry about that right now. He needs to think about Angela. He hasn't told anyone yet about going into her room – about finding that all her stuff is still there; at least he thinks it is, she may just have taken a small bag and only the things she really needs. But it makes no sense that she would abandon her investigations just like that, does it? All her equipment is still set up. Her log books are still there.

He doesn't want to admit it yet, but he has a very bad feeling about it all. Something has happened to her. It must have. He needs to check her room once more, properly this time. He needs as much information as he can before he goes to the police. They'll never take him seriously, otherwise.

'Oh, Angela,' he whispers, staring up at the darkening sky. 'Where on earth are you?'

37

Ali

Back in their bedroom, Ali steps back from the window. She knows that Smeaton has seen her. She could hear what was going on down there. He's going to come and question her again, she's sure. He's not just going to accept that Angela has gone. He's going to want to check on Jack, too – if he doesn't resurface soon. It'd been a mission to get him back from the north wing, but she'd managed it – half guiding, half dragging him along the corridors, trying to make sure that they weren't seen.

Jack has been in the bath for half an hour. She's checked on him, more than once – partly to make sure he hasn't fallen asleep and drowned himself, although perhaps that might not be the worst thing ... It would be a good way out of this mess. She could say he confessed to killing Angela, told her where he'd left her body then killed himself. She could lead them to Angela, act out her best distraught wife act, and end up the hero of this game after all. But so far he hasn't drowned, and there has been no indication that anyone – any*thing* – has tried to drown him. The more she thinks about it, the more she knows that she must've imagined the strange feeling of being pushed underwater. That the footprints she's seen disappearing were just a trick of the light. There's been no ghostly boy in the kitchen, and the pond drained itself just as it has every other time since they've tried to fill it. They were doing something wrong, or else the ground just isn't suitable.

Perhaps *she* should drown Jack. Would it be so hard to hold him under the water, for just the right amount of time? He is so weak, since she's been administering the drugs again, and he's quickly lost most of the strength he'd started to build since he came here. She has him under control again. He's not going to do anything stupid. And yet she has a strong urge to get rid of him. She can tell everyone about what he's done, have the police investigate the dead hitchhikers. And she will be free to start afresh. Alone.

Not here though. That was clearly a mistake. She's tried, she really has. She thought she could change her attitudes, thought she could succumb to the principles and guidance of the place – let herself be led by the guru. But, despite Smeaton's gentle approach towards teaching enlightenment, she now knows it was never going to bed in for her. She's just not that sort of person. Spirituality and self-help, finding the path to enlightenment, has never been her thing, not even as vague interest. As someone told her once, when she started her research into the mind – no one can make you change, no one can brainwash you into things you don't want in your life; no matter what you might be told, you are always the one in control of your own mind. No one can change you unless you want to be changed. And she did not want to be changed. She came here to get away from her past, to hide somewhere that no one would ever think to look.

Coming here made her feel less guilty about Jack too. About the things she has made him do. Because when it comes down to it, she hasn't made him do anything – he's chosen the path of a follower – he *wanted* to do what she told him to. He hasn't even taken a lot of convincing, most of the time. Something inside him was made that way, and it was just unfortunate that he met someone like her, someone keen to exploit his nature and use him as her personal guinea pig.

Poor, weak, Jack.

The drugs helped, of course. It was sheer luck that the drugs trial for Hycosamex, which she'd been working on at her hospital, had gone wrong – it was discovered that the drug was causing people to lose control of their actions, causing a lack of inhibition and leading them to take unnecessary risks. The drug, of course would be more thoroughly tested now, to find new uses for it – just like back in the sixties when they experimented with LSD on the military, or the discovery that Viagra was a lot more than a heart drug. Hycosamex had started off as a drug for motion sickness and when they found out it could also reduce seizures, it was rolled out into a global trial for people with epilepsy.

But then there were the side-effects – acute depression and mania, complete amnesia, people climbing up tall buildings and throwing themselves off...

The trial was halted immediately, for a serious safety review. The drugs were recalled – supposed to be returned to the manufacturer to be accounted for. But it was easy to misunderstand, amidst the underlying panic; to say that she had destroyed them in the mortuary crematorium instead. They had raked through the ashes and found no trace, but that's because the place was thoroughly cleaned after every burning. So they had to accept it. The main thing was, none of the patients had the drugs in their possession anymore. She returned the blister packs and the boxes. She made sure that she had accounted for every single box that had left her clinic. No one knew that she'd walked out of the hospital with the entire stock of Hycosamex tablets in a canvas shopping bag, hidden beneath several packets of crisps and bars of chocolate from the hospital vending machine.

No. She will not kill him like this. There are other things that she could do – keeping him at just the right dose of medication will do until she finally runs out.

And she needs him for a little bit longer.

38

Angela

It's a beautiful morning, and I've been sitting on the bench by the flower garden, admiring Julie's roses. We had plans to make perfumes and soaps. Not just from the roses, the other flowers too, and the herbs. I'd ordered a couple of books on it all; they're probably sitting there in Mary's shop now, waiting for me to collect them. Eventually, Mary will open the packages and send them back ... when it becomes clear that I'm not going to need them anymore. I wonder if it will help things along – maybe it might be something she can take to the police, once Smeaton has discovered the rest.

I know that he will.

I'm not angry with him for not going to the police straightaway, or for trying to put Mary and the others off. It's not because he doesn't care. It's not because he's not worried about me. But if Smeaton went to the police about every disappearing waif and stray he's come across in his life, he'd never be off the phone to them.

He liked to tell me stories about them all, sometimes, when it was just me and him. Sitting in his office with tea and homemade shortbread. He told me about the people who were around when he was a child, how they would disappear and reappear whenever the mood took them, and how no one ever looked for them because, as his father had told him one day – after his mother had run away, he later found out, with his father's best friend – 'Everyone is free; no one is joined to another; if someone is meant to be in your life, they will be in it, and if they are not then you should never spend a sleepless night, but accept that they are where they want to be.' His mother had returned, of course, but the best friend had not. Smeaton had asked his father about him many times, but no one seemed interested in his whereabouts. It wasn't until years later – when Smeaton had left his home and travelled to other communities around the world, seeing how they worked, making plans, honing his own spiritual beliefs – that he had found out that the man had died of a drug overdose many years earlier ... and that was why his mother had come back. It had rocked him, for a while. Shaken his beliefs in what his father had taught him. Would his mother have returned if her lover had stayed alive? Were people really so free that you shouldn't even look for them when they disappeared?

I know he must be in turmoil right now, wondering about me. Wanting to believe that I left because I wanted to, trying to convince himself that he was right to accept this, to take my 'note' at face value. But he knows I wouldn't leave like that, without saying goodbye. He knows, and he will accept that soon – and then he will go to the police.

In the meantime, all I can do is hang around, watching the others living their lives. Trying to find a way to let someone know that I am still here, and that I'll remain here until they find my body and let my spirit truly be free. That's what I'm hoping, at least.

I wish I could smell the roses. I wish I could touch their velvety petals. Just one more time. I climb off the bench and walk over to the rose bushes. There are many different colours, from the palest pink to the brightest yellow, peaches and cream, and one that is just off scarlet. They have exotic French names like Belle Epoque and Avec Amour and old-fashioned ladies' names, like Beryl Joyce. Perhaps someone will create a new breed and name it after me. Fairy Angela. It would be a lurid pink with pale-yellow edging, and an almost iridescent sparkle, as if it had been sprinkled with glitter.

There's movement out of the corner of my eye. A figure appears from one of the side doors. Dressed in black, hood up. Carrying something. A box. Intrigued, I move closer. I'm using my feet as normal, but as always, now, I can't seem to feel the ground.

It's Ali.

She's moving fast, away from the house, towards the trees. She glances around furtively; her expression is set hard. She doesn't want to encounter anyone right now. I move faster, so I am side by side with her. She glances back once more. Her breath comes out in short, ragged pants and she walks faster towards the woods. Now I can see that she is carrying two boxes, not one. I recognise one. I spotted it on her bookshelf, back when they first arrived. The one full of newspaper clippings, which she wasn't able to fully explain. The other one, I haven't seen before. But I suspect it is also full of something that she would rather not explain.

The woods are silent. I can't feel anything, but I would be able to tell if there was a breeze. The beeches have only just got all their green leaves – and they would be swaying now, if there was anything to sway them. Ali slows as she passes the hollow oak. Glances down to the dark, bare hole where she and Jack left me.

Do you feel me now, Ali? I wonder. She glances around again. Stumbles on a root. Swears under her breath. She's nervous. Skittish. In front of her now, the tyre swing hangs from the thick branch above.

Swing, I will it. *Swing*. But it remains immobile.

Ali keeps going.

I follow her to the dense copse at the far end of the wood. She crouches down, takes something from her pocket. A glint of metal shines, caught by the light of the fading sun. There's a shearing sound as she slices the trowel into the mulchy earth and starts to dig. I move closer, listen to her rasping breath. She's using the other hand to pull more earth out of the hole. She wipes a hand across her forehead. Then she stops.

'Hello?' she says. 'Is anyone there?'

She turns around, and I am crouched there, her face inches from me. I blow out a breath, slow, gentle. I wonder of it smells of my death. Of decay, and beetles and crushed twigs from where my face lay. Cold and alone, until they came back for me.

She mutters something, then turns back to her task. I can't touch her, I can't reveal myself to her, and yet somehow it comforts me that she is spooked. I think on some level, she knows that I am here.

She opens the boxes and tips the contents into the hole. Pieces of paper flutter down into the shadows. Other things, too. A scarf, a necklace. A wallet.

What are these things? Who do they belong to? I move closer, trying to make out the names on the clippings, trying to see what other items she has thrown in. She moves, blocking my view. Reaches into her pocket again.

There's the spark of a match. The crackle of the first flame. She fans it with her hands and it takes, easily. The paper dry and brittle, just the right amount of air. I want to push her over the hole, stop the flames, stop her from getting rid of this stuff. But I can't.

I shrink back, powerless, as the flames whirl and dance, lighting her face in reds and yellows. Her small smile, her expression saying, 'I've got away with it.'

No, I think.

No.

Dr Henry Baldock's Journal – 30th July 1955

We were visited today by a crowd from the village. Four of them, telling us they were going to the authorities; that what had happened to Jessie was a disgrace.

Telling us that there's no way that young George's drowning was an accident either.

They say the husband – Thomas – is in a bad way, and who can blame him?

I was allowed to sit in on the meeting, only because I believe now that Dr Throckmorton and the hospital administrators are worried that they're about to be found out. Throckmorton questioned me today – asking why I chose this place for my project, asking was I really a 'spy' for the board, and trying to laugh it off when I'd looked uncomfortable. I could tell he didn't believe what the villagers were telling him.

Mrs Samuel, who runs the village shop, said she was a relative of Jessie's, and that they'd both descended from Alice Samuel and did we know who that was?

I had to confess that I didn't, but Throckmorton and Miss Jaynes, his secretary, went quite pale. He tried to tell me afterwards that this was of no consequence, that Jessie's long-dead ancestors had no bearing on what had happened to her. But at my insistence, he told me who this Alice Samuel was, and why she's still known by name locally, despite having been dead for more than four hundred years.

She was one of the infamous 'Warboys Witches', the case that seemingly led to the Witchcraft Act of 1604, which, incredibly, was only properly repealed four years ago. Alice had been the victim of a cruel child and her crueller siblings, who'd conspired against the woman seemingly to attract attention, and this had spiralled into the accusation that she had bewitched and led to the death of Lady Cromwell – the grandmother of Oliver, the Lord Protector of the English Commonwealth. Alice and her family were tried and accused of witchcraft, and eventually, hanged.

Despite what we all know now – that there were no witches, only misunderstood and ill-treated women – it's a story that's remained important in the community, its legend living on, and for some it's an excuse to meddle in people's lives, even now.

Jessie had been taunted for her ancestry, Mrs Samuel said. And Mrs Samuel herself had suffered the very same – although she was stronger than Jessie, she said. Jessie was always a sensitive little soul. And when George had been born they'd said he wasn't her husband's but the Devil's son, because he had a strangely shaped birthmark on his forehead, that they were convinced was the Devil's Mark. They had bullied poor Jessie and forced her to reject her own son. The poor lad had suffered, too, being bullied and taunted at school, and none of them wanting to be his friend at all.

Mrs Samuel surmised that the drowning was no accident at all – more that it was those cruel boys, playing a dunking game – testing to see if the young lad was a witch.

Throckmorton laughed at that, but Miss Jaynes had gone paler than I thought it possible for a woman to turn without passing clean out; and I knew it all to be true.

That poor woman and her poor, poor boy.

These small communities might give an impression of being one big happy family, but they can be a danger, too, I can see. Rumours and nonsense and all sorts have gone on, and look where we are now. And yet despite all this making perfect sense to an outsider like me I know that Throckmorton will take it no further and will ensure that the whole thing will be recorded as nothing more than a tragedy.

He's a local, an upstanding member of this community. He'll not want anything to bring his own name into disrepute. I suspect he'll let the dust settle, then he'll leave his post here and retire. He'll get away with this, just as he has got away countless times with all manner of shocking crimes against his patients. None for which, sadly, I have any real proof.

39

Ali

Her clothes reek of smoke and she feels dirty, soiled. She doesn't know what to do about the car. At first she thought of burning that, too, but it would raise more issues than it would solve. Someone in the house would start asking where it is. There is no need to do anything about it right now. She eyes it, sitting there in the drive. It is filthy from rainwater and muck. She has no need for it now, and it is almost out of petrol. Maybe she can say it's broken down, get a scrapper to come and collect it. Hope that they take what they need from it and turn it into one of those neat cubes of metal like she's seen them do on TV. For now, the main thing is that she has got rid of all of Jack's stupid little souvenirs. But there's something else she's forgotten, of course. The rug, from the boot. Damn.

Rose calls her name from somewhere near the herb garden, but Ali pretends not to hear. No time for that right now. Yes, she resolved to be nicer to Rose, and that still stands, but for now she needs to get herself cleaned up before anyone wonders where she's been and what she's been doing.

Jack is in bed. He hasn't got up since the previous day. She dutifully went down for breakfast, saying he was still sick. Smeaton wasn't there, but some of the others were concerned; Richard commented that perhaps she was coming down with something too – she knew she wasn't looking her best. Angela's absence is making them all a bit skittish, but for the time being it means they're not overly concerned about what might be wrong with Jack. The part of her that still cares for him recognises the depression in him and knows that he needs help, but the part that despises him doesn't care. The part that despises him wants to grab him by the shoulders and shake some life back into him. She stares at him. Feels ripples of repulsion crawling over her skin.

She remembers the night when things changed, when it all shifted up a gear. They'd been coming back from a night in the West End, a show, post-theatre drinks. He'd been fun for a while, then he'd wanted to get the last train back, just as Ali had started to warm up.

'Let's stay – we can go clubbing ... or get a cheap hotel and drink in the bar?' she said.

'I'm tired, Ali. We can do this another time. I'll have a look, book us something nice.'

She stopped walking, stepped back into a shop doorway, letting the people behind them pass. 'I want to *play*, Jack.'

He glanced around, checking that no one had overheard. 'I'm not sure I can, tonight.'

'Since when do you say no? Come on, Jack ... please? I've got an idea.' She took a bottle of water out of her bag, something else out of her pocket, wrapped in a tiny plastic bag. 'Take one of these. It'll perk you up.' She offered him one of the capsules, popped the other one in her mouth and took a big swig of water.

He frowned. Took the capsule she was offering him and grabbed the water bottle out of her hand.

She watched his Adam's apple bobbing as he swallowed the medication, then turned away as if she was blowing her nose, depositing the other capsule, which she'd kept hidden in her hand, into a tissue.

'Let's wait here for a few minutes,' Ali said, pulling his arm.

They sat in a doorway, in silence, for nearly ten minutes – until Ali was sure that it was starting to work. Jack wasn't able to give her any indication, other than a glassy-eyed stare. She'd read up on this drug as much as she could from the previous trials. It was fast-acting in capsule form. It had to be if it was to help treat seizures. The dosage in her trial had most likely been too high, and even at lower concentrations it was known to interact with alcohol. It was dangerous, giving it to him like this – but that was part of the thrill.

She grabbed his hand, hurried them into the Tube station before the metal folding doors were pulled across. Somehow, it was more fun, knowing there was a chance that they might not be able to do it.

Ali headed straight for the escalator, but slowed down, waiting as she heard the sound of barriers crashing behind them, and a bunch of last-minute travellers running up behind them.

It was perfect.

'Be careful,' she said, under her breath … and then to Jack. 'Push.'

He stepped onto the escalator in front of her.

'Now,' she said in his ear.

Jack leant forwards and pushed. The man in front – one of the last from the group that had just barrelled in, shouted out in shock before he fell, knocking into another one like a skittle, sending him flying down the steps.

Ali grabbed Jack and ran down the left-hand side, as the guys piled up at the bottom, shouting, screaming at each other.

They didn't wait to see if anyone was badly hurt. Ali ran down the tunnel, still holding onto Jack, dragging him close behind. They jumped onto a waiting train, and the doors slid shut behind them.

They were out of the station, on the way home, before anyone had a chance to work out what had happened; and in the morning, when Jack woke late – thinking he had a hangover worse than the amount of drinks he'd consumed warranted – Ali was pleased to find out that he couldn't remember a thing.

After that night, Ali knew she could push her little experiment as far as she chose, and to avoid any reluctance on his part she would make sure to give him the drugs mixed into a drink, or food – and then there was no way that he could object. She was looking forward to publishing her findings, even if she could never put her name to them.

Now she turns on the bath taps, tips in some of the lavender salts. She realises that she has not had a proper bath since the night they moved in – preferring to wash with water and soap in the sink, or occasionally using one of the showers in the communal bathroom at the end of the corridor. But she longs to soak. She remembers the weird feeling from before, when she thought someone was trying to drown her. *Idiot*, she thinks, then lets the thoughts slide away, along with all the other odd things that have been going on lately. She recognises the symptoms of her own ailing mental health. Knows that she is hallucinating, imagining, becoming paranoid: the boy ... the pond ... the woman in the grey dress. Stress – too much stress. She will deal with it soon – once she's sorted out Jack, and maybe got rid of that damn car. All this stuff with Angela is adding to it all, of course. But all she can do is hope that Smeaton continues to swallow the story that she has gone off travelling.

She dips a toe into the bath, pulls it out fast. Too hot. Another flash of paranoia hits her. What if Smeaton knows what really happened? What if he's just biding his time, gathering information before he goes to the police?

She turns off the hot tap, leaves the cold running. She pops her head around the door, checking on Jack. Maybe they should just grab their stuff, jump in the car and disappear? She's sure they could make it to Felixstowe and onto a ferry before Smeaton realises they've gone. And if he's not actually suspicious – he wouldn't call the police anyway, would he? He's said it himself – this place isn't for everyone. People can come and go as they please. Didn't Angela say that a couple of occultists left after two weeks?

She sits on the edge of the bath, turns off the cold tap. It must be ready now. She sticks her finger in to test the water again, pulls it back quickly. She turns on the cold tap, but all it does is emit a high-pitched squeal, and no water comes out.

Damn it.

She sighs, closing her eyes, and runs the tips of her fingers back and forth across the surface of the water. Then she feels a slight tugging, as if something is trying to grab hold of her fingers, pulling them in. It's too hot, and she panics. She opens her eyes and pulls her hand out of the water. It's cloudy from the bath salts, but she's sure she sees the tips of dirty fingers, just as they vanish back under the surface.

Breathe, just breathe, she tells herself. Clearly this was a mistake, and anyway, there's no way she can get into that bath, even if she wanted to. She'd be boiled alive.

She goes back through to check on Jack once again. He is semi-coherent, turning himself this way and that, pushing off the covers.

'Too hot,' he says. 'I'm so hot ... help me, Ali. They're coming for me now...'

She pulls the covers off him. He is wet with sweat. He smells worse than she does, despite having washed earlier. There are toxins leaching out of his skin. Are the drugs poisoning him? Is *this* why they were recalled by the manufacturer? She tries not to breathe too deeply. She forgets about the bath. '*Who* is, Jack? Do you know where you are?'

'Them! You know them, Ali. You know!' he shouts the last word and she has to lay a hand over his mouth, trying to quiet him. Oh, how easy it would be to grab that pillow from her side and smother him to death right now.

'Jack, no one is coming for you.' She wants to believe this, she really does. 'You just need to sleep a bit longer. You're ill, I think. You have a fever.' She lays a hand on his forehead, as if to confirm this. He is clammy, warm. But it's not a fever. He's ill, but not like that.

She goes into her bedside cabinet and takes out the carrier bag from the back of the drawer. She opens it. Takes a deep breath. There are still a few capsules left.

She could give him too many ... no one would know what he's taken. No one knows that these drugs exist. But no. Not now. Not like this.

'I killed them,' he says, his voice is a coarse whisper. It makes the hair on the back of her neck stand up. 'I killed them, Ali. I killed them and no one knows ... no one knows it was me.'

She takes out two of the capsules, hands them to him. He takes them with a shaking hand, swallows them dry. He doesn't question her. He never questions her, because he trusts her.

I know, she thinks. *I know what you did. And it's me who's had to clear up the mess behind you.*

She thinks of Angela, lying there in the hollow of a rotting tree. She thinks of her now, hidden away, but not for long. Someone will find her, soon. Her broken and rotting corpse, lying in a ditch. Dirty water and debris covering her like a blanket.

Just like all the others.

A wave of repulsion hits her again.

He is so weak. So unquestioning. So compliant.

She wants to shake him until he breaks open, and all of his weak little bones snap into pieces. She wants him to yell at her, to protest – to say, *I didn't do it – it wasn't me!*

But it was you, Jack, wasn't it? If only you had said *no*…

She walks back through to the bathroom and peels off her stinking clothes. She puts her hand into the water, but it is still too hot. She sits there, naked, on the edge, breathing in the steam. At least no one can try to drown her tonight. Not if she can't get in the bloody bath. She's tired. She aches. She can't keep doing everything to keep them both safe.

The game is no fun anymore.

40

Angela

I wonder how far I can stray from where I was killed. Perhaps I can visit places where I was happy? I know where I would like to be ... The sun is shimmering over the fields, and I feel no resistance – it seems to take me no time at all to get to the village.

Despite all that's happened recently, nothing looks different here. It looks just as I imagine it did hundreds of years ago. The pond is still there, looking pretty with its border of neatly planted pansies and well-kept grass; the small section under the arched bridge, with its blue and white wildflowers and the little plaque in memory of the women who were accused of witchcraft and cruelly mistreated many years ago. Now officially pardoned by the government, of course, not that that's much comfort to them now.

Across the road, the village square is devoid of people apart from an old man whose name I've never known. He sits on a bench, feeding pigeons from a bag full of bread scraps, and doesn't see me. Doesn't sense me.

So far no one has.

I think there's only one person that might. Mary might style herself as a cynic, but I think she's got more psychic ability than I could ever have hoped for, and it's time for me to put that to the test. I think the day must be warm as people further up the street are walking around without cardigans or jackets, and the door to the shop is standing wide open.

Mary doesn't like to leave the door open, she likes to be alerted when someone comes in. But it gets hotter than a furnace in there, and all the fans in the world don't help. Sometimes she has no choice but to let the fresh air in, and keep her beady eyes on the open door for those who like to take advantage. I hesitate outside, feeling strangely worried about going in. I can see her behind the counter. She is serving someone, chattering away as usual. I can't hear her clearly, but what she is saying sounds serious. It's not like her to sound so downbeat. I can't quite see the person she's chatting to. One arm is resting on the counter, and a carrier bag looped over the other. I can see a bit of trouser leg, and I'm pretty sure it's a man, but that's about all I can tell from here. I need to go inside.

I'm about to step inside when an old woman I recognise turns the corner and comes walking down the street towards me. She's staring straight ahead, on a mission. I've been in the shop when she's been in there before. She's not a chatterer. She likes to come in with her list, get what she needs, and go. I step back a little so that I'm not obstructing the entrance to the shop, and when she arrives at the step she pauses for a moment, and her expression changes from determined to confused. She glances behind her then back towards me. She is looking straight at me. I smile, and quietly say, 'Hello.'

She frowns, and then rubs at her arms, as if she's suddenly felt a trickle of a breeze.

My eyes scan the square, across the young trees lining the boundary. Their leaves are not moving at all. If there *was* a breeze, it wasn't widespread, and it didn't last for long. I remember how it feels on your skin when you're excited, and I wish I could feel that prickling now. The waves of goose pimples running up each arm. I don't feel it and yet somehow I do. A phantom feeling. A memory of what it should be, like amputees who still think they can feel their missing limbs. Did I cause the breeze? Am I exuding some sort of electrical field that has somehow reached this old woman? She glances around once more then hurries into the shop. A moment afterwards, the man who was at the counter comes thudding down the step, and he turns the opposite way from me, not sensing me at all. He's whistling a tune, something from one of those old war films whose name I can never remember. He disappears around the other corner and he's gone. My brief feeling of elation sinks.

I go up the steps and into the shop. The woman from earlier is hurrying around the aisles with a basket balanced on top of her tartan shopping trolley, as she always does. Except she seems to be talking to herself, muttering something. I can't quite make out the words. She's going even faster than usual, rushing around, throwing things into her basket willy-nilly, her list seemingly abandoned. I follow her around, keeping a safe distance. She glances around again, and I try another smile. She practically runs to the till.

'You're quick today, Mrs Maybold,' Mary says.

I stay hidden behind a display stand of cereal, jams and hot chocolate. I poke my head around, just slightly, and as I do the old woman rubs her arms again.

'Can't stop, lots to do today.'

I step out into the aisle, giving Mary a clear view. She looks up from the till, and her eyes scan the shop. A brief wash of concern passes over her face and then her usual smile returns.

'Don't suppose there's any news on the girl, is there?' Mrs Maybold says, stuffing things into her tartan trolley.

Mary looks alarmed. 'Not like you to ask ... What brought that on?'

'I don't know. Nothing.' She shrugs. Puts her purse back into the little pocket on the back of her trolley. 'Something just made me think of her today.'

Mary crosses her arms; her expression is pinched. 'You know I don't believe she's run off, Phyllis,' she says, conspiratorially. 'She wouldn't do that. Not without telling me.'

The old woman nods. 'I agree. It would surprise me if she'd done that, right enough. Anyway, I really am in a rush today.' Phyllis Maybold grabs her trolley and darts out the shop before Mary can say anything else.

The door closes behind her with a bang, as if a gust of wind has caught it, knocking the doorstop clean out of the way. It's one of those little wooden wedges. Sometimes they just move, if there's a vibration on the floor, like if a lorry has trundled past on the main road. But there are no lorries today. Mrs Maybold's rushing around has probably dislodged it, but Mary looks uncomfortable.

She staring straight at me now. She wraps her arms around her chest, rubs herself warm, as if she too has felt an unexpectedly cool breeze. Her eyes are wary.

I take a few steps towards her. 'Don't be scared, Mary. It's me. You're right, you know. Don't let them stop looking for me. Please. I haven't run away. You know I haven't.'

'Oh Angela, I do miss you. I wish you'd come to me. I'm here for you, wherever you are.' Mary closes her eyes, places her hands on the counter. A single tear runs down her face, dropping onto the pile of newspapers on the counter beneath her.

She can't see me. It hits me, almost like a physical slap, even though I can't feel anything anymore. I thought at first that maybe she just wasn't ready. But now I realise the truth. She's a fraud. She's no more of a psychic than I was. I want to be angry, but I'm not. It just helps me to understand her. She is even more like me than I thought. All she wants is to feel it. All she wants is to believe that something else exists. Because if there is nothing but this life, then what hope is there that we will ever have something more?

41

Ali

Ali is still sitting on the edge of the bath. The water doesn't seem to be cooling at all, and when she tries the cold tap again, still nothing comes out of it. She picks up her dirty clothes from the floor and puts them back on.

She can hear the sound of Jack snoring through the bathroom door. Bloody Jack. She envies him right now, him and his oblivion. Maybe she should just give in, take some of the medication herself. Maybe the pair of them can just drift off together. This wouldn't be such a bad place to die. She does wonder if there is any point in going on. What are they going to achieve now? The game is well and truly over. Unless...

Unless she adds a new player. She sits down on the floor, leaning back against the bath. She stares out of the window, watches the cloud formations. The fat puffy ones like marshmallows; *cumulonimbus*? Is that what they're called? They drift slowly by, as if they're on a conveyor belt, forming weird shapes and turning them into animals as they go.

She sighs. Life could have been so simple ... but simple was never enough for her.

She has always had to take risks, push things too far. Taking the drugs from the hospital had been such a thrill. She wasn't even sure at the time that she would do anything with them, but walking out of there that day with a bag stuffed full of illegal, unlicensed drugs was the most thrilling thing that she'd ever done; and she'd done a lot of things.

Jack had done a lot of things.

It turned out that he never really did need much persuading, except for when things took a darker turn than even she hadn't fully expected. He'd been genuinely upset after the escalator incident, once it came back to him a few days later, as a horrific, sweaty night terror. She tried to convince him that it didn't happen, but he didn't believe her. He said that he wouldn't play her game anymore. That it wasn't the game for him.

She kept telling him, over and over ... nothing *really* bad happened; that guy had been fine. People fall down escalators all the time. He was drunk. There are signs all over the Tube stations telling you not to run. It happens, it was an accident.

But of course she knew that it wasn't, and deep inside his muddled head, he did too.

The first time they killed someone was a surprise in many ways. She remembers when she first had the feeling ... the urge that came over her as she drove along that road late one night. Saw him standing on the verge, his homemade cardboard sign asking if someone could, please, take him to Leeds, with a smiley face drawn on beside it. That real smiley face of his own. He was so happy when she pulled over ... and she really thought about doing it herself, there and then. But she came to her senses, sped off again, Jack screeching in her ear. Asking her what she was doing. She caught the man's furious face in the rear-view mirror, smile gone, two hands raised, middle fingers pointing to the sky.

She laughed so hard she had to pull in at the next services to calm down. Had to rush to the toilet before she wet herself. All the time, Jack fuming at her, berating her. Angry. She waited until he went off to the toilet himself, before emptying one of the capsules and stirring the powder into his coffee.

She debated this with herself many times over the course of her work. Should he be fully aware that he was taking the drug, or did it have to be a secret, so that he had no idea that it was a drug that was helping him to do the things that she wanted him to do? They still had to be things that he wanted to do, deep down, didn't they? She was still working on her theory. Still trying to work out if she truly believed that true coercion was real.

She wanted to believe that free will *always* prevailed, somehow, but when drugs were added to the mix, who knew? This was the whole basis for her research. Could someone be completely controlled? Could they become willing participants in risky, dangerous acts? Was it possible to *make* someone evil? In some ways the drugs complicated things more than she expected. She wasn't sure that she could entirely prove her theory at all – but the experiment evolved. That was what happened in science, wasn't it? It was still an important piece of research – and besides, the addition of the drug did make it much easier for her to manage.

Further research revealed that the drug acted faster when mixed with hot liquid. She hadn't actually done that before. She had sprinkled half of one over his dinner one night, but she'd never put it into a hot drink in case it deactivated the ingredients. But as she read more and more about the mode of action, it seemed that hot liquid might be a good base for it after all.

That first night, by the time they got back to the car, he said he was feeling tired and a bit strange.

'I might just have a lie down in the back for a minute,' he said. 'I think that coffee has done something to me. You know what I get like sometimes.'

He climbed into the back seat, and Ali climbed into the front. As they drove out of the car park and back onto the motorway she said, 'Jack, are you awake?' and he grunted something unintelligible in reply.

'I'm going to pick someone up, and I want you to do something for me. There's a pack of dishcloths down the side door. Take them out. Once I pick someone up, you need to do it.'

'Do what? What are you talking about?' His voice was slightly slurred, and she was worried that she'd given him too much. That he wouldn't be able to do it.

'You know what. What we talked about before. I'm going to pick someone up, and you're going to kill them for me. Aren't you Jack?' Another grunt. He sat up. 'I don't remember saying that.' His voice was thick with confusion.

'Lie down ... you need to lie down. You need to be asleep when they get in, and then when it's time you get up and they fall back a little, like they're about to have a nap. Then you'll lean over the seat and you'll hold the cloth over their face, stuff it in their mouth and hold their nose. Keep doing it until they stop moving. You *know* what we agreed. You said you would do this for me. Don't try and pretend you've forgotten. Come on Jack ... After that, we'll stop at a hotel up ahead. You know what I'll do to you once we get there don't you?' She gave him her best seductive voice. She was already turned on, just thinking about it. She knew he would be too, he just didn't know it yet.

She could see the figure up ahead. They'd obviously come down from the last slip road, walked as far as they could along here, then given up. It's a man. She'd hoped the first one would be a woman, just because it would have been easier, but then again, this guy wasn't very big. If Jack did what he was meant to, it would happen quickly.

She indicated left and pulled in to the layby where the man stood, waiting. Headlights shone in his eyes and he raised a hand, lowered his cardboard sign. She'd already read where he wanted to go, and knew he wasn't going to get there. She almost felt sorry for him, but the feeling quickly passed. He was about to become part of an important experiment. Before she opened the door she glanced around at Jack one last time. 'You need to be ready. Don't let me down, Jack.'

'I won't. I'd never let you down, Ali.'

The door opened and the young man climbed into the car. She grinned at him. 'I'm Ali,' she said. 'That's my husband Jack in the back. Don't worry about him, he's sleeping off a hangover.' She rolled her eyes for good measure, then indicated right and pulled back onto the road.

'Jarold,' he said. 'Just travelling around the UK for a bit, ran out of cash. Gonna head back up to Edinburgh, bit by bit...'

'Well, we're only going as far as Newcastle,' she lied. 'But I can drop you there and you'll find someone else for the last leg, I'm sure. Someone waiting for you up north, is there?'

He shook his head. 'Nah, just fancy getting up there for the festival.

Plenty of stuff happening, you know. No one waiting for me. Free as bird I am.' He laughed easily and she felt a lurching in her stomach. *Wrong place, wrong time, Jarold.*

'Here, do you want a drink of this? Sorry, I lost the lid ... Don't worry, my mouth's pretty clean,' she laughed, and offered him the bottle of Coke she was holding in her right hand. She'd dissolved a couple of capsules into it earlier, when Jack had been in the toilet.

'Sure,' he said. Smiled. Took a sip.

'Finish it,' she said. 'I'm done.'

He'd smiled again, drank the rest of the bottle. It only took a few minutes to kick in. The gas and the sugar seemed to make it work quicker, too.

'I'm just going to have a quick nap,' he said, groggily, rubbing his face. The bottle dropped from his hand.

She glanced in the rear-view mirror, just as Jack slowly sat up. His face a picture of pure concentration. He was holding a white cloth in his hands. They made eye contact, and Ali smiled.

Ali leans back against the bath, smiling at the memory.

42

Smeaton

Smeaton is worried. He knows that there is something wrong. The villagers are right. He needs to go to the police about Angela. The note, despite sounding like her, just doesn't add up. She'd been trying to warn him about Ali and Jack, and he had dismissed her concerns. Mary is worried too. She doesn't believe that Angela has just gone off somewhere without telling anyone. She'd never even mentioned any desire to go travelling, being happy enough to listen to Smeaton's tales from around the world – even if most of them were completely made up.

They all agree that it's just not like her. Despite all her little quirks and eccentricities, all Angela really wants is to be part of a proper family. Smeaton sits down at his desk and opens his laptop. He takes the small mobile router out of his drawer and plugs it in. He rarely uses the internet, and he knows the device won't be charged. None of the residents have internet access and that's how he prefers it. He tries as much as possible to stay offline himself, to stay away from the real world, with all the madness that is happening out there right now. He knows he's burying his head in the sand somewhat, but it worked for his parents and it's working for him. If he can be happy here, why worry about the rest of the universe as it falls apart?

The problem is, this is meant to be a safe place, and now it is falling apart too.

He waits a moment for the wi-fi connection on his laptop to find the router. It doesn't always work first time, as if it knows that it is not an important item. It's important today though, because he's going to do something now that he should have done right at the start. Angela had asked him. She asked him if he had checked out Ali and Jack's stories, or had he just taken everything at face value. He has to admit now, to himself if no one else. That that's exactly what he did. Fool.

He opens up his email program, and after a moment it refreshes and a bunch of new emails appear. Most of them are junk. Despite not spending much time online, he still seems to find himself added to various mailing lists and in receipt of copious spam and nonsense. There are a couple of emails in there from people enquiring about Rosalind House; he will deal with those later. He makes it clear on the website that people should not expect a fast response by email, but he purposely does not include the phone number because he does not want to have to deal with those things on any immediate level. If people want to live here, they have to realise that the pace is very different. If they can't handle that, they're not likely to fit in. It's the first of his tests.

It had been luck – or as some might think destiny – that he had been online when Ali's first email had popped up. He'd opened it straightaway, something about the subject line intriguing him. She had introduced herself politely and concisely and told him that she knew that this wasn't the way things were meant to work, but they had just had such a run of bad luck that they needed to get away. She offered him money, and despite his belief that Rosalind House should not be one of those places that relied on the residents' funds to make it work, he could hardly turn it down. The boiler was on its last legs. And they needed funds to complete the ornamental garden, so that they could try again with opening it to the public. He'd have found the money in time, but Ali's offer had come on a day when he'd felt like things were piling up, becoming impossible. He'd accepted the offer gladly.

A big mistake now, he realises.

He can't bear to read the emails again. Some of Angela's scepticism has already invaded his thoughts, and he can't really believe anything that he has already read. He does, however, remember enough of the details to do some investigation of his own.

He opens a browser window then pauses, his hands hovering over the keys. Who first? Ali or Jack? He has a feeling that Jack will be more straightforward. The man's mood swings and the fact that he has been confined to bed for the last few days, barely seen anywhere, confirms what Ali had said about him taking medical retirement due to stress. Maybe it is really as simple as that.

Maybe it isn't.

He types Jack's name into the search bar. Then deletes it, changes it to *Detective Inspector* Jack Gardiner. He immediately gets plenty of results, and just looking at the first ten, he thinks he's got what he needs. He clicks open the first one, an article from the *Evening Standard*, one of the London newspapers. The headline reads 'Baby Z Detective Inspector Leaves under a Cloud'. Smeaton sighs. He rubs at his face; his eyes feel tired suddenly. As if they are already worried about what he's going to read next. He skims the article with a sense of relief. Mistakes made, vulnerable child put at risk, mental-health issues, unusual behaviour, falling asleep at work, suspicions of drug misuse unfounded, union rep, medical retirement ... blah, blah, blah. Nothing there that he doesn't already know. Jack, it seems, is clean.

He tries Ali next, adding *nurse* after her name in the search box, hoping that it will throw up nothing apart from her bio on the website for the hospital where she used to work. But it throws up more than that: it turns out she was involved in a clinical trial that was cancelled due to the medication causing serious side-effects, and the whole thing was pulled by the pharmaceutical company. She was the clinical nurse in charge of the trial at her hospital, one of the main investigative sites, and she had made a statement about it. The side-effects reported ranged from dizziness and confusion and narcolepsy, to extreme paranoia, psychosis and in three cases, suicide.

Something about this gets Smeaton's senses tingling; a drug that resulted in sleepiness and confusion? And her husband suffering similar symptoms, leading to him being removed from the police force? Smeaton is worried that he is adding two and two and making fourteen. Is he just seeing what he wants to see now? Is he looking for a problem when one doesn't exist? He clicks back to the main search, scrolls down further. Clicks onto the next page, and there it is: a link to an abstract for a proposed academic paper. A poster from a psychology research conference. The paper is about the psychology of coercion and control, an exploration of the works of Dr Henry Baldock and several others. Ali is listed as one of the key authors. This was her research, then – the official research. But did that lead her to commence *another* experiment of her own? An experiment with only one trial subject...

Smeaton feels sick. He takes the small notebook out of his desk drawer – the one he'd collected from the locked records room. He knew he recognised the name. He flicks it open to the first page, reads the careful, curling handwriting – almost too neat and legible for a doctor. *The Journal of Henry Baldock, dated 2nd March 1955.* This was the man who was sent to investigate abuse within the hospital. The man who went on to write an important paper about controlling behaviour in a hospital setting, which included several case studies where patients had been forced to believe that they had done things that they hadn't done – and other cases, where they were coaxed and cajoled into doing things that they did not want to do.

Ali didn't find this place by chance, on the commune network's website, did she? She lied about that. She no doubt lied about many things.

Smeaton feels a chill run over him as he thinks back to the times just after they'd first arrived, when it had seemed like Jack had been looking at Ali with adoration, like he'd do anything she asked him to ... And then, for a few weeks, he'd seemed positive and happy – embracing his new life. But now he is nowhere to be seen, and only Ali has access to him ... feeding him ... nursing him...

Oh Ali, he thinks. *What exactly is it that you've made Jack do?*

Angela was right. There is something very wrong with Ali. If only he had listened when she tried to warn him, Angela might still be here now. He knows now, it all makes sense. Angela hasn't run away at all. She must've found something out, and made the naïve mistake of going to see Ali.

He locks the notebook back in his desk, and goes off to find Ford.

43
Ali

She sits back on the edge of the bath, dips a finger into the bathwater again – still too hot. The plug will have to stay in for now. She'll have to ask Smeaton about the cold water – maybe there's a blockage somewhere? She remembers something that Angela said, about some creepy doctor drowning himself in a rain barrel, and she shudders at the thought.

Angela...

She closes her eyes for a moment, feeling tired all of a sudden.

An image floats into her vision, and she tries to open her eyes, but she can't; it's as if they are glued shut. She panics, remembers the bath – if she falls in she will be scalded. She tries to stand, but she can't. Strong hands grip her upper arms, and she hears whispers. She's not in the bathroom anymore. In the vision, her eyes are open and she is walking across loose gravel. She can see the pond in the distance. She is pushed, roughly, the grip on her arms released. In front of her is a wooden rain barrel. Water is overflowing, running down the sides. She walks closer, unable to stop herself. The water is dark. She reaches out a hand to dip her finger in, and a face floats up to the surface – pale and bloated, dark holes where eyes once were.

She stumbles back, falls. She tries to scream, but there is no sound coming from her. She edges away, as the barrel tips over and the water gushes out towards her, the bloated corpse floating on the wave and she screams again and this time she can hear it.

Her eyes fly open, and she is curled on the bathroom floor. Water is overflowing from the bath, hot, splashing, leaving a warm pool around her. She comes to her senses, gets onto her knees. Leans over and turns off the hot tap, smarting from the heat of the boiling brass. She takes a breath. The water sloshes gently from side to side, spilling a little more over the sides, then it stops.

She stands up, hurries out of the room, closing the door tight behind her. Her heart is still hammering. She thinks she might faint, but she forces herself to take long, slow breaths. Eventually the panic subsides.

Jack is awake. 'What's going on in there?' he says. His voice is still groggy. There is no urgency. He would not be able to help her if anything else was to happen.

He's of no use to her now.

'Get dressed, I'm going to show you something.'

He turns over, faces away from her. 'Just leave me alone, will you?'

Ali balls her hands into fists. Feels her nails cutting into her palms. 'You can't just lie around in bed all the time. People are asking questions. It's only a matter of time before someone comes up here to check on you.'

'Tell them then.'

The rage starts to burn, from her hands, up her arms, into her chest. 'Tell them? *Tell them?* Have you completely lost your mind, Jack? Do you want to spend the rest of your life in prison? Do you want me in there, too? You'll never see me again. I might be able to survive a life in prison, but you sure as hell won't. You'll be someone's pet before you've even spent a night in there. You know what they do to weak, pathetic little yes-men in prison? You know what they do to ex-cops in prison? Jesus Christ, Jack – you know what they do to serial killers?' She blows out a breath, starts to pace the room. 'They won't believe you did it anyway. They'll never believe it. You – pathetic little you – you killed all those hitchhikers, did you? You carried their bodies out of the car and tossed them into ditches? They'll know you could never have thought this one up yourself. Because you have no fucking imagination, Jack. No drive. No wonder you were the laughing stock at work. Useless piece of shit. They didn't want you working with vulnerable cases – you were a bloody liability. If it hadn't been for me giving you some sort of *purpose* in life, you'd still be nothing. Weak, pathetic little Jack, hanging on the coat-tails of everyone else—'

'I got *you*, didn't I? Loads of the lads wanted you. But it was me who got you...'

She laughs. 'You think you had a choice in that, do you? I picked you out right from the start. I could see you were a follower. You were always a step behind your cocky mates. Letting them make the moves, finding the girls to chat up – and then they'd send you for the drinks. Didn't you notice that, Jack? You were never first on the scene, so to speak – were you? How you made it as far as DI, I will never know...'

He appears momentarily lucid. 'Hang on, you're saying you picked me? You planned all this?'

'Planned all what? The Game? You enjoyed it, didn't you? It was a damn sight more exciting than the rest of your life ever was. Don't deny it...'

'I'll admit it was fun at first. It was a buzz. And we always had such amazing sex...' He pauses, scratches his head. 'When did that stop? I can't even remember...'

'You don't remember because of the pills, you idiot. You made me give them to you. Said you couldn't deal with the nightmares, the flashbacks.'

'Did I? I can't remember...'

'I took a big risk getting those drugs for you. You could at least be grateful. I can't help it if they messed with your ability to get it up, can I?'

Jack starts to cry, and Ali is horrified.

'I can't remember it anymore, Ali. I can't remember what I've done ... I just know ... I know it was bad. When we came here, I started to dream again...'

'I know you did. That's why I started giving you the drugs again, you idiot. I thought maybe you could go cold turkey here – that maybe your sex drive would come back – but it wasn't working. I could see how confused you were. I was worried you'd tell someone – like Ford, maybe. He was suspicious. And bloody Angela, too – although she's been dealt with, at least.'

'Are they still looking for her?' he says. And then so quietly she can hardly hear, 'Where is she?'

'Where is she? You clubbed her over the head and tossed her in a ditch. You can't have forgotten that, surely?'

'No ... I can't – I can't have done that. You're lying.'

'You remember the hitchhikers, don't you? Four of them. Do you remember their names?'

He shakes his head. His face seems to clear. 'Not their names ... but I kept things—'

'I burned them, didn't I? Jesus Christ. You can't keep that stuff, Jack. The news clippings either. No one has worked it out yet – that they were all murders. That they were all done by the same person. Using the trial drug was genius; no way they can find it on a tox screen, because it doesn't technically exist in its current form and they don't know what they're looking for—'

'You drugged them? But I—'

'Of course I drugged them ... bottle of Coke. Every time. Never take drinks from strangers, Jack. Or lifts.' She laughs again, and it sounds strange and alien. Not like her laugh.

She needs to end this. She's come full circle, it seems ... Her parents, then Jack and now she's losing grip on reality, too. She knew it as soon as she arrived in this place. She's always been in control – of herself *and* others. But now ... now, she can't stop the visions, the voices, the sense that something here, something more powerful than her, is taking control of her.

'Come with me, Jack,' she talks slowly, calmly. Tries to soothe him again after the turmoil of the last few minutes. The revelations that he is struggling to process. 'I've got an idea. A way to get you off the drugs, so that you don't have to think about all the bad things anymore. You can move on, live your life. We can enjoy it here.'

He sits up, swings his legs over the edge of the bed. He is shaking. Nervous. But there is hope in his voice when he says, 'What are you going to do?'

'You just need to come with me, Jack. You trust me, don't you?'

He nods his meek little lamb head, and follows her out of the room.

Dr Henry Baldock's Journal – 5th August 1955

I just happened to be in the office when the call came. I answered it, and for a long while afterwards, I couldn't stop shaking.

It was Mrs Samuel who visited just the other day. She told me that Jessie's husband had been found hanging in his brother's barn; he had climbed onto the hay bales and knotted a rope around the beam.

I can't quite believe it. Jessie, George and Thomas Samuel are gone. The whole family wiped out in such a short space of time. A chain of horrific events, leading all the way back to something that happened more than four hundred years ago. Small town rumours with devastating consequences.

I don't believe that Jessie should ever have been in here. She should have been cared for by her husband and her family. And yet she was brought here supposedly suffering from hysteria, when what she was really suffering from was being overworked, overstressed and terrified at being a mother, helpless against the cruel bullies who refused to leave her and her son alone.

By all accounts, her husband had tried his best, but he wasn't the recipient of the jibes and taunts. He'd come from another village. He had no idea what he'd walked in to.

I think it's critical that we look into the mental health of new mothers, to give them more support than they currently receive. There has been some research done already, and this is becoming an area of interest. But I'm not sure if this would have helped Jessie. The church-going villagers had turned against her because of her background, and her son was just another of their victims. The poor boy had existed in a world where he was convinced that no one loved him at all.

I will be sending my findings to the board about all this, as a separate note, not just part of my report on the whole operation of the place. This is an issue that is too big to ignore. The community here seem to be holding a collective hatred against a family based on ridiculous superstition, and the hospital had somehow become complicit. This is something that should have been addressed long before now.

I remember seeing the nurses giving Jessie the cold-bath shock treatment, and I wonder if that is really what they were doing after all. Could it be that those women were testing her to see if she was a witch, just as those nasty children did to her son?

On a more rational note, it is my belief that had Jessie been given better care, then not only would she be alive now, but so would her husband and her son. But then there's no way to account for the bullying that her son received – the taunting and accusations from the other children. I do wish that there was a better system in place to deal with vulnerable children.

Don't people realise how dangerous superstition and gossip can be?

44

Smeaton

Ali stops walking when she sees them. She turns, as if about to disappear in the opposite direction, then seems to decide against it. Her face flits from surprise to panic before she appears to gather herself together and gives them a small smile.

It's too late though – she looks guilty. Smeaton is confused. He opens his mouth to speak, but Ford gets there first.

'Where's Jack?' Ford's voice is filled with venom.

'He's sleeping, he's—'

'He's been sleeping a lot these past few days.' Ford says. 'What exactly is wrong with him?'

Ali sighs, looks away. 'Look, I didn't want to tell you when we arrived. He's ... he's had some issues. Some mental-health issues. The doctors were trying to label him, drug him – take him away for evaluation – all of that. I – we – didn't want it. That's why I brought him here. I thought it was all stress, you know? I thought the fresh air and the change of pace would sort him out, I thought—'

'That's bullshit, Ali. You've been drugging him, haven't you? I could tell the difference. I'm not stupid. The first few weeks with me, he was completely fine. He seemed happy. Then recently something changed. He became spaced out. I asked him what was wrong and he said he got confused sometimes. That he couldn't remember things...'

'Maybe we should go and sit downstairs and have a nice cup of tea,' Smeaton says. 'Discuss this calmly.'

Ford ignores him. 'You know what I used to do before I came here, right?'

Ali shakes her head.

'I was in the Met. North of the river. Major Investigations. Burned me out. Too much shit, so I gave it up and found this place. I needed a complete change. Jack was the same, yeah? He told me. West London – child protection. More awful stuff than anyone ever needs to deal with in their life.'

'That's right,' Ali says. She sounds confused.

Smeaton is confused too. 'You knew him?' he says.

'No. Of course not. Do you know how many officers are currently serving in the Met? Besides, I'm at least ten years older. I was gone long before Jack started to run into difficulties.'

'What do you mean, *difficulties*?' Smeaton is worried now. He hopes his imagination is running away with him.

'I did a bit of checking. Asked a couple of mates still in the force to look him up. I was intrigued. Don't ask me why. He was reluctant to talk about stuff, and I started to wonder if he was lying – about having been police.'

Ali shakes her head. She's smiling now. Looks relieved. 'Why would he lie? He didn't do anything wrong. He had a clean sheet. The pressures got to him. Hardly surprising.'

'Mate of mine told me his sheet wasn't quite clean. That there were mistakes. Questions asked about why a vulnerable child was left in a home with an abusive father. Jack was acting strangely, they said. Made some poor decisions.'

'I told you, he was stressed. They sent him for all these tests. Couldn't find out what was wrong. You're right, he wasn't himself. He was confused, his brain was mashed. It happens.'

'And yet he got pensioned off without a blot on his record. This stuff was all off the record, right? My mate says there was talk of him being an addict. Says his division wanted to keep it quiet. Wouldn't look good for them if a vulnerable child getting her legs broken by her junkie dad could've been avoided if the DI in charge of the case wasn't off his head too.'

Smeaton is taken aback. 'Is this true, Ali? Is he an addict? Is he still using drugs? Because you know our policy on drugs here ... We have people in recovery. We don't have the facilities to deal with addicts here...'

'You've got it all wrong, but it doesn't matter. We're leaving. You people are not for us. This place is not for us, that's clear.'

Ford looks as if he wants to say something else, but Smeaton lays a hand on his arm.

'Let us see Jack, maybe we need to call the local GP to have a look at him. Get him seen to before you leave.'

Ali shakes her head. 'There's no need. Really. He'll be embarrassed now, knowing that you know. He's struggled to deal with it all. He hates it. Feels powerless. Please, just let me go to him now. Then tomorrow, we'll pack up our things and we'll be gone. I don't think we've brought you any good feeling, have we? We seem to have unsettled everyone. Angela running off like that...'

'Did she tell you she was leaving?' Ford's anger is bubbling again. Smeaton can tell that he is trying hard to keep it in check.

'Of course not. We didn't even get on. She didn't like me.'

'I don't think that's quite true,' Smeaton says. 'She told me she'd tried, but that you weren't receptive—'

'To what? Her crazy babbling about ghosts? Of course I wasn't *receptive* to any of that nonsense. A grown woman, going on about spirits and crystals and witches, for goodness' sake. She was a fantasist, that's putting it mildly...'

Smeaton sighs. 'Maybe you're right to leave. This place isn't for everyone.'

'Maybe once you're gone, the girl will come back,' Ford says, and Smeaton gives him a look.

'No chance of that happening,' Ali says. It's under her breath, but Smeaton is sure that's what she's said.

Ford balls his hands into fists. 'What do you mean by that?' He's clearly heard too. 'Do you know where she is?'

Smeaton lays a hand on the other man again, trying to keep him calm. 'Go and see to Jack, Ali,' he says, 'then get some rest. We'll see you at lunch, and maybe we can decide on the best course of action, OK?'

Ali nods. Her hand is on the door handle. Smeaton sees the key in her hand.

He places a hand on Ford's back, guides him gently away.

45

Angela

I watch Smeaton and Ford as they disappear down the corridor towards the stairs. Ali stands at her door, key in hand. She waits for a moment, then she slips the key back into her pocket and turns back the way she came, hurrying along the corridor, away from her room, away from the men.

'No, no, no!' I scream, but no one hears me.

Now I am torn. Do I follow Smeaton, try to find some way to alert them – or follow Ali, to see what she's up to? Maybe prevent her from doing something terrible ... because there is no doubt in my mind now. Ali is up to no good.

I don't know if it was Ali or Jack who killed me, but I know now that they were both there. They both took my body away in the car, dumping it in a cold dark place, far away from home. From my friends, from my family. I wonder if I was wrong to stay in the woods when they drove off, maybe I should've tried harder to follow them. It seemed impossible at the time, but maybe I *could've* climbed into the boot with my body? But despite losing several of my senses, I knew I wouldn't be able to cope with the sadness of what they were about to do.

Why did they have to do this? I was no threat to them. All I know for sure is that whatever they did, they have done it before.

I'd thought that Jack was the bad one, when I'd found those newspaper clippings. Why did I assume it was him – just because he's a man? I can see now that I was very wrong about him. If he did anything, it was because his horrible wife made him. I had never thought it was possible for someone to be controlled to the extent that they would commit murder, but thinking about it now, it does makes some kind of sense. I don't know how she did it, if it was all mind-games or if she drugged him too, but Ali obviously had a hold over Jack that he couldn't break.

But where is he now? I don't believe he's in the bedroom. I'm certain that he is in danger. Ali is panicking; she seems desperate and I believe that she will do whatever it takes.

I hurry off in the same direction as Ali. I can hear her footsteps, soft, urgent. I turn the corner and see that she heading off to the staircase at the back of the building. I follow her downstairs and outside, then watch as Ali pulls a key out of her pocket.

I recognise it. Realise that she had it in her hand upstairs, too. It wasn't her bedroom key – it's the key to the north wing.

Ali opens the door and steps quickly inside. I manage to find a burst of energy to propel myself in behind her before she closes the door in my face. Ali locks the door, then she pauses. Cocks her head as if she is listening for something. She slips the key into her pocket, then rubs her arms, glancing round. She shakes her head, then starts walking again. She is muttering something almost too low for me to hear. I concentrate on moving faster, until I am right behind her. I breathe out a long, slow breath, but I am not sure if there is anything coming out of me. After all, my lungs have no function anymore.

'Stop it,' she says. To herself? 'Your mind is playing tricks.'

I smile. Have I finally managed to do it? Have I caused an energy shift that Ali is picking up? I move faster, passing Ali, then I turn, quickly, and look straight at her.

Ali stops dead. Her eyes dart from side to side. She whirls round, and then back. 'Who's there?' she asks.

I let her pass then continue to walk beside her, matching her pace. I want to reach out, to try and touch her but I'm too scared about what will happen. I don't want to upset the way things are and disappear. Not yet.

I need to know where Ali is going first. Find out what she's up to ... and then – it's so obvious now ... then I can go back and find Smeaton, and I can disturb the energy around him too. And him and Ford, they'll find Ali ... but no. No, damn it! It won't work, will it? It is only Ali who has mentioned feeling strange things in the building. Smeaton has never experienced a thing. He refuses to believe it's possible. Why would he start now? Unless he knows ... and unless he's always known, and he's been trying to protect us all. Because I know that I'm not the only ghost who's been trying to make contact with the living residents of Rosalind House.

I think about Jessie and her son; their sad, sad story that Mary told me – that I had her tell and retell. I wish I could have seen them. I wish I could've helped them leave this place. Be in peace. The whole time I lived here, I never felt anything of their presence at all – and then Ali appears and she feels it straightaway. It's not fair. None of it is fair. And now I am trapped here, not sure what I am meant to be doing – not sure if anyone will ever feel my presence here at all.

Ali is at the end of the top corridor. Most of the rooms up here are old treatment rooms. Some are too dangerous to enter, with most of the floorboards missing. There was always a horrible feeling in this part of the building, but now it just looks desolate, cold. She pushes open the door and I hurry to make sure I can slip in behind her. But I needn't have worried. There seems to be something wrong with the automatic door closing mechanism, and it stays open. Good. I can follow her in, and I won't be trapped in there with her.

'Shh, now,' she says. 'It'll all be over soon.'

Someone else is in there. If my heart was still beating, I'm sure it would be hammering hard in my chest right now, but as it is, I feel strangely hollow. I go inside. Ali's back is to me, and I can see that someone is strapped to something like a dentist's chair – hands and feet bound by restraints. Something on the head ... and, oh, I see now.

Circular pads are attached to Jack's temples, wires leading out to the machine that stands by the bed. It's an ECT machine. My eyes follow the leads at the back, to the wall, where it is plugged in. I can't imagine it will work, after all these years. Maybe she is just trying to scare him? But I don't know why. I stand closer, trying to see what she is doing.

She is standing close to him, saying something to him, whispering it in a low voice and I can't make it out.

Jack's eyes are closed, but I can see tears on his cheeks. I need to stop this, but I don't know how. I lean forwards, and I touch the bed. Jack's eyes fly open, and he screams, 'I'm sorry, I'm sorry!'

I jump backwards, and Ali grabs something and stuffs it into his mouth, muffling his screams. She glances around, her face confused, then she turns back. Picks up a strip of fabric from the small table next to the machine, and wraps the blindfold around his head. Jack thrashes his arms and legs, tries to spit out the rubber pad from his mouth, but she holds it firm with one hand, and presses down on his chest with her other.

'You need to calm down, Jack. You're only making things worse. Can't you see I'm trying to help you?'

This is not the help he needs, no matter what it is he has done. I run out of the room, and hurry down the corridor, down the stairs. I panic for a moment, thinking that she has closed and locked the door outside – but it is wide open, a chair holding it open.

Someone else has been here. Smeaton? Ford? Or perhaps they've sent one of the others? I haven't got time to find out. I run out of the door, across the gravel, into the other building and along the corridor to Smeaton's office. The door is ajar, and I hear voices inside.

'Are you sure it's a good idea to have Fergus roaming around in the north wing? He's said before how much he hates that place.'

'We all have to muck in now,' Smeaton says, 'until we find out what's going on. I think you're right that Ali was up to something earlier. She was jumpy, not herself. We should go back up there and check on Jack.'

'She knows something about Angela, I'm sure of it,' Ford says.

Ford is sitting in the comfortable chair – I'm quite upset that I won't be able to enjoy that chair again, or my chats with Smeaton. Smeaton is leaning back in his chair, arms behind his head. He's staring at the wall beside where I am standing, and I move into his line of vision, but he doesn't react. He doesn't see me. I turn to see what it is that's he's staring at.

The map.

There is a map there of the whole hospital. It's been engraved out of a thin brass plate, and there is a name and a date on the bottom. It was a gift to the hospital from a local businessman whose wife was treated there in the 1940s. He was grateful to the hospital for fixing her, and letting her go home. One of the hospital's success stories. There's a circle of light in the middle, from where it is bouncing off from the reflection of the ceiling light. It's highlighting the kitchen.

Yes, I think. I think I can do this...

'Let's have another walk around,' Ford says. 'Maybe Jack's in one of the other rooms. He seemed a bit out of it last time I saw him. Maybe he's got lost, and Ali's too embarrassed to say – or she's worried, given that Angela's gone too. Doesn't want to panic anyone?' He turns and looks at the map, and I seize my chance.

I try to squeeze everything inside me together. I stare up at the ceiling light, willing it to move. I squeeze tighter, and I keep staring. I close my eyes. Squeeze. Open them again. The light is swinging, ever so slightly. I turn to the map, and I see that the circle of light on the brass is moving, too – only a fraction, but it is definitely moving. I am shuddering with the effort. I ball my hands into fists, and I see my skin become more transparent, as if I am using all the energy within myself. I can't burn out, not yet. I have to let them know where Jack is.

The ceiling light swings faster, back and forth, then it starts to circle slowly around. The light on the map moves with it, pulsing and circling, passing over the lounge, the foyer, the entrance to the north wing.

'Jesus, do you see that?' Ford says.

Smeaton's mouth hangs open in shock. He looks up at the ceiling, back at the map.

I squeeze harder. The tops of my hands disappear, and I can see my fingernails curled beneath. I keep squeezing, and my fingers vanish too. I stare at the ceiling light, back at the map. Both of the men are standing now, eyes wide with shock. And finally, it happens.

The light shines over the far end of the north wing, right at the spot where Ali and Jack are right now, in the treatment room. I stop squeezing, and the light stays right there on the same spot.

'What the...?' Ford says.

The lightbulb explodes, and shards of glass rain down onto Smeaton's desk.

'The north wing treatment rooms,' Smeaton says. 'Let's go.'

I follow them out into the corridor, where the lights flicker overhead, and I glance at my hands and see that they have returned, fully formed – just a little bit paler than before.

46

Smeaton

Ali springs away from the chair and backs herself into a corner of the room. Her eyes are darting wildly, and Smeaton takes a few careful steps towards her. He is not sure what to do. Ali is far more unpredictable than he'd realised. Dangerous, too, it seems.

'Jesus Christ!' Ford throws himself towards the chair, yanks off the electrodes. Jack's temples are blackened, the skin of his forehead red and blistered, as if it has been boiled from within. Ford feels for a pulse in Jack's neck.

Ali's face remains blank, impassive. She is muttering something under her breath, and her eyes are darting wildly.

Ford takes his hand away from Jack's neck. He turns to Ali. 'You've killed him. You've actually killed him, you utter—'

'I'm going to call an ambulance,' Smeaton says. 'I think Ali needs our help right now, not our judgement.'

Ford shakes his head, stares at Smeaton with an expression that says: *You've lost your mind, too.*

Maybe he has. In all his years, Smeaton has never come across anything so messed up, so utterly terrifying than this. And what was all that with the flashing light in his office – coincidence? Was someone – or something – really trying to alert them to this – to tell them that Ali was here?

But it was too late for Jack, wasn't it? Thankfully his eyes are closed, a thin blindfold over them. He has a small rubber plate in between his teeth, too, to stop him from clenching his teeth, grinding them into pieces. Ali has done these things to protect him – and yet she has killed him. A thin line of drool runs down the side of Jack's cheek.

'I didn't mean to kill him,' Ali says, her voice barely a whisper. 'I was trying to fix him ... But you've got to understand – he was a bad man. He was a very bad man.' She slides down the wall to the floor, hugs her knees to her chest. She rocks gently; dirty tears smear her cheeks.

Smeaton crouches down in front of her. 'Ali ... it's OK. You're safe. I promise—'

'It's not her who needs to worry, is it?' Ford spits out the words, paces back and forth. 'What the hell is wrong with you?'

Smeaton raises a hand, trying to placate him. He's not sure if he's shouting at him or Ali now, or who he is more angry with: Ali for doing what she did, or Smeaton for trying to soothe her. But does Ford not realise what he is doing? He has to try and keep her calm. They have no idea what she's capable of. He wishes he could alert someone else, so that they could call the police and the ambulance while they keep Ali here to try and find out what's going on – but there is no one coming. No one knows they are here. There was no sign of Fergus on their way in, so clearly he is no longer in this part of the building.

Ali sniffs, drops her head into her hands. Ford finds a sheet from a pile of discarded laundry at the back of the room, and drapes one over Jack. Then he folds his arms and leans back against the far wall, away from Ali, and away from Smeaton.

Smeaton mouths a silent 'thank you' – he's glad that Ford hasn't left him alone here with her. He starts again. 'Ali ... you're safe here. Jack can't hurt you anymore. Now please, you need to tell us what this is all about. Can you do that? Can you tell is what Jack did? He hurt you, am I right?'

Her head flips up, and her eyes are dark again. 'Hurt me? As if that pathetic wimp would ever have dared lay a hand on me. He could barely tie his own shoelaces without my help.' She points at Ford. 'You must've noticed, surely? Did he ever take any initiative when he was out there in the woodshed? Or did you have to tell him how to do everything. Every. Bloody. Thing?'

Ford drops his arms to his sides, his face is crumpled in confusion. 'He didn't know how to do anything. I had to teach him ... There's nothing wrong with that?' He looks across at Smeaton, and Smeaton shrugs.

Ali continues, 'He can't think for himself, he never could. He watched his mum push his dad around and he just let it happen. He joined the police because they wouldn't let him into the army – not fit enough. He needed a job where they give you a role – where you know where you fit.'

'I was in the police, too, Ali. I can tell you now, that's not how it works. You need initiative. You need skill ... and balls. He worked in child protection. You can't tell me he wasn't brave to do that?'

'He did what he was told. He followed protocols. He was too bloody literal. If he'd shown some initiative – if he'd shown some *balls* – then he might've saved a little boy's life. You know, he joined that division to try and help families, because he knew what it was like – and there wasn't all the help, back when he was a kid. But did he help anyone? No.'

'I don't get it though,' Smeaton says. 'He sounds like a good man. What did he do? What changed?'

Ali snorts. 'He met me.'

Smeaton and Ford look at each other. They have no idea what she's talking about.

Ford crouches down beside her now, 'Ali—'

'He pushed a man down an escalator. He broke his leg.'

'Perhaps it was an accident,' Smeaton tries, 'maybe—'

Ali sits up straighter. 'He killed four hitchhikers.'

'For fuck's sake...' Ford says. 'This is ridiculous. You can't expect us to believe—'.

Ali cuts him off, ignoring him. 'He smothered them as they sat in the passenger seat. Then he threw them out, left them hidden in the undergrowth at the side of the road. Discarded them, like they were nothing – dumped them there with the banana peels and drink cans...'

Smeaton feels a chill run down his spine. He doesn't want to hear the rest of it, but he knows he has no choice now.

Ford asks the question that Smeaton dreads. 'If he smothered them while they were in the passenger seat ... who was driving the car?'

Ali grins, and Smeaton can see now that she's gone. Her eyes are glazed. Her face seems to have contorted itself into something else, someone he doesn't recognise at all. She's hidden this well all along, managed to fool them all about her own mental state, but now she's completely snapped.

'Who was driving the car, Ali?' Ford is holding her shoulders now, his face close to hers.

Ali bursts away from the wall, knocking Ford over. She stands, pushes Smeaton out of the way. Ford has fallen back, but quickly rights himself, and he grabs her before she can get any further. He grabs her by the throat and pins her up against the door.

'Stop it', Smeaton shouts, grabbing at Ford, trying to pull him off her.

'It was me,' Ali says, her voice dripping venom. 'Who the fuck do you think was pulling his strings?' She laughs, and it echoes around the room, sharp and hollow.

'I don't understand, Ali. Why? Can't you at least help me to understand why? I saw you listed on a paper...'

She sneers. 'You looked up my thesis, didn't you? That was just the start of it. What got me interested. I was exploring the psychological effects of coercion and control. I was trying to prove that evil wasn't inherent, that it could be manufactured. Then I took things to the next level. Jack was a good subject.' She glances across at the bed where he is still strapped in, draped in a sheet. 'But he was spent. It was over. The original experiment fell apart when I decided to go down my own route. I couldn't ever publish the new findings under my own name, not after the things that he had done. Besides, the drugs weren't controlling him anymore, all they were doing was knocking him out – and they weren't going to last forever, so I brought him here and I made him go cold turkey. But then Angela started poking her nose in, and I had to start drugging him again to keep him calm. What was I going to do when they ran out? All he wanted to do was sleep. Getting rid of Angela broke him, and he was ready to confess to the whole thing. He couldn't see the damage that would cause. I don't want to spend the rest of my life in prison. Although I'm sure I'd be able to find plenty of new playmates in there...'

Smeaton has heard enough. He slaps her across the face.

Her only reaction is a smirk.

47

Ali

Ali lands in a heap on the floor. Ford had not cared about being too harsh with her, dragging her out of the treatment room, manhandling her along the corridors, throwing her into her bedroom like a discarded rag doll. She sits up, rubs at her arm from where it has slapped hard on the wood. There is a sharp pain and a strange kind of buzzing on her skin and she wonders if she has broken her arm, or dislocated something. She holds her forearm, pressing tentatively. The pain doesn't ease.

'Bastard,' she shouts. 'You're not going to get away with this.'

She's not sure what she can do about it, now that she is sitting here on the floor, locked in the room, but she's not quite ready to give up yet. All this fuss for poor little Jack ... oh, and poor little Angela, too. That fairy really has flown away for good. She hopes they realise that.

'She's not coming back, you know,' she shouts towards the locked door. 'Interfering little cow got what was coming to her.' She thinks back to Angela's shocked face when she confronted her in the woods. She was so confused. Didn't see it coming when Jack came up behind her and cracked her over her stupid little head.

Ali stands up and walks towards the bed. She feels tired, all of a sudden. Like a thick blanket has been dropped over her from a height, trapping her beneath. She lies down on the bed.

'Just a minute,' she mutters, 'then I'll sort everything out. OK, Jack? I'm sorry. Things all got a bit out of control. Just let me rest for a bit, then I'll pack and we'll be out of here. We'll do what you said. We'll go away – properly away. Abroad. Where no one will find us.'

The bedsprings creak as she turns over.

'Jack? Where've you gone? You can't leave me here on my own in this place. We're in this together, remember? Jack? Jack! Where the fuck are you?'

She jumps out of bed, starts to pace around the room. Her arm is throbbing now. It's definitely broken. Damn it. Damn it all. She crouches down and pulls out the box from her bedside cabinet. She has bandages in there, maybe even a sling. She pulls it out and everything spills on the floor and her arm sings with pain. She closes her eyes, falls back against the bed.

When she opens her eyes, there is someone sitting on the floor opposite her.

She stares at the girl. Ratty blonde hair, ring through her nose. Blue eyes like the sky. She'll never forget those eyes. The girl's face is expressionless. She's holding her hands together, fingers entwined, like a small cradle. She lifts the cradle forwards and Ali leans in, to see what she is holding in her hands ... and as she leans, the girl's face changes ... A dark-haired man with peacock-green eyes and soft, red lips smiles at her, and when he opens his mouth into a grin, a stream of writhing black insects falls from his mouth and into Ali's outstretched hand and she pulls away, screams. Closes her eyes. 'You're not real. You're not real,' she keeps saying it, keeps rocking back and forwards. When she opens her eyes, she is alone again. The swirling image of the dead hitchhikers is gone. She breathes out a long, slow sigh. Her arm starts to throb again, and with her good arm, she scrabbles around the floor, tossing things aside, bandages, dressings, cotton wool – until she finds the bag. Why did she hide the bag? Was it from Jack, or from herself? She opens it and takes out a handful of the small white pills. Stares down at them.

Hears Jack's voice, 'You might as well join me, Ali ... there's nothing for you here.'

'Of course there is,' she says, angrily. How dare he say that? What does he know? 'Shut up, Jack. You were never going to see this through to the end, were you? You're weak ... useless ... you're...'

She stops talking. Jack is sitting in front of her, cross-legged. He's wearing a Kings of Leon T-shirt, and his hair is gelled into a quiff. It's how he looked the night they met.

She reaches for him. 'What are you—?'

'I'm dead, Ali. You killed me, remember?' He tilts his head to one side, then the other, and there are scorch marks at his temples. 'You fried my brain, didn't you? You bitch.'

She shuffles back, crushing herself against the bed. 'No ... you. You killed all those people ... You're the bad one, Jack. You did it all. You.'

The pills are still in her hand. She closes her eyes, tosses them back. Swallows them dry. When she opens her eyes, she is alone again. But there is a scent in the air – a smoky, sandalwood scent. Jack's aftershave. She remembers inhaling that smell, that first night, when they kissed. It was just a game then, wasn't it? She never really thought it would work. It was never supposed to end like this. She thinks back to all those years ago, her mother and her father, in and out of hospitals – trying to fix their defective brains. She wanted to fix them. She wanted to fix everyone – that's why she trained as a nurse. She thought by dealing with it head on, it would never come to affect her. That her dodgy genes wouldn't give her away. But it didn't work out like that. Somewhere inside her head, she knows that something has broken. Snapped, like the filament on a spent lightbulb.

Using her good arm for balance, she twists over, rolls onto her knees and stands up. The brief moment of clarity has passed. Her head starts to feel fuzzy, and she can't quite remember what it was she was going to do.

'Jack?' she says, glancing around again. But there's no one there. The room swims in and out of focus. She stumbles forwards. Lurches towards the bathroom. She remembers. The bath. She aches. She stinks. She's so, so tired.

She needs to get into the bath.

48
Angela

First there was Smeaton's voice, calm, but full of fear – and then Ford's – I could hear the anger in his. I heard the rumbling tones of him berating Smeaton as they locked the door and left Ali inside. 'You shouldn't have let them come here. This is all your fault.'

I don't think it is Smeaton's fault.

He was being kind, letting them come here. Giving them a chance.

I can hear them, still – in the corridor outside. 'What she's done to Jack, it's nothing short of barbaric.' Ford's voice.

'The voltage was high. I don't think he would've felt anything.' Smeaton, now. 'I'm calling the police. Let them deal with it.'

What did you do, Ali? What else did you do?

I sit by the window, waiting.

Eventually, the door opens and Ali staggers into the bathroom. She is smiling, but her eyes are unfocused. There is no sign of the tears that I had imagined from the sounds that she was making only a few moments earlier. Yelling at the men outside the door. Telling them what she thought of them. Yelling at someone else – as if people were in the room with her. I wanted to go and look, but I was scared of what I might see. I don't need any more trauma. Ali is carrying enough for us all.

I can see it in her eyes now, quite clearly. She is deranged. She has lost her mind.

Perhaps this was how it was all along? If I am right, then she is the one who made Jack kill those hitchhikers. An experiment – can good people be forced to do bad things? Disproving the theory of inherent evil.

But she has done the opposite. For *she* is evil. She is incurable. She is sick and twisted and vile and awful, but that is the way she was made … and who knows what she did before she started her experiments on Jack – her puppet. Her plaything, to be moulded into whatever she wished.

I wish now I had spoken to him after I found the newspaper clippings. Maybe, with Smeaton's and my help, we could've stopped this – the rest of this. Maybe I wouldn't be here now, sitting on the window ledge in her bathroom, waiting for her to see me.

The bath is full of water. She must've filled it before and then forgotten about it. She dips a hand, tentatively, into the water. She frowns, then reaches down to pull out the plug. She is humming a tune, quietly, but I can still hear it clearly. I know what it is. It's 'De Noche', one of the Taizé chants. One of my favourite songs. It is beautiful, soothing. I don't like her having it. I don't want her to have it. Half of the water has drained away now. She stops humming. Glances around.

'Hello?' she says. She looks scared. I want to scream. I want to scare her. I open my mouth, but no sound comes out. She turns on the taps, and the water judders and spurts. Hot steam slowly fills the room. She smiles, starts humming again. She seems at peace with herself, and for a moment, I am fooled.

But then I wonder … what is she doing? She talked before of being afraid here, in this room. Is she trying to take the easy way out? If she is gone, then no one can find out the truth.

The truth of what she is.

She pours in lavender bath salts and they meld in to the steam, and I am sad that I can't smell them. I always loved the smell of lavender. She tests the water, dipping in a hand. Turns off the taps. Her expression changes and I realise something else: she is in pain – she is cradling one arm with the other. She winces. Glances around again.

Has she sensed me, after all?

She struggles to undress, the bad arm difficult to manoeuvre, She leaves her clothes in a pile on the floor, steps carefully into the bath, lets herself slide into its depths. She goes under, stays there for just a moment too long. I imagine myself feeling panic – fluttering in my chest – imagining it is a poor substitute for the real thing, but of all the senses I have lost, it's still the sense of smell that I miss most.

She resurfaces, and she is still smiling. She is humming that tune, still.

No, I think. You don't get to have this serenity.

I concentrate hard, willing it to happen. Not sure if I can do it, or if it will happen anyway, as is inevitable.

And then...

Her expression changes. The humming stops. She slides herself backward, as if trying to push her way out through the back of the tub. The water swirls in front of her, and it becomes cloudy, discoloured. Tinged with something dark, green. Slimy.

A small hand appears, breaking the surface.

Then another.

The small hands grip on to the sides of the tub, and Ali pushes herself back as hard as she can, tries to stand. She's struggling. It's too slippery. Too many bath salts have turned the bottom of the bath to slime. She places a hand on the side of the bath, tries to put weight on it and forgets it's her bad arm, in the panic. It gives way, her hand slips, and she slides awkwardly, crashes down and falls face first into the water, her back seems to have bent at an unnatural angle. Her legs poke out, kicking uselessly into the steamy air.

The boy's head appears through the dank green murk. He is clothed, his hair plastered to his small, pale face. He starts off transparent, becomes opaque, before he takes on an almost solid form. Although I know that he's not, of course. Like me, he is no longer real. He sees me, and he smiles. A small shy, smile. I think I am his first sighting, as he is mine.

Ali has not resurfaced. Her body thrashes, her head almost breaking the surface more than once. But then I see them – lots of hands, women's hands, pushing her, pulling her under.

The boy stands.

The green murk swirls, the fronds of pondweed and algae disintegrate. Now all that floats is Ali's hair, spread around her like feathers.

She is still face down, only her pale legs stick out at odd angles over the edges of the tub.

The boy climbs out of the bath, and I know who he is. He's George Samuel – he drowned in the pond over sixty years ago, and he is here, now.

He walks towards me, and as he does, his sodden clothes start to change colour – the water draining away, until he reaches me – and he is bone dry. His hair fresh and clean, neatly parted and combed to one side, revealing a strangely beautiful scarlet birthmark on his fore-head. He is wearing smart grey shorts and a lemon-yellow T-shirt with a collar. His face is white, his lips tinged with blue. He gazes up at me, and I smile back at him.

I take his hand, and I can almost feel it, as if he is real, as if I am real, and we are together – and he is saved. And I was right, all along, about the existence of ghosts – but I was wrong about one thing. It's not only the bad who can see them. The good can, too. But only when they are a ghost themselves. And only if they have love to give to those who most need it.

We both need it.

I pull him up onto the window ledge beside me and we turn, facing outwards. Out at the fields beneath, out into the beyond, out to wher-ever we want to be.

Now, I think. *Concentrate. Do it. Push through. Together. Let's fly into the wind.*

I squeeze his hand, and feel him squeeze back. Nothing happens. We aren't going anywhere. We can't leave. Not yet. But we are together now. We … whatever we are, we are real. But we are not free. Maybe one day we will be.

Until then, we will stand here – staring out into the thick, dark night; and although there is no reflection in the glass for us to see our-selves – if you were to look upwards now, from the grounds of this sad, crumbling place, you will see us. Standing quiet and still. Holding hands.

Smiling.

Dr Henry Baldock's Journal – 10th September 1955

It is with a heavy heart that I must write my final report and present my findings to the board. The details that I will include on the official document will be quite different to the ones that I must record here.

My recommendations are simple. There must be an urgent, independent review of all cases. All patients. All diagnoses, treatments, prognoses. I know that there are people here who should not be here. I know that there are staff here who have failed to move with the times, still favouring superstition and barbaric treatment methods over the new recommendations that the board seeks to bring. This is not something that can be dealt with quickly, but I would wish to see that the chronically ill and seemingly untreatable be taken to alternative hospitals straightaway; and that those with more minor conditions be reviewed in a non-psychiatric setting, where possible.

It is time for change. Time for reform. I wish to be part of it.

But despite what I have said, what I have recommended to the board – what my rational, medical mind knows to be true – there is more to it than simply this.

If it were possible immediately, then I would want it to be so: this hospital – Rosalind House – carries a darkness within its walls. I am concerned that my presence here has unsettled it. There is something unearthly here. Something paraphysical, that I am no expert to explain or rationalise. If it were possible, I would desire more than anything that this place be closed down. Razed to the ground. The land returned to the farmers, to the villagers, who have far more understanding of it that any outsiders such as I will ever know.

For I believe there to be entities within these walls. Sad, unsettled beings: Alice Samuels and her family, unfairly tried and unjustly hung as witches; Lady Susan Cromwell, their accuser, who died shielding her own guilt. Then Jessie Samuels and her family, victims of rumours and bullying and unnecessary tragedy; and the nurses who contributed to their deaths through their own ignorance and fear. They all want their voices to be heard. Some of them want justice, some retribution, and until they get it they remain here, waiting – silent and calm. Lurking in the shadows, shielding themselves from the light.

Lingering.

Until something, or someone, comes and awakens them once more.

Acknowledgements

This story developed from a combination of several ideas: my real-life ghost story, the Holliday fenland history, my real-life job in clinical trials, my mum's old job as a psychiatric nurse, and a visit to an exhibition at the V&A on counterculture, which led to my interest in communes (thanks for the ticket, Ash!)

As far as research goes, a huge thank-you to Julia for the Warboys and Baldock history (and for telling us where to buy the witch stickers!), to the Findhorn Foundation (who didn't know I was there researching this book), to Will Shaw for *Spying in Guru Land*, and to Abz for telling me how child protection works. Thanks to my mum (aka Ali Gardiner) and dad – the former, for telling me all about her (often grim) time at Rosslynlee and other psychiatric hospitals where she trained in the 1970s, and the latter for almost being brave enough to scale the inner fence. Our urbexing skills need a bit of work... Thanks also to the Ghost of Arthur's Bridge Road – I hope you're happy now.

Big thanks to my nephew and niece, Cody and Aimee, who named several of the characters, including Smeaton Dunsmore and Fairy Angela.

Thanks to Ford Swanson – a colleague of my dad's from many years ago, who had no idea that his name would always be lodged in my mind and would eventually make it into a book.

Hugs and kisses for A.K. Benedict, who almost got me to go on a ghost hunt and continues to try to convince me that ghosts don't exist, and for Steph Broadribb, whose encouragement and early reading convinced me to carry on with the ghosts (which are totally real, by the way).

Massive thanks to Richard Latham for his generous CLIC Sargent bid – I hope you like your and Julie's characters! And to Sam Carrington and Leila Solomon for their generous bids via the TBC Charity Auction; I hope you enjoy the book as much as the chocolate.

You would not be reading this book if were not for my wonderful agent, Phil Patterson, and my fantastic publisher, Karen Sullivan. Their insights and suggestions, along with astute editing by West Camel, took this from spooky to creepy AF. Thank you to all at Marjacq and Orenda. You're all ace.

To my readers and supporters, friends and family, fellow crime writers and brilliant book bloggers: thank you for your enthusiasm and for always sticking by me. And for drinking the wine at my launches.

And the last paragraph, as always, goes to my other half – Mr JLOH – who never stops believing (and is much more of a scaredy-cat than me.)

⁞⁞⁞⁞⁞

You can find out more about me and my books on my website, *www. sjiholliday.com*, where you can also sign-up to my mailing list for exclusive news and updates, and find links to my social media accounts. If you enjoyed *The Lingering*, I would love to hear from you!

'Totally addictive.
Like *Fight Club*,
only darker'
S.J. WATSON

One crossed wire

Three dead bodies

Six bottles
of bleach

WILL CARVER

Good Samaritans

'A great blend of crime thriller and the darkest imaginable domestic noir.
I loved it' SARAH PINBOROUGH

AN EPISODE OF **SIX** STORIES

CHANGELING

MATT WESOLOWSKI

'Wonderfully horrifying ...
the suspense crackles'
James Oswald

'Impeccably crafted and gripping
from start to finish...'
Doug Johnstone, *Big Issue*

THOMAS ENGER

INBORN